TWINKLE, TWINKLE, LITTLE BAR

ISABELLA MAY

Copyright © 2021 by Isabella May
Print Edition

Editor: Alice Cullerne Bown
Artwork and design: istock.com by Getty and sam_4321, Fiverr

All rights reserved.

No part of this book may be reproduced in any form or by any electronic or mechanical means, including information storage and retrieval systems, without written permission from the author, except for the use of brief quotations in a book review.

Acknowledgements

There are always so many people to thank each time a new book launches. To all my usual support crew, *thank you*! And an extra special THANK YOU must go out to Sue Baker, Fiona Jenkins, Emma Hawkes and Heidi Swain for being absolute superstars in recent months XX

"Cocoa and spice make Christmas so nice"

CHAPTER ONE
River

RIVER JACKSON WAS living a lie. It wasn't a deceit of the big, fat, hairy and scary kind, but it was hardly a microscopic English Riviera grain of sand-style fib either. Rather it was a slow and steadily growing lie, whose fuse had been lit when River had witnessed the application of jam to a scone.

To be clear, that's to say the application of jam first… as in *before* the cream. *Never!* Not when you were Somerset born and bred, anyway.

It was sacrilege, in his book. Whatever next? Layering Cheddar cheese on your sliced white bread first, and then smothering that with butter?

River felt so let down. And to think that Cornwall was on so many people's bucket lists! His growing sense of disillusionment had ended with him donning a pair of the darkest wraparound shades whenever he set foot outside. If he saw just one more thatched roof and rose-festooned country cottage that looked like it'd dropped off the front of a clotted cream fudge box, he swore he would punch the owner.

River wasn't even violent, he couldn't bear to squish an errant ant. It could only mean one thing – he was done and dusted with Cornwall. Truly, madly, deeply over his two-year love affair with England's southernmost county. And herein lay the *slight* downside to him waking up and smelling the Cornish coffee… (yes, even coffee was a foodie, all right, drinkie, *thing* in these perfect parts). River's fiancée, Alice, probably wasn't sharing his thoughts.

Alice had her horses in Cornwall.

Alice was living her dream life in Cornwall.

Meanwhile, the denim-blue-eyed, shoulder length brown-tressed and bearded River was marooned in his cocktail bar in Cornwall. As helplessly stranded as the tourists who foolishly walked across the causeway to the historic attraction of nearby St. Michael's Mount just before the tide sneakily cut them off from the mainland.

Gawd, the cocktail bar. Gawd, the world's greatest mistake. Gawd, the humiliation.

No, it wasn't quite as catastrophic as the White Stripes splitting up, Tom Cruise jumping on Oprah's sofa in a cringeworthy declaration of love, or the distinct lack of class and imagination involved in giving cocktails names like Sex on the Beach and Screaming Orgasm. Still, for a former rock star who'd once given the British and American press as many daily column inches as a Spanish bartender would add rum to a Cuba Libre, it was fair to say that River Jackson had publicly screwed up good and proper.

Granted, River's first cocktail bar in Glastonbury had worked, when he'd quit the band, Avalonia, and returned home to set it up in earnest a couple of years ago. But that was only because Glastonbury's high street had been crying out for a little after-hours variety; something different from the poles-apart extremes of gung-ho cider and skittle alleys, or the other, slightly more eccentric pastimes the town was famous for.

The quaint Cornish market town of Pasty (yes, that really was its name), on the other hand, neither wanted nor needed his wares. People came here on holiday, to relax in said chocolate-box cottages, self-sufficiently lugging a week's worth of food and alcohol with them after shelling out a small fortune on accommodation. And people also camped inland, beyond the tourist-swamped sand dunes, nibbling takeaway salads and tubs of couscous, and clinking BPA-free champagne flutes full of the local M&S's finest offer-of-the-week prosecco.

As for the other kind of people – the locals. Well, if River had thought half of Glastonbury's population had glasses of fizzy apple welded to their hands, he had a rude awakening with all of Pasty's inhabitants. Here it was go hard with the microbrewery pints… or go home. Fancy beer or nothing.

Why hadn't he done his research, spending some time in this niche part of Cornwall? Why hadn't he tested the waters with his futuristic fusions and their dry ice pomp and ceremony before committing to the move?

But it was too late for regrets. In a matter of months, River had scared away all and sundry. His savings, which had been mammoth after pocketing millions from his ten years in the band, had started to dwindle. And time was ticking on; forty was waiting smugly for him on the horizon, as if the irksome number had always known this was going to be River's fate.

He tossed a coin high in the air.

Heads and he'd have to come clean, tell Alice how he felt, be true to the both of them.

Tails and he'd pretend none of it was happening. Just for the moment. Just until the New Year. Things were always clearer in January. The first of November was no time to be hatching new plans. Not when the love of his life had already decked the bows of the bar with holly… and mistletoe… *and* the glitteriest tinsel you ever did see.

And Alice knew River didn't 'do' the dreaded T-word as far as drinks went – he was as far removed as he could be from those bartenders who flounced their plastic straws with a halo of tinsel as if the customers were on a golden oldies cruise.

Ping. The coin landed.

River couldn't bring himself to look. Oh, crap; it had bounced off the edge of the bar anyway, on a trajectory of its own like a rebellious bouncy ball straight out of one of Enid Blyton's Noddy books.

"Look after the pennies and the pounds'll look after 'emselves," chortled Jimmy, River's one and only punter of the afternoon, as he dived awkwardly for the coin. He seized it, then gripped it heroically, arm outstretched like a small child who was proud of his treasure. He meandered toward River, and finally, painstakingly, nudged the coin across the counter.

Shit. It was tails. River was officially stuck in limbo then. Not that he'd have been overjoyed to see the coin land on the stalwart profile of HRH the Queen, but the royal seal of approval would have provided a definite sign. One that he couldn't ignore.

A familiar noise started up. River brought a hand to his forehead. Jimmy had pulled his spoons out of his pocket – as he was prone to do most afternoons of the week.

"Will you stop playing with those blasted things? They're

scratching the table!"

"I don't see a juke box or a *rock band* offering me an alternative to accompany my cocktail." Jimmy shrugged and moved the spoons to rest on his knee. He closed his eyes, lost in his rhythm as he started on a new piece of percussion.

River did the only thing he could. Smiling fake-serenely at his solitary, sarcastic and stubborn customer, he fixed himself a Frisky Bison. The jaded rock star-turned-mixologist's answer to a cup of tea. And then he lifted his glass high, toasting the remains of the greyest Monday he'd ever known.

CHAPTER TWO
Alice

PASTY.

Sure, Somerset had its share of curious village names: Star, Queen Camel, and Wookey Hole to name but a few. But a new start in a small town named after a pie filled with meat? A small town that, charming as it might be, didn't quite have the dramatic allure or the coastal excitement of St. Ives or Newquay? It should have rung alarm bells from the get-go. Not to mention the fact that Alice was a veggie!

It was no use trying to ignore the growing feeling that something had to give. Like, preferably, a sinkhole which would take her, River, and her beloved horses back to Glastonbury. None of which was to snub Cornwall. It was a gorgeous place.

It was just that Alice missed her perfectly imperfect roots. Which wasn't a reference to her glorious head of hair. Alice was blessed with long, ethereal, honey-blonde curls that had somehow retained their childhood hue, making her look as if she'd been plucked from a cornfield. Paired with the most unusually emerald eyes, she possessed a breathtaking beauty most women could only dream of. That said, she prided herself on her modesty, and really rather hated it when people assumed that she couldn't have any substance beneath the bewitching style.

If only things were as peachy as her looks, when it came to going back to Somerset. Sadly, it was too tall an order to expect she'd ever be able to patch things up with her preposterous parents and snobby sister. Well, in this lifetime anyway. Yes, you could definitely say they had broken the mould when they'd made the Goldsmiths. True, her father had managed to sneak away from Alice's overbearing mother, to offer his guidance on all things property-related when she and River had initially upped sticks to Cornwall. But the hints he'd dropped to River, that he would invest in a smallholding enabling his daughter to pursue her love of horses, had turned out to be nothing more than lies. Which wasn't to paint a picture of poverty, *but of the blatant inequality between his two daughters.* Alice would be eternally punished, and cut off from her inheritance, for 'bringing shame on the family'. She had joined a rock band right when, according to her parents, she should have been training for the British Olympics.

What were they like? *She'd never quite achieved that level of grace on horseback!* Meanwhile, her older sister, Tamara, and her ever-growing brood were positively showered with benevolence (aka anything and everything money could possibly buy).

Whilst Alice couldn't really say she missed her old family, she definitely missed her new and kooky one: free-spirited Aunt Sheba and her incredible intuition, River's mum, Heather, and her husband, Terry (slightly overlooking his fatherly link with besotted Blake and ghastly Georgina, though they had thankfully moved on). Oh, and then there was Blossom, Aunt Sheba's irresistible tortoiseshell cat.

It wasn't just family, though. Alice missed the Glastonbury locals, too. She missed Lee and Jonie, who had taken over River's flagship cocktail bar on the high street. Their enthusiasm and verve were infectious. And oh, how she missed The Cocktail Bar's customers, a bunch of people you simply couldn't replicate anywhere on earth if you'd tried, more was mostly the pity.

All right, she didn't miss Lennie, their former band manager, who had randomly turned out to be River's dad. She didn't miss her other former band members who'd developed terminal laziness. And Alice Goldsmith certainly did not miss the paps. But mercifully they had their Taylor Swifts, Sias, and Ed Sheerans to run after nowadays. On the giant snakes and ladders game of the music industry, Alice and River had slid down the longest reptilian tail, to a guesstimate S list, since quitting the band and going into relative hiding. A newfound status that suited them both just fine… meaning, surely, it would be safe to return to Glastonbury now?

Surely they could be as free as Cerys Matthews from Catatonia, or the cute, floppy-fringed bassist from Blur who had turned himself into a farmer? Nobody could say Alice and River hadn't given this new life a go. But, at the end of the day, they were just too far away from all the people who mattered. Practically at the tip of Cornwall's toe. Any further and they'd be in the sea!

Obviously the second loves of her life, her horses, had been great (she'd managed to rent some stables), and so had the literal breath of fresh air that Alice had so desperately needed away from the limelight. But River's plans for his second cocktail bar – as adventurous and appealing as they'd felt at the outset – had gone spectacularly Pear Bellini-shaped. Apart from Jimmy, Rio and Justin, who'd recently moved into the cottage down the road, the occasional 'date night' traffic, and the monthly book club meet-up, customers were a rarity.

The trouble was, if Alice knew one thing about her boyfriend – the man she was dying to hear the pop of a certain question from – it was that he wasn't going to give up on his pipedream without a fight. His Magical Mañana cocktail hadn't even been ordered yet, let alone made its way to the lips of his patrons! But how much longer could they wait for that to happen? *Would it even happen?* Two whole years and not a soul had uncovered it, buried in the middle of the menu. Or maybe they had, but nobody liked Tequila. In cocktail terms, this modern day mystery was one part unbelievable, two parts unfathomable, with a generous dash of frustration. Something River'd had to suck up reluctantly, with a very large straw.

In desperation, Alice decided to call Sheba, River's adorable, quirky aunt. She needed her angel cards read.

"I don't like to read them over the phone," said Sheba in her broad Somerset accent. "The energy doesn't flow as well. It would be preferable if you could get here in person."

"I know," Alice replied. "I can't get away this week, though. I haven't got any helping hands at the stables, and Cotton Candy has a vet's appointment. Besides which, River would be asking too many questions. Sorry, I know he's your nephew and all. Don't think I'm being underhand. We're still as loved up as we've ever been! I really wouldn't ask... but I need urgent clarification."

A strange and indecipherable sound could be heard down the phone.

"Sheba? Are you there?"

"I'm cutting your cards, Alice. Do please chill out."

"Oh, okay."

Evidently Sheba didn't have much time for small talk. A long silence ensued.

"Well? Are you going to tell me when to stop?" Sheba said.

"Oh, right, yes: STOP," Alice shouted.

"No need to be quite so forceful, my child," said Sheba, and the shuffling came to an end. "From where in the pack would you like me to take the cards?"

"Erm." Alice screwed her eyes tightly shut and tried to envisage the backs of the beautiful, intricately painted pack, whose wisdom hadn't let her down yet. "I'll go with the very first card on the left, one as close to the middle as possible, and the l… last… no, the second from last card on the right," she said decisively.

"Hmm, let's see what we have here, then." Alice heard flicking noises and could imagine Sheba laying out the cards, turning them over, spacing them apart, picking Alice's three and analysing their depictions to extract their pearls of wisdom. She stayed quiet, waiting for Sheba to start talking.

"Straight off the mark I'm getting a strong travel theme here, Alice."

Alice groaned inwardly, willing the story to change once Sheba studied the cards in more detail.

"The Angel of Displacement has come forward first. Blimey. Things are shifting like quicksand, my girl. Roots are no longer secure. Trying to tether them back down will prove fruitless."

Wow. Bold. Sheba wasn't one to hold back, but it seemed neither were the cards.

"The Angel of Voyage is staring me in the face next. That's some pattern, huh?"

"Huh, yes. I guess it is," said Alice, her mobile-gripping hand shaking in response to Sheba's words.

"And finally, surprise, surprise, we have one of my favourites; the fortuitous Angel of New Beginnings. In summary, my dear: there's not much you can do but lean into the winds of change, and surrender."

Alice thanked Sheba as quickly as she could. Then she marched to the stables, as if that very action might free her from the contemplation that now shrouded her like a Bodmin moor fog that was closing in fast.

The theme of those cards was not only travel, but travel on some kind of vast and currently incomprehensible scale. The kind of travel that didn't just mean a move back to Glastonbury. And it was imminent.

Shoot.

Which was hardly a strong enough word…

This couldn't be right! But Alice knew in her heart of hearts that, since the news had been relayed to her by Sheba – and at her own flipping request – it was. She wanted nothing more than to settle back in Glastonbury – and then stay right there. She'd spent a decade on the road, touring the world in a band. She'd graced the stage in every imaginable dot on the globe; from Rio de Janeiro to Reykjavik. Nowadays when it came to the letter R, all she wanted to do was *relax*… and maybe *raise* some little *rascals*.

All right, definitely raise a brood of mini-Rivers. He was her soul mate, he'd been her band mate – and frankly, while flimsy and questionable pieces of women's and men's underwear had heaped up at his feet on the stage while he'd crooned Avalonia's greatest hits, she'd waited long enough to have him all to herself.

Besides, how would more travel lead River to propose? No, they'd made their bed in Pasty. Now they'd just have to lie in it.

CHAPTER THREE
River

THE FUNNY THING was, River didn't think the coin really had landed on tails when it hit the floor and stopped careening. Sure, his thoughts went with the fate-must-have-had-Jimmy-intervening-for-a-reason story at first. But soon River suspected that Jimmy was just being Jimmy. Aka, the same annoying Jimmy who thought a pair of spoons was a kosher musical instrument. River scowled at the idea of his customer flipping the coin in his hand, meddling with destiny, all so he still had a bar to frequent.

Why else would he suddenly receive a letter from his landlord to inform him he had put the premises up for sale?

River would have thought it serendipitous, if he wasn't feeling like such a failure. Alas, the pinnacle of success he had fallen from made his current situation plain embarrassing. It was just as well he wasn't pursued by the media nowadays. He'd gone from being one of the most acclaimed (and no, that wasn't just his ego inflating itself) rock stars in the world, to a moderately notable mixologist and cocktail bar owner in England's most mystical town, to his current situation – invisibility.

He was a failure, who had now broken his promise to

Mercedes and the goddamn mission. Which was another story, and a long one at that. Suffice to say River's lengthy travels with his band had ignited a giant passion for cocktails. But cocktails with distinction, cocktails with a difference, cocktails with a twist.

One gig had seemingly melded into another at the tail end of his stint with Avalonia. The band were spending month after month together on the road, without as much as a break. But for some bizarre reason, the cocktails didn't all merge into a giant pitcher of oblivion, along with the music and motels. Each and every tipple River had sampled, he had lovingly and joyously committed to memory. And then he had also started a giant scrapbook, referred to as the Bible, with all the ingredient and flavour combinations he had crammed into his head.

During a particularly long and arduous South American tour, River and his band mates (including Alice… who'd been dating that twit of an actor back then) found themselves in Guadalajara, Mexico. Scratch that: River was the only member of the band who wasn't comatose that glorious morning, and had been blissfully aware of his co-ordinates. He'd stepped over the litany of bodies strewn like dominoes inside the posh hotel's suite, opened the curtains on the early morning sun streaking the city's streets with golden light, and decided to explore his surroundings for once.

Except he'd taken things a little bit far… hitchhiking to Tequila, consumed with an unshakeable desire to visit one of the town's famous distilleries. Well, he didn't quite get there. But he did meet a little old lady in the agave fields *en route*; a little old lady who'd somehow known of his future cocktail bar plans before he had, entrusting him with a bottle of special elixir to use in said future cocktail bar; a super intuitive little old lady by the name of Mercedes.

River had listened to her wittering away as if they'd known one another all their lives, rapidly blinking at the realisation he'd either completely lost the plot and wandered into a parallel universe… or set foot on the path fate had always intended him to walk that day.

The rest was history. Literally. Because the bottle of elixir Mercedes had entrusted him with hadn't seen the light of day since he'd traded Glastonbury for Cornwall; since he'd unpacked it and hidden it in the store cupboard in his second bar, waiting for the perfect moment – or, more precisely put, for three random customers to order the Magical Mañana cocktail from the middle of the drinks menu, as per Mercedes' precise and non-negotiable protocol.

Whilst the moment had quickly come to pass in his unconventional hometown, the occasion had never materialised in perfunctory Pasty. It was all the more tantalising as the elixir was special stuff, which would make the hopes and dreams of the three who imbibed it come true almost instantly. But it was hardly surprising, when footfall was currently as thin on the ground as visible flooring in Raffles' famous Long Bar. One of River's favourite cocktail bars, it was customary to litter the floor there with peanut shells as one sipped on a refreshing Singapore Sling.

River could only dream of emulating this Singaporean success story, serving a throng of eager customers. Instead, he picked up the brown envelope hiding the landlord's notice, took a deep breath and thrust it equally deeply into the back pocket of his jeans, silently begging the universe to provide him with the moment of least resistance to break the alarming news to Alice.

Except he feared that, just as the moment had never come for his special and life-changing Magical Mañana cocktail in his latest venture, the moment to let down the love of his life would prove just as elusive.

Cornwall was perfect for Alice. River couldn't possibly fudge his relationship with her, after all it'd taken for them to finally get together – another incredibly long story. Gah. The bloody fudge word. It crept into everything.

THE WORLD WORKS in mysterious ways. River had kissed Alice goodnight that same evening, turned out his bedside lamp, thoughts swirling like giant and toothy sharks inside his head, putting paid to any notion of sleep. Or maybe it was the elephant (letter) in the room (bedside table drawer)? River could almost feel the guilt seeping from his pores and soaking itself into the mattress. Soon it would be so obvious that he had a terrible secret that Alice would be sure to confront him. He shut his eyes anyway, determined to swap the predators infiltrating his head for sheep. Who on earth had been crazy enough to think that counting woolly animals jumping over fences would send a stress-ridden human being off to the land of nod?

River didn't have to ponder that idea for long. His mobile phone rang and he reached across to mute it, which was futile because Alice was now as wide awake as he was.

"It's gone midnight, Riv!" Alice tutted. "I can't believe someone's calling you now. What's the matter with people?"

How Alice would have laughed at herself if she'd come out with that little gem just a few years ago, when an early night was a 2:00 a.m. finish.

"Looks like it's my mum." River squinted at the incoming caller ID. "I don't get a very good feeling about this. I hope everything's okay. She'd never normally call me so late."

River pressed the answer button and put the phone to his ear to take the call, but Heather's panic-stricken voice could already be heard and now Alice was sitting bolt upright in bed by his side, her arm enfolding him already as if she sensed he'd soon be needing comfort:

"It's your aunt Sheba," said Heather, her own Somerset accent stronger than ever as it broke through her tears. "My beautiful sister is dead."

CHAPTER FOUR
Alice

ALICE WAS BESIDE herself. She should have detected something was off during the angel card call. Sure, she'd thought that Sheba seemed a little put out, a little reluctant to do the reading over the phone. But nothing could have forewarned her that Sheba would suffer a short, sharp stroke that same evening. And that would be that.

Now, of course, her mind was racing; tripping with guilt that she'd unwittingly stressed River's aunt out. But surely nobody had died from shuffling a few cards? The readings were always steeped in love and positivity, no matter which cards were pulled from the pack. It wasn't as if they'd been playing poker and she'd made Sheba bet every last penny of her savings!

Alice couldn't possibly tell River that she'd only spoken to his aunt a few hours ago. This was not the time to start dissecting their life decisions. Besides, as she'd said to herself earlier at the stables whilst she was grooming Lemon Drop, Pasty is where they had made their bed. There was no doubt they were currently lying in it.

River returned to the bedroom with a tray of tea and biscuits. Another layer of guilt settled on top of the first one:

TWINKLE, TWINKLE, LITTLE BAR

Alice should have been fussing about after her boyfriend. It was his aunt who had died. Technically, she could only call Sheba by her name since Alice and River weren't yet married. But Sheba had been more of an aunt than any of her own relations. The Real Deal. A more wonderful, caring and flamboyant family member you couldn't hope to find.

"Here." River took a cookie, snapped it in half and popped it into Alice's mouth. "Food may seem crazy but sugar is always important when you've had a big shock. Part of me feels like knocking us up a tray of shots from the bar... but no, Aunt Sheba wouldn't have approved. She was always more of a herbal tea girl. I think my mother and her weakness for Ginger Rabbits put paid to Aunt Sheba ever visiting our Glastonbury bar – other than the official opening."

Alice laughed and then cried and then laughed some more. It was true, River's mum's penchant for Ginger Rabbit cocktails was legendary, and the only reason he agreed to feature them on the menu; the violet infused Crème Yvette was definitely an acquired taste.

"I'm just so relieved that your mum and your aunt patched up their differences before it was too late. Sometimes it's difficult to have those conversations, you know?"

"I know what you mean," said River, tenderly brushing a crumb from Alice's cheek. "You put them off because you have imagined all sorts of awful scenarios in your head; your words being misconstrued, the disagreements..."

"The disappointment," Alice chipped in.

"Speaking of which—"

"Look, I know this is really not a good time, but—"

Alice looked quizzically at River and River reflected her

expression right back at her, both of them trying to say something that sounded spookily similar at the same time.

"You go first." River gestured with a smile. "As long as you aren't breaking up with me. Today would definitely not be a good day for that."

"Okaaaaay."

"You're not breaking up with me, are you?" He rubbed at his chin and frowned.

Alice chuckled heartily: "Of course not. Come here you sexy rocker."

She kissed him gently on the lips. River's response told her he could easily be persuaded to take things a whole lot further (what was it about grief and sex?) but now was definitely not the moment. She playfully pushed him away and took a much-needed swig of her tea. Her man might be a mixologist but he could also brew a better cuppa than anything purveyed at The Ritz. In other words: River Jackson was a keeper and had nothing to fret about.

"Now where was I?" she said, running a hand through her unruly curls.

"At the okaaaaaay bit."

"Ah, yes. Hmm. Well, the thing is." Alice took a giant inhalation of air before gabbling her current thoughts about leaving Cornwall out in the open – omitting the angel card reading and Sheba bits. She covered her face with her hands, afraid to peep out for fear of catching the despair creeping over River's face.

The last thing she expected to see was a smile so genuine that it had soon shapeshifted into roaring laughter.

"Riv?"

"Oh my God! This is the best news, Alice!"

"It *is?*"

"Totally!"

"Let's move back to Glastonbury. Let's do it before Christmas."

"Well, I want to get back soon, but there's the slight matter of the horses and the stables… of your erm… bar?"

"There's got to be a solution. We'll work around it."

"You think?"

"*I know.*"

Alice settled into the crook of River's neck, intermittently sipping her tea and sniffing. He handed her a tissue. For a former rocker he was so flipping practical. What a rollercoaster of emotions they'd been through in mere minutes, though. She couldn't deny how good it felt to remove the mantle of distress she'd been wearing all these weeks – even if that was now replaced with sorrow.

She would miss Sheba so much, despite the fact they'd barely seen her since the move.

Sheba had given them a safe haven at the time in their lives when they'd needed it most, taking Alice and River under her wing and setting them up with the very best static caravan on her campsite so they could cocoon themselves from a hideous onslaught of media intrusion when they'd first quit musical life and moved back to Glastonbury – not to mention the unwelcome pursuit of their band manager/the guy who turned out to be River's long-lost dad.

In death, it seemed, Sheba still had the uncanny knack of bringing the two of them closer together… until they were most definitely singing from the same sheet – even if this one was made of cotton and studded with a pale blue star design, as opposed to lines of musical notes.

Alice had no doubt that Sheba would currently be surrounded by all of the angels from her cards.

"This isn't right," Alice announced, snapping River out of his watery-eyed trance, no doubt reminiscing about the fun times they'd shared with his aunt.

"What? Please don't tell me you've changed your mind already! I promise we'll find a way."

"Silly." Alice patted his knee as if to reassure him that Glastonbury was still very much on the proverbial cards. "I'm referring to celebrating such a momentous and exciting decision so tamely. We need to mark it with something stronger. I insist. In spite of what you said earlier about Sheba's inclination for a brew, only a cocktail will do."

"All right then. Let me rustle something up," River was easily persuaded.

They might not have many customers but there was a certain, undeniable beauty in living above a swanky but unappreciated Cornish cocktail bar.

CHAPTER FIVE
River

WELL, THANK BLEEP for that. No, not Aunt Sheba's passing. River definitely wasn't chuffed about the loss of his favourite aunt. In fact, he couldn't bear to think about how much he would miss such a sage and reliable constant in his life. Or how his mum would cope without her. Instead he was just relieved he didn't have to mention the landlord's letter. Which wasn't such a hurdle anymore, after his girlfriend's surprising and happy revelation, true – but it would still be infinitely easier to let Alice think this upcoming move had been her decision. As soon as she'd set her sights on a midnight drink and he'd fixed them a pair of cranberry and rum warmers, her curiosity as to what River had been about to say had evaporated like a liquid nitrogen cocktail into the ether anyway.

Alice had already started making enquiries with her equine friends as to possible contenders to take her horses, and several of them were, ahem, champing at the bit. The corniest of puns but it was true. Whilst River and Alice wanted to view the return to their Glastonbury roots as a permanent thing, there was still that lingering possibility that they might retrace their steps, only to decide once more that the grass was greener in another of England's fair counties. It had happened in their early twenties, and it had happened all over again only a couple of years ago. Yes, they were both fed up with feeling like yo-yos, but working out where they fitted in had turned out to be not such a small matter.

In other words, River was petrified as to how Lee and Jonie would react. No way would he be taking the cocktail bar off them. This also meant he couldn't possibly set up a spin-off drinking den of his own. His friends had worked their backsides off to keep business booming, and the town was too small for competition.

It was a dilemma and a half and he was tempted to pour himself one of his beloved Frisky Bisons, but the habit was starting to inch its way into his daily routine and it had to stop. Besides, what the thick, luscious layer of snow outside truly called for was a hot chocolate. The most decadent one he could construct himself, at that.

He pottered about in the upstairs kitchen pulling bits and pieces off the shelves and out of the drawers of his well-stocked pantry. River was meticulous for keeping a clean and organised culinary ship – just as he was with his open-plan bar-stroke-kitchen downstairs. Heating creamy Jersey milk in a copper pan, adding the richest and darkest of 80% cocoa chocolate, a little sugar, blood orange zest, and a dash of Grand Marnier, he'd soon fixed himself one hell of a hot chocolate. He took it to the cushioned window seat to savour it fully, admiring the fluffy, cotton wool flakes of snow that were adding to what already looked like the icing on a Christmas cake in his small back garden.

Whilst the moment was utter bliss, akin to meditation by

virtue of the way the combination of chocolate and snow seemed to block all external thoughts from his head, there was something profound about it too. If only he could bottle the taste sensation hitting his tongue, flooding his veins and filling his belly, River couldn't help thinking he could make a lot of people very happy.

The door opened and Alice jolted him out of his daydream. She was clutching a box of gingerbread in her hands. It was only River's favourite Christmas treat!

"I know it's a bit early for festive food, but Rio and Justin had a kit leftover from the Saturday class they did with the kids up at the town hall, and they thought we might like it."

River's heart nipped. Aside from Jimmy, who was actually, when the chips were down, impossible not to love, it was Rio and Justin he'd miss the most when they packed their bags and left Pasty. The couple had swiftly turned into not only his most loyal customers but his and Alice's friends. They were constantly bringing them the most thoughtful surprises. They must have intuitively known River was a gingerbread fiend as he couldn't recall any of them previously serving up ginger-infused desserts at either couple's dinner-for-four invites. Rio and Justin had definitely done the most hosting in that department. Rio's roast dinners were epic and Justin was a pro with all things pudding. The guys made the perfect pair. Oh, and they put on inspirational and fun-themed drama and craft workshops for children at Pasty's town hall, when they weren't being commissioned by the BBC to write a new primetime TV drama.

"No time like the present," said River, shapeshifting into a child himself, excitedly bounding over to Alice and opening the box to start building himself a gingerbread mansion. Okay, shack. The imagery on the box was not quite in keeping with the flimsy panels and minimalist decoration kit inside. Luckily, there was another drawer in River's kitchen island that would take care of that. Soon he was pulling out tubes of edible silver spheres, mini candy stars, M&Ms, hundreds and thousands sugar sprinkles, a rainbow of food colouring, chocolate-covered mini pretzels and peppermints.

Alice giggled. "You never need much encouragement to get into the spirit of the season! Although, I suppose that's not such a chore today given the weather conditions outside." She moved over to the window seat, to admire the winter wonderland she had already spent the morning embracing. On the way she picked up his half-full hot chocolate mug and inhaled deeply. Her eyes lit up.

"Go on, try it," said River.

Alice took a cautious sip. Now a megawatt smile accompanied the dancing eyes.

"That is *inspired*, Mr. Jackson. Heaven in a mug."

A chocolate moustache coated her upper lip, but River thought it was too cute to point out. Alice would go nuts when she looked in the mirror later. He chewed back a grin. Now that she'd seen to the horses, he'd have his girl all to himself. Well, except when he went downstairs to open up for the evening. He'd already given up on running an afternoon bar, apart from on Saturdays. Mainly because this approaching one would see them host the town's monthly book club get-together.

River's suppressed grin became an actual grimace when he acknowledged how much things had changed in that regard, how desperate for business he'd become. Back in Glastonbury he'd had the audacity (and what he considered the class; a mixologist's respect for the cocktails) to limit his clientele – the book club included – to just two drinks of an afternoon or evening. How they'd complained! That little protocol had sailed straight out the window and into the Atlantic ocean when it came to this place. It was all he could do to get punters through the door, let alone coax them to stay for more than one drink.

Alice brought him back to the present again. As had become habit on a bitterly cold day, the kettle in this place was constantly in action. Now she deposited a steaming hot mug of tea before him. While he'd been musing, River had whipped up a batch of his own royal icing (not trusting the solid-as-a-brick looking stuff in the box). He'd separated it out into small bowls, and dotted each batch with a different colour to inject some much-needed theatrics into the beautification of his little Hansel and Gretel hut.

The irony, when he loathed Christmas decorations in general. But gingerbread houses were the exception to the decoration rule. They were meant to be magical, toothsome and exquisite. Like little fairy-tales. They had something of the intricacy and attention to detail of brightly-coloured, hand-crafted cuckoo clocks. They were as indulgent as rich cheese fondue and glossy, luxurious Swiss chocolate – taking River back to Avalonia's picturesque tours to the many cities located in and around the Alps.

Tinsel was tawdry and garish. Brash like a cheap pub full of fruit machines and dart boards. It reminded him of his so-called father – and former band manager, Lennie – and his penchant for tacky bling medallions.

Yes, gingerbread *and cocoa* were different.

And, like Rio and Justin, they came together to create something rather splendid. Now River was itching to do something with both ingredients in the bar. Sure, gingerbread biscuits could hardly be infused with alcohol. That would taste vile with anything but Bourbon! But paired up with a subtly alcoholic hot cocoa… and now you were talking.

What was the point, though? All his efforts to concoct a Christmas-themed menu would end up in ice-blue flames like the halo around a lit figgy pudding. He couldn't expect Rio and Justin to keep him in business. Try as he might, he couldn't convince Jimmy to trade his customary Tom Collins for a Test Pilot. What hope did he have of hooking him on hot buttered rum-infused cocoa?

"River?" a familiar voice cut through yet another of his daydreams. Alice, tea towel over one shoulder, mobile phone in hand (and cute chocolate smudge still firmly in place above her sweet lips), was gesticulating wildly. "I know it's been a strange few days but I do worry about you sometimes! It's your mum." She cocked her head toward the phone in her hand. "You must have switched your mobile off again, she's ringing on mine. It's sure to be about the funeral. Shall I take it?" She nodded her head jauntily again – this time at the icing-encrusted and food dye-stained state of River's hands.

"Would you? That would be ace. Thanks honey."

River snapped himself out of his festive foodie trance once and for all. He scrubbed his hands at the sink while Alice chatted to his mum. By the time he'd cleaned himself up, though, the call was over.

"She's too busy arranging everything to talk to you so she quickly left me the details. The funeral will take place on Monday afternoon at two-thirty in St. John's Church. No black. No flowers. Sheba's wish was that donations be made to Greenpeace."

"Monday? That's a bit soon!"

"That's what I thought," Alice agreed. "I suppose the undertakers are keen to get things going at this time of year... what with the holidays approaching."

"I guess we need to get packing, then."

RIVER AND ALICE took the last remaining seats in the church. Right at the back. Both of them felt terrible for not making the service in time to comfort his mum with a hug. But they had got there. That was the main thing. Never again would River make the mistake of making a Monday morning departure in partly slushy, partly black ice-coated conditions on the roads leading to the motorway from the tail end of Cornwall. It was a wonder they weren't at their own funerals.

Last time River and Alice had been here, it had been for a merrier occasion; Lee and Jonie's wedding – though sadly they had been seated apart as it was during their tumultuous will-they-won't-they-get-it-on phase.

Still, it was important to find the pockets of joy today, to celebrate Sheba's life. Looking around and taking in the vibrantly-dressed sea of people who had turned up to pay their respects, it was clear that River's aunt had been overwhelmingly adored by the townsfolk and wider community. This snapshot in time was as beautiful as it was melancholy.

Once the service was over, and River and Alice had been sufficiently mobbed and mauled by well-meaning friends, his mum flung herself at them both, holding onto them for dear life. Heather stayed that way in St. John's small churchyard, and she stayed that way as close family members followed the hearse in a solemn limousine procession up to Wells Road, where Sheba would be laid to rest.

"She's been bottling this up for days," said Terry, Heather's relatively new husband, once everyone had been deposited back onto the high street after the emotional burial. "Sorry, River, I should have called you too. It all happened so unexpectedly. Your mum took most of the arrangements on herself, thanks to that eejit Tony leaving Sheba in the lurch last year."

Heck, River had forgotten about him. They'd called him 'Uncle Tony' on welcoming him into the fold. He had never been in the picture much anyway, He and Sheba had got together later in life, but his long haul lorry-driving job had either taken him to the other side of Europe for weeks on end… or he'd be in Sheba's bungalow on her caravan site sleeping, eating, and binge watching blasts from the past on UK Gold. River could count the number of times he'd encountered the guy on one hand. Then Uncle Tony had met a new woman in Bulgaria and never returned. "I tried to help," Terry continued. "But Heather wanted to take the reins. You know how fiercely independent your mum can be."

"Come on, Mum, let me straighten you out and look at you properly," said River, trying, in vain, to unpeel Heather, dressed in canary yellow, from his blue vintage Dolce and

Gabbana suit at last.

Reluctantly, Heather relaxed her frame and allowed her son – and Alice – to take in her frail form fully. River tried not to gulp at the weight she had lost... or the blinding yellow shimmer of her dress. Heaven only knew which Glastonbury atelier had bewitched her into purchasing the thing.

"Well, aside from the panda eyes, you're still looking as youthful as ever," he lied.

At least she would have been, if she'd been eating. His mum was svelte at the best of times. What the heck was going on? He made a mental note to take Terry aside at the wake. It was a given she wouldn't have eaten much in the past week since the terrible shock, but she must have been skin and bones for some time before that. Maybe Terry hadn't noticed, since winning his exciting contract with a small-time DIY television programme. His growing painting and decorating company now renovated local stately homes and it was clear that it required him to work all the hours – even if the influx of money was welcome.

River and Alice propped up either side of Heather and made haste for the wake at the bottom of the high street, with Terry just behind them chatting with his son Blake and his new girlfriend, Ali (hopefully a permanent fixture, now he'd finally stopped making eyes at Alice).

River had met Ali before – on another TV show, of all places, when he'd been invited to put in a one-off cameo appearance along with Alice – but he sensed that if she did become family and his step-brother married, the two-women-with-similar-names-thing could get very complicated. Especially after a cocktail or two. Which was exactly where they were headed now. River took a deep breath. He felt Alice's hand loop its way around his mum's tiny frame with a reassuring squeeze.

This would be the first time either of them had returned to the Cocktail Bar since he'd left it in Lee and Jonie's capable hands. He didn't want to make anybody paranoid about his first impressions of the not-so-new ownership, particularly as he had practically wrapped the bar up and gifted it to Lee and Jonie with a big red bow on top, but he knew he wouldn't be able to trust his emotions the moment he stepped over that threshold and back into his former business. Despite Sheba's preference for a cup of tea, she'd apparently insisted that her wake be held there – she had recently updated her funeral arrangements. It seemed a bit morbid, and made one wonder if she hadn't foreseen the event with her cards. Instead River chose to believe that perhaps, even though he no longer owned the bar, she'd been proud of her nephew's achievement (having no children of her own) and she'd wanted to celebrate that on the day that everyone had come together to celebrate her life. Well, the sentiment was nice anyway.

He took another mammoth breath of air and pushed open the door. Heather, once again, sandwiched between himself and Alice.

Without further ado, River wove the three of them through the throng to the front of the bar, depositing Heather on a stool, and quickly catching Jonie's attention so he could put in an order.

"River!" Jonie looked genuinely delighted to see him, and the ever-curly, red-headed Lee waved frantically in the distance, signalling he'd be over to catch up just as soon as things quietened down. It helped put River at ease immediately and he felt his shoulders relax.

"Hey, Jonie! You and the bar are looking amazing... all right, *and the guy behind it,* I suppose."

"Thank you. And back at you all. I'm only sorry to see you here in such upsetting circumstances. What can I get you? You lot look parched."

"Would the Ginger Rabbit still happen to be on the menu?" River chanced.

"Well, of course. I can't say we sell as many of them since you left town, but your mum does still pop in with Terry from time to time."

Heather smiled through glassy eyes and put her hands in a praying motion to thank Jonie.

"What about you two?" She looked from River to Alice.

"I'll have a Coco Loco, for old times' sake." Alice smiled.

It had been her favourite tipple when the bar had belonged to River. He'd never thought to include it in his Cornish menu, preferring the two establishments to have their own completely unique identities – from the décor right through to the drinks on offer. Maybe that had been his mistake.

"I would say I'd have a Frisky Bi... but, you know what, I'm after something chocolate-infused. Something wintery and *hygge*. I don't suppose you happen to have anything?"

River hadn't even looked at the menu and couldn't assume that all of his creations would remain there untouched.

"I'll knock up a chocolate Martini. Will that do you?"

"Perfect." He grinned.

And it was. For some reason, this whole chocolate-alcohol-gingerbread malarkey was as firmly stuck in his brain as royal icing. Even if he had long since devoured his Hansel and Gretel shack.

The crowd at the bar thinned out as people found themselves tables and comfier chairs, but River and co were keen to stay close to the action. It was great to catch up on snippets of gossip and trade-talk with Lee, between him taking orders. River found it strangely invigorating. Lee's zest for cocktails, life, and the locals was something else.

Alice was in her element, too. Sometimes River had worried that so much time with the horses and stable crew would made her forget how to interact in other settings – especially since his own bar was rarely buzzing. But he needn't have given it a thought. She was back in her element chatting away to Hayley, Glastonbury's favourite taxi driver, and then Zara, owner of the former organic bakery-turned-chocolate shop next door.

"Last orders," cried Jonie, with the ring of a bell.

River felt a stab of envy. He didn't need to use any musical instruments in his Cornish concern. But he could just imagine Jimmy insisting the spoons would be an excellent last orders medley, and found himself mentally eye-rolling the notion.

"I'm going to take your mother home now," said Terry. "She's a bit squiffy so I think it's best."

"Right, erm, listen, Terry." River wasn't sure how to come out with his worries without sounding like the quintessential interfering stepson. "Will you do me a favour and make sure you cook Mum up something substantial, to soak up the alcohol?"

"Of course, pal."

"And will you do me another favour, and make sure you cook Mum something daily?"

"What do you mean?"

"You might not see it, but I do. She's lost a heck of a lot of weight, Tel."

"You reckon?"

"I know." River pulled his most startled expression in a bid to convince Terry. "Sometimes it's hard to see what's going on when it's right under your nose. But even her cheeks are hollow. That yellow number she's in today looks more like a tent. Far be it from me to stick my oar into your affairs, but do you guys ever sit down and dine together… or are your work commitments eating into dinnertime? Excuse the pun."

Terry frowned, biting on his lip.

"You're right, son. Come to think of it, your mother always puts something back for me, insisting it's a replica of what she's made for herself. Now you mention it, well, I'm doubting that's been the case. I should have twigged sooner. But I'll have words as soon as she's sobered up. Don't you fret."

"Thanks Terry, that would be…"

"Everything okay here?" Heather appeared with a sultry purr. Eyes bright like jewels. See, this is why he'd capped the cocktails at two per customer when he was running the place. How many blimming GRs had Heather knocked back this afternoon?

"Sweet as pie," said Terry, proffering River a conspiratorial wink.

"That's what I like to hear. My two favourite men in the

world are getting on."

"Talking about getting on, Mum," said River. "It's probably best if you make tracks now and let Terry fix you up with dinner. The organic canapes were a lovely touch, but I think the volume needed to feed this lot," he gestured at the rapidly diminishing crowd, "was slightly underestimated."

"That's my fault," Heather admitted. "I budgeted for a couple of nibbles per head but I'd no idea that this many people would pack the bar."

"Aunt Sheba was very popular."

"That she was," said Terry. "And yes. Never fear. Speaking of the aforementioned pie, I'm going to dust down my trusty recipe book and whip up a hearty one of those tonight." River pretended he didn't clock his mum's anguish at that announcement. "River, you and Alice are more than welcome to join us. There's plenty to go around. Blake and Ali won't be there, by the way. Not that you and my formerly grumpy idiot of a boy haven't patched things up, but on a day like today, I sense a more intimate family supper would work best." He patted River matey-style on the back.

River breathed an invisible sigh of relief. He and Blake were civil nowadays, for sure. But there was only so much one could expect, given the fact Blake had smashed up this very bar in a torrent of fury a few years ago upon learning River'd had the audacity to swan back into town and turn Terry's former drinking den and skittle alley into *'a cocktail bar that nobody had ever asked for'*.

Yes, the Cocktail Bar used to be the most British of public houses, Stella Artois and Strongbow its masterpieces.

"Normally we would love to," said River. "You know

that." He hoped he sounded reassuring but the only intimacy he wanted tonight was with his girlfriend. "It's just that I've booked us a table at Cagnola's this evening. We'll check in at the hotel and then meander down there for dinner. Alice is stoked. It's her favourite pizzeria in the world. Pasty doesn't really have much in the way of pizzas."

"Figures." Terry snickered.

"We'll catch up in the morning before we head back, yeah?" River looked pointedly at his wobbly mum, fighting with the instinct to shake his head in reprimand. He needed to go easy on her. Her sister had passed away, after all. But it was a fine line between refraining from preaching and asking the necessary questions to get to the bottom of her apparent extreme dieting. He certainly hadn't seen Heather snaffle any of the hoisin and sesame tofu bites circulating the room, and he doubted she'd eaten breakfast.

"Come on then, love." Terry opened Heather's fawn coat out ready to bundle her up in it – and give everyone a welcome reprieve from the bright yellow – but she tsked and hooked her arm through River's, taking him aside to whisper in his ear.

"Obviously the will is yet to be read, and all of that side of things will take time. But Sheba has left you a note. We found it on her bureau, next to her angel cards. We had to call into the campsite office with one of her members of staff, who was concerned that she seemed to have an increasing number of personal belongings cluttering up the desk."

Blimey, the campsite. River hadn't given a thought as to what would become of his aunt's business, quiet though it must have been at this time of year, because few fancied camping in nigh on Arctic conditions. He felt something being pressed insistently into his hand. His mum curled his fingers over the edges of the paper, willing him to open the note a little later, away from prying eyes. So he stuffed yet another envelope deep into his pocket and tried to keep the curiosity at bay until he and Alice were in the hotel room.

Alice's own curiosity was piqued then. She caught River's eye, made her excuses and broke away from Zara to cross the bar and say goodbye to Heather.

"What was that all about?" she asked once Heather and Terry had left.

"You tell me. Sheba left me a note, apparently."

Did River imagine it, or did Alice blanche at his remark?

"Wh… how…?" Alice began blinking most rapidly. "She died of a sudden stroke, Riv."

"Tell me about it. It's like she somehow knew it was going to happen. Why else would she leave me this?" He tapped at his pocket. "And why else would it be sitting next to her cards?"

"No, no, no. The two things can't be related." Alice looked alarmed. "Angel cards wouldn't reveal those kinds of things. Not that I know much about them. Tarot cards, yes. But Sheba didn't do those, did she?"

"Who knows. All I do know is my aunt's sixth sense was stronger than absinthe."

Alice's eyes became saucers now and he swore he detected a shudder.

"And that's time," shouted Lee, ringing the bell.

Gradually everyone started to weave their way out of the bar and Alice started to look more like her usual self. River couldn't help but notice Jonie whispering into the ears of a very select few people around them. Until she approached him and Alice.

"We wouldn't normally do this, though it isn't breaking any trading rules, except our own. We're pulling the blinds down and having a wee lock-in. Just a handful of us. We'd love you to join us... unless you have other plans?"

River was torn. He so wanted to read the mysterious note and feast on one of Cagnola's trademark *calzones,* followed by a chunk of *tiramisu.* Like, yesterday. So much he could feel his aunt's words burning a hole in his pocket. But catching up properly with good friends was important too. Especially as he needed to start slotting plans into place and putting feelers out.

"We're cool with that for an hour or so," Alice answered on his behalf. "Zara, come join us!"

River and Alice took the window seat, not that anybody could now see out of it, anyway. River contributed to the conversation where he could, as Alice and Zara picked up from where they'd left off when his mum had said her farewells, but mostly he was marooned in another of his epic trances. When he did zone in to the small talk, it was to hear, to his astonishment, that the glossy, chestnut-braided and mega-fringed Zara was shutting up shop.

"I've tried to carve out my own niche for years." Zara blew her sultry bangs out of her eyes and sipped on her cocktail. River noted she still had a thing for B52s. "But I had no choice but to reinvent myself and go on a chocolate-making course, turning my back on the cakes and the bread," she said, the exasperation ringing out loud and clear in every word. "It worked for a while when I made the change last winter. I guess it was the novelty element, the seasonal thing. I mean, I *love* chocolate, don't get me wrong. But actually, baking is my real passion. There are a surprising number of organic and allergy-free bakeries dotted about town now, though. I couldn't put myself out there again only to fail." Zara sighed and her sad, molten chocolate eyes conveyed how the situation had tired her out. "And also my landlady has hiked up the rent by a whopping fifteen percent." River refrained from making a loud tut. What was it with people renting out business premises? "And a string of beyond shitty relationships that I can't seem to stop bumping into." Oh gawd, yes. How could River forget? Zara and Blake had been an item the last time he'd been in this bar! "I have to draw the line somewhere, so it's time for me to set off for pastures new. It's just a shame I don't know quite where those pastures are."

"Whatever you do, don't go to Cornwall," said River – unhelpfully, going by the pointed look Alice gave him.

"Zara can go wherever she likes," Alice corrected him. "The sky's the limit and the world's her oyster. Cornwall is a great place to live and to work, actually."

Wait, what? Alice better not be going back on their plans...

"So, what are you going to do between now and, when? January the 5th, did you say?" Alice continued.

"I honestly don't know, but I'll have to think of something now I've handed in my notice," Zara replied with the most downcast look on her face, chin slumping on her hand. "I'll be at a bit of a loose end in December, I guess. I don't intend to keep shop hours so I'll probably set myself up online via Facebook and become a bespoke Christmas ordering service. Not that there's exactly a shortage of places offering up gluten-free, lactose-free and dairy-free chocolate in the vicinity. Now I know how all the crystal and incense shops feel every time a new one sets up. The rivalry here has become savage." She knocked back the rest of her short drink. "It makes me so sad. I mean, I was one of the first to do what I'm doing, but somehow my formula hasn't worked as well as other bakery owners... who have also started their own lines of chocolates, by the way. Or maybe it's just that I have the high street's most stingy landlady and I need to charge slightly more to keep the business afloat? Either way, my work here is apparently done."

This was too depressing. On top of such a sorrowful day, too.

River extricated himself as politely as he could to snap up the local paper on the free table to the right. He wished he had some business advice for Zara but his head was all over the place. He couldn't even sort his own life out. At least Alice was giving the woman a shoulder to cry on.

Lee approached him on cue with a Frisky Bison.

"How are things, mate?"

"You don't want to know." River wasn't going to bullshit him. "I'd rather hear about the obvious success you're making of this place. Seriously, dude, I'm made up for you and Jonie. I've never seen so much passion and enthusiasm turn into a vision that consistently delivers. It's beyond impressive. You're an inspiration."

"Hey, cut yourself some slack, Jackson. If it wasn't for you, none of this would have come to pass and you know it.

We're truly grateful. But we'd also understand if you ever wanted this place back. It's not like we haven't got a couple of million tucked away in the bank. We could move to Wells or Street, set up another bar in no time. Easily done."

It was true. Lee had been one of the lucky three who'd stumbled across the Magical Mañana in the menu, his life becoming unrecognisable overnight. He'd proposed to Jonie and she'd shouted an overjoyed YES. Oh, and he'd won the jackpot in the lottery. Lee and Jonie's joint prowess also meant it would be a doddle to replicate their success in a neighbouring town.

It was true, but it didn't make it right. "Never!" River finally replied after taking a refreshing gulp of his drink. "But you can expect to see me here a little more often as of approximately next month… Alice and I are fed up with Cornwall. We're moving back."

"*Maaaaate!*"

Lee was up on his feet, beaming from ear to ear, dancing a merry jig and pulling River into a hug in no time. His skills in that department had upped their game too. Last time he'd attempted it, he'd ended up patting River liberally on the back after coming over all awkward, making River feel like a baby being coaxed to bring up wind.

"Lee, can you help me collect the rest of the empties?" Jonie chirruped from across the bar.

Instinctively, River stood to lend a hand, too.

"No way. You're to sit right there and get that beauty down you." Lee did something magician-like with his hand, gesturing at the cocktail glass. "I'll be back. And then you can tell me all about your plans."

Well, that wouldn't take long. River didn't have any. Damn. Lee's Frisky Bison was almost on a par with his own – which wasn't being egotistical, River had made considerably more of them, that was all. He relished the apple pie-ness of his tipple, the sharp tang making his taste buds come to life. And yet... what he'd have done for another of Jonie's chocolate Martinis. It was enough to make him fear he'd turned into a full-blown chocoholic. Except the really weird thing was that he'd taken several slurps of his mum's Ginger Rabbit when she wasn't looking, as well. Of course he'd tried said cocktail before. Everything on his former menu was vetted (pun not intended – but apt in this case) by River. Ginger in a drink had never been his bag, though. Until this afternoon, when it suddenly, totally, completely and utterly had been.

Here we go again, he thought. Chocolate and ginger on the brain! Was this some kind of epiphany prior to his taste buds changing? At least he assumed they'd change at forty. He recalled how his mum had woken up on her fortieth birthday and started devouring olives, despite having loathed them from the ages of two through to thirty-nine because they reminded her of beetles.

River flipped open the local paper as he continued to sip. He wondered what he could say in answer to Lee's question. '*Bumbling around*' somehow didn't seem like a fulfilling enough reply. Although, judging by Lee's initial reaction, River was probably making far bigger a deal out of his and Alice's decision than was necessary. His friend seemed genuinely thrilled at his news. Surely, no matter what he decided to do – or not do – he'd be happy and make them feel welcome.

The gazette talked about this and that: profits were up at the retail outlet, the weekly Christmas market had begun in earnest, a group of meddlesome tourists had been drinking and littering Glastonbury Tor, pavements needed resurfacing. Same old, same old.

He turned the page again and his eyes settled on a rather disturbing double spread. Oh...

The reporter had written a special feature on the closure of local village pubs. Woah. This was an absolute disaster. How could it even come to pass? Some of these establishments were centuries old. River guessed a mixture of increased brewery prices and outsiders from the cities were pricing villagers out of their heritage. He winced at the latter. Isn't that exactly what he and Alice had done in Pasty?

On the other hand, he couldn't deny that he suddenly felt a bit better about his own rubbish situation. For all of five minutes, anyway.

He browsed on. Birthdays/deaths/weddings, classified ads, football news. He wondered... if he surreptitiously held the paper at a certain angle, could he...? River delved into his pocket with one hand while keeping the paper steady with the other. He quickly pulled out the letter, opening the envelope as best he could. Was anyone watching?

Lee was suitably distracted with his glass collections, Alice was engrossed in conversation with Zara. He knew his mum had told him to wait until he got back to the hotel but (no offence Lee and Jonie) this was the lamest lock-in River had ever experienced. Chiefly because there were only eight people here, including the couple behind the bar.

He unfolded the paper. Goodness. It was written in calligraphy (bless his aunt) and deserving of a much more serene reading place. The town's atmospheric Chalice Well, the Abbey, and the Tor all immediately springing to mind.

'Dearest River, There will be significantly more coming your way when the will is read,' was Sheba's opening. River swallowed hard. *'But between now and then, I'm entrusting you with the ownership of my beloved Volkswagen camper van. She may be ancient but she was my pride and joy, and, as you know, darling nephew, I rarely got time to take her out for a spin. Promise me that will change now she's yours. Enjoy her. But let others enjoy her too. Her renovations were a labour of love that never got their moment in the spotlight. It's time to take her out into the community and fulfil that potential. I'll leave it to your wild imagination to work out exactly how. Atma Namaste, your loving aunt Sheba.'*

River brought the Frisky Bison to his lips. With a remarkably steady hand he downed the remnants in one swift go.

CHAPTER SIX
Alice

ALICE HAD PUT in a hard morning's work at the stables. The grooming and tack-cleaning had been endless, but luckily the snow had now stopped. In fact, for mid-November, the temperatures were positively balmy. Later she'd be treating herself to a hack in the fields.

Time alone with her six horses (Cotton Candy, Lickety Split, Blossom, Minty, Applejack and Lemon Drop – yes, she'd named them after the original *My Little Pony* gang) had also given her the opportunity to think about events earlier in the week. Whilst Sheba's funeral had been as sad as expected, the delight Alice had felt at being back in Glastonbury had brought good tears to her eyes. There was no mistaking it, the town was where she and River both belonged. But whenever she thought about her horses, predicting her immediate future felt like looking into a very murky crystal ball. She couldn't bear to be apart from them.

She decided to skip lunch with her stable hands. She felt guilty. They'd brought in huge flasks of homemade soup and rustic soda bread today. But it was important that she caught up with River and the latest developments in his Glastonbury rental search. So far nothing had come up and they could hardly impose themselves on Heather, or move all their clobber into a hotel room. She guessed winter, and the run-up to Christmas, was a crap time to be looking for half-decent property to let. Perhaps they could investigate long-term Airbnb possibilities. Now there was a thought. It put a spring in her step as she did a mental stocktake of the contents of the fridge, wondering what she could rustle up for lunch.

Alice turned her key in the back door, admiring the thyme bushes that somehow managed to thrive despite the earlier caking of snow. She de-shelled herself from her huge winter coat, hung it up, toed off her boots and braved the cold floor of the hallway. She knew River wouldn't be in the bar yet so she quietly climbed the stairs in case he was catching forty winks. Last night had been a surprisingly late one for cocktails. Rio and Justin had somehow managed to gather together an impressive group of friends who were *en route* to a festive cookery course further south and had decided to stay in Pasty for the evening. Its solitary hotel must have been as ecstatic as River at the prospect of all that unexpected trade.

As she reached the creakiest step near the top of the staircase, she stopped. She could hear River talking on the phone. Maybe it was a letting agent? She didn't want to burst in and intrude on his train of thought. There was nothing worse when you were trying to talk business. She carefully avoided the noisy step and camped outside the door. It was slightly ajar and she found she had the perfect listening post.

"Come on! Can't you give me a little longer? Be fair, Mr Twiggs. I'm not going to resort to saying, do you know who I am… but do you know who I…"

Mr Twiggs?

That was their stinking-rich landlord. What the hell was going on? Alice tried to hold her breath so she could hear River's words more clearly.

"I appreciate that, but I didn't think you were serious."

River was pacing the wooden floorboards.

"Yes, I know it was an official written notice, but you're not just making us homeless as of November the 30th – I run a business from this property too, you know!"

Alice's heart thudded. River was shouting now. She needed to get some fresh air and fully digest what she'd just heard. And yet it was no use running away. River had to be confronted. Immediately. How dare he keep all of this from her! She knew he'd had a lot on his plate and the loss of his aunt must have shaken him up more than she'd realised, but they were a team. In it together. If she couldn't trust him…

Dammit. Who should fly into her head, the moment she had that thought, but Georgina bloody Hopkins? Alice had assumed she'd packed her up in a suitcase in the recesses of her mind (aptly since the bitch had moved to Spain), locked it, and thrown away the key. She was the woman who had claimed she was pregnant with River's baby. Was this the way it was going to be, every time he kept even the smallest of secrets from her?

Being effectively chucked out of their accommodation was *not* small, though. The cheek of him. It was enough to propel Alice through the door. She stood fiercely in the entrance so her boyfriend had no escape, and no choice but to face her head on as she waited, foot tapping, hands welded to hips.

CHAPTER SEVEN
River

THE DOORBELL RANG just as River was on the top rung of the stepladder, reaching for the row of antique cocktail shakers. Thankfully, he'd already stashed away the secret bottle of elixir that had never graced the Magical Mañana, triple-wrapping it in bubble wrap. Dropping that would have been the mother of all disasters, not that he knew quite what he'd do with the bottle when he moved on from Pasty. Heart in his mouth, River cradled the copper and steel collection to his chest and reversed down the rickety steps, cursing himself for choosing that very moment to pack the shakers away in the removals box. A sombre act at the best of times, but all the more so when you didn't know quite *where* you were moving to.

It might be Alice. He knew this was highly unlikely since she still had a set of keys but this was no time for second-guessing. Perhaps that's how formal their relationship had become. Reduced to a tinny doorbell chime.

His heart sank back into place – and then further still. He could see from the silhouette at the window that it was Jimmy.

"I'm not open. Come back later."

"This is a social call and I've trekked half a bleddy mile to make it. Let me in, Jackson!"

River sighed. He gently placed the cocktail shakers on the bar top and unlocked the front door to what would soon be his former premises. Another former premises.

"Here." Jimmy thrust a casserole dish at him. "I shouldn't give a monkey's, old fool that I am. This is my Cornish fish stew special."

"Oh, right. Thanks. That's... it's totally unexpected." And Jimmy transporting it here on foot in the current conditions was totally dangerous. After a brief hiatus from the cold snap, the county had iced over again. Jimmy's cotton wool hair sported an extra dusting of white from the light but fresh snowfall, and his cheeks were so red they could rival any Santa on a Christmas card. "Come in. It's freezing out there. And yes, you're quite right, you shouldn't care. The way I speak to you most afternoons is bang out of order. Beyond rude. If it wasn't for you and a handful of others…"

Now River's words had frozen in the air.

"You're right about that much, lad. But you're the kind-hearted soul of an idiot. I can see beneath the facade. That's why I made you this."

River proffered a small smile of gratitude. "How did you know about my current predicament, anyway?"

"Bit of a double whammy, isn't it?" Jimmy stated, summing up the pitiful extent of things.

Now River gritted his teeth. He shouldn't give a monkey's himself about the local gossip mongers but something told him the whole of Pasty had now been filled in – and not with beef, potato, swede and onion, but with the state of his relationship, abode and career.

"You could say that." River sighed deeply. "Fancy a mulled wine?"

"Get on then," said Jimmy. "I'm more of a Tom Collins man, truth be told."

"Really? I can't say I'd noticed."

Jimmy chuckled, removing his spoons from his pocket. It was lucky he refrained from playing the things, because River couldn't really bite the hand that was currently feeding him. Not that he couldn't knock himself up something substantial to eat. It would be beyond hypocritical of him, when he'd given Terry that telling-off about feeding his mum.

"So, what happened? You can't be doing much right to have your woman walk away and the landlord kick you out, all in the space of a week. I bumped into Justin yesterday and he was concerned."

"Cheers for the vote of confidence." River sighed again. "Justin's a good friend. Today it's you and your stew full of protein and vitamins. Yesterday Justin popped by with one of Rio's mountainous roast dinners."

"You're a lucky man. Just not so lucky with the ladies, it seems. Pour me the wine and spill," Jimmy instructed him as if he were River's grandfather, all ears for the woes of his precious descendent.

River fixed their drinks and suggested they take the comfy seats at Jimmy's usual table.

"I took the liberty of trying to protect my girlfriend and… it sort of backfired," River began in earnest.

Jimmy nodded, encouraging him to get the whole story off his chest.

"I know I should have been truthful with her. We'd decided to move back to Glastonbury in any case." Jimmy looked shocked and then hurt. For a moment, River thought Jimmy was going to go through the five stages of grief, so he semi-sugar coated the blow by adding, "Rio and Justin showed a keen interest in taking over here for a while. Both of them were after a career change and uncertain as to what. Looking after this place and putting their own spin on it would have been perfect as a stopgap. Of course, I would have driven down now and then to check everything was running smoothly until we were sure that the move would be permanent, until there were new tenants. Sadly, since the landlord started to apply the pressure, that's no longer an option. He's planning on turning the place into one of those giant antiques emporiums. He's gutting the cocktail bar and the living quarters upstairs, then he'll build into the garden too."

Jimmy's face fell again. "Bloody Twiggs!" His forehead creased, making him look antique himself. "That family'll be the death of Pasty. They've been ripping off Cornish folk since they were in nappies and now we'll have scores of the mega rich and the celebrities flocking here to furnish their posh homes."

River gulped. He pretty much belonged to that category himself. He fretted that his friend might have a funny turn. Now the rest of Jimmy's face was burning up, not just his cheeks, and it was all glowing a shade of mulled wine claret! Best to quickly share the rest of his tragic tale and try to persuade Jimmy it was all for the best.

"To cut a very long story a bit shorter than it needs to be,

I had an opportunity to show Alice the landlord's note a few weeks ago. But then my aunt died. Alice, simultaneously, had been itching to move back to Glastonbury. She brought it up first. Just as I was about to. Like, literally. All of which seemed to render Mr. Twiggs kicking us out of here as obsolete. At least I assumed we'd have time to do things of our own accord. I had the romantic notion of being back in Somerset by Christmas day."

River took a quick glug of his mulled wine, closing his eyes momentarily as if it might make the shambles of his life vanish into thin air. "We went back for the funeral, but then my aunt left me a note to say I've inherited her ancient relic of a Volkswagen camper van."

"Nice!" Jimmy interrupted.

"Yes and no. The wording of the note suggests Aunt Sheba wants me to turn a pumpkin into a carriage, and do something for the community with it." River was back to sighing. "I couldn't find the words to tell Alice what was in *this note* initially. Which probably sounds a bit *déjà vu*. The day of the funeral was a long one. There was lots to drink. We went out for dinner that night and still I couldn't find the right moment."

"Well, that's a bit silly. You're talking to me about it now without a hitch," said a mercifully calmer Jimmy.

"Yes, I know. I guess it was a lot to take in when I first read it. I was emotional. I needed to turn everything over in my mind."

"So, when did she find out?"

"Oh, she'd completely forgotten about my aunt's note. I guess all the drinking on the day of the funeral clouded her memory too. It was only when I pulled the landlord's note out of my jeans pocket, after she'd overheard me yelling at Twiggs on the phone… I'd erm… well, I'd made the dumb mistake of putting Aunt Sheba's note in my pocket with it."

"Heck. That would look as if you were keeping both things from her."

"I've totally messed up. It's reignited all sorts of trust issues between us about stuff that I thought was dead and buried. I'm not sure what to do. She read both notes in quick succession, asked me if I cared to reveal a third, fourth, or fifth note that had 'conveniently slipped my mind', packed a couple of bags and said she needed some space; she'd be back in a couple of days. That was four days ago."

"Give her time, River. She could have packed a suitcase, rather than a couple of bags. It sounds short term to me. Trust that it will all work out. And make sure you *never* keep anything from her again, no matter how small or insignificant it might seem to your good self." Jimmy took a tentative sip of his wine. "S'good, much better than I expected," he declared with a grin and a demi-toast that went unreciprocated. "Listen, you haven't robbed a bank or hopped into bed with another woman, lad. At least I hope not… Maybe she has her own issues to work through and wants to be sure about the move? Let's finish these drinks and I'll give you a hand with the packing."

RELUCTANTLY, RIVER CAUGHT the train to Taunton alone to pick up the VW, cursing inwardly at the burden. He really didn't need this complication in his life. That sounded ungrateful but he had a car (the infamous mustard bucket) and a pair of feet: he liked to keep his transport options simple. Despite a fleeting and fanciful idea about a leisurely trip around Europe the other day, he – and Alice, if they ever patched things up – had spent enough time clocking up the kilometres on the great roads of the world to last several lives.

Although it wasn't such a long train journey, it was full of stops and changes. With that in mind, and knowing it wouldn't be a patch on his last hot chocolate, River treated himself to a takeaway version of what was fast becoming his favourite drink. He sipped at it watching the landscape float by as the train sped from Cornwall into Devon and then up to Somerset, his home county. Finally it was his stop and he alighted at Taunton, ridiculously aware of the kids walking in front of him munching on a bag of gingerbread people. River wasn't too sure where he'd position himself on the vast spectrum of all things woke, although he tried every day to be a better human, but this culinary upgrade he completely agreed was well overdue. Why should it always be a male gingerbread biscuit getting its bits gobbled up?

Hayley, Glastonbury's taxi driver extraordinaire, was ready and waiting for him as he made his way outside the station. She raised a giant placard aloft and pointedly looked either side of her to check who else was reading it, completely ignoring her client who was walking straight ahead.

'*RIVER JACKSON!!! YES! It's REALLY him! The lead singer from the band, AVALONIA!*' it screamed.

Bloody hell. How many exclamation marks could you fit on a piece of card? And talk about a sudden swarm of bees.

This was exactly what River had been terrified of. In no time at all fellow travellers lunged at him left, right and centre with their outstretched mobile phones, desperate to get a snap of his beanie hat-covered head.

"Thanks, Hayley. Very thoughtful of you."

"Well, you've been away for a couple of years. I thought you might not recognise me so I'd best make a sign just in case."

"Erm, you saw me at my aunt Sheba's funeral a few days ago."

"So I did."

River wasn't having the wool (or the beanie hat) pulled over his eyes. Evidently, Hayley had wanted to do a spot of name dropping in the lobby of Taunton's station today. He gritted his teeth as she prised his case away from him, insisting on carrying it – despite the fact he could manage, despite the fact it had wheels. It was impossible to win when it came to Hayley.

They made polite conversation as she expertly navigated them out of Somerset's county town and *en route* to Glastonbury. "D'you really think that King Alfred geezer burned his cakes up there on the hill, as legend would have us believe?" she asked as they cut through the picturesque village of Burrowbridge and she pointed out the famous ruined church on the pear-green hillock to the right of them as if River were unaware of its existence. "Seems a bit far-fetched to me. What King would be cooking, for a start? Even in the olden days there were cooks to run around after the Haves."

But River's thoughts might just as well have been hidden in the bulrushes fringing the bumpy moors road that was gradually leading them to Glastonbury.

"Cat got your tongue?" Hayley pressed.

"Come again?"

"Most unlike you not to have said a word. I've virtually reeled off my life story with Bob since we passed Pizza Hut."

"I'm tired. That's all," River replied, although he was glad she and Bob were still an item. He was the TV producer who'd taken Terry and his team on for the budget DIY show that went about renovating posh manors and the like in the West Country. Something told River that if Hayley ever did split up with Bob, she'd insist Terry and his workforce did the same. In other words, it never paid to argue with her.

"Tis the people that make a place."

Now they'd moved on from a one-way chat about history to Rumi-style poetry. Give him strength.

"That's hardly original."

"Cut your losses, Riv." Hayley lifted a hand off the wheel, flicking her arm about as if she were in an opera. "So you ballsed up, moved where the sand might be blonder than Weston-super-Mare, but you and Alice, you're both miserable as sin and you can't even give a Screaming Orgasm away." She snorted.

"You know full well I don't sell those revolting things."

"I also know I'm right, though."

River knew it, too. But if only it were that simple. For the hundredth time, he berated himself for not showing Alice the letter from the outset. Either letter. No wonder she felt so unsettled. In many ways the move was a bigger deal for her. River was only attached to the bricks and mortar of a bar. Alice had her horses. Alice had *a lot* of horses.

"People go on holiday to the Seychelles, but it doesn't mean they could stick living there."

"I don't need a lecture, Hayley. I'm grieving, in case it'd escaped your notice. My aunt's just died."

"Grieving my arse." Hayley snubbed him. "Sheba had a good life. She wasn't old but she wasn't young. You only went to see her when it suited you. Don't make out you were Tequila and lime."

River suppressed the urge to sigh again. The world's most annoying taxi driver was spot on. And then he bollocked himself once more for thinking that way about his friend. Yeah, she wasn't the most conventional choice for someone who'd trodden his varied career path, but she was one of the most solid companions he had. No two ways about it. What you saw with Hayley was what you got. No pretence. No bullshit.

Eventually they reached his aunt Sheba's campsite. A member of staff wearing a burgundy 'Baa Caravan Park' fleece, complete with a giant motif of a sheep jumping over Glastonbury Tor *and a rainbow*, greeted River.

"Sorry, I did try to get hold of you but nobody was picking up," he said. River patted down his pocket and felt for his phone. He suspected he'd stupidly packed it in his case. "Heather, your mum," the campsite worker added that piece of unnecessary clarification for River. "Well, she thought the VW was here. I mean that figures, of course, but no. Sheba had it stationed up at the campsite in Wookey Hole."

Great and how totally random. Come to think of it, how totally Aunt Sheba.

"I can give you the keys." River baulked as he was handed

yet another envelope. "If you hurry there now you'll catch someone before the office is shut and they can take you to the van."

Thankfully, Hayley had nothing else on her agenda that afternoon. River jumped back into the taxi with his case, clocking a forlorn-looking Blossom – Aunt Sheba's cat – meandering up the drive, seemingly in pursuit of them as they sped off for Wookey Hole... via Glastonbury high street, via the Cocktail Bar. He couldn't help but wonder what would happen to the cat now. His mum was allergic to pet hair so she couldn't take Blossom on. He willed the cute feline out of his head. She was not his problem. Surely the caravan park could keep her as a 'working' cat.

"You can't take any of it back." Hayley stated the obvious as they sliced through the high street, passing the nostalgia of the bar. River swore he could see Lord and Lady Rigby-Chandler cosied up inside, as had become their freeloading habit when he'd run the place and they'd made their Happy Hour tipples stretch through to closing time. "That wouldn't be fair. It's theirs now," she continued. "They might not be as enigmatic as you and Alice," River was impressed at Hayley's vocabulary, though at this moment in time he doubted he could ever ooze any kind of aloof magnetism ever again. "But they're doing all right, Lee and Jonie, pulling in the crowds, keeping things ticking over in their own little way."

"Do you think I don't know that?" he sulked.

His head told him he'd made the biggest mistake of his life, giving his premises away to his friends. His heart told him this was just one step on a journey. Soon the rest of the path would reveal itself. He needed to be patient, go with the flow and trust.

Soon River was eyeing up the impressive edifice of Wells cathedral as they trundled through yet another high street.

"Why are we going the scenic route? Surely we should be looping around Wells? It would be a heck of a lot quicker."

"Because I need a favour." Hayley pulled the taxi over onto double yellow lines. "Jump out and get me a quarter of salted caramel fudge from the shop on the corner there, will you? Here." She handed him a crumpled note.

Some things never changed. River smiled as he did as he was told. He'd intended to pick up Hayley's quarter as quickly as possible, so they could be on their way, but the sweet perfume made him cave in within moments. River reluctantly allowed the magical contents of the shop catch his eye. The rectangular stacks of other-worldly fudge were exactly what you'd hope to see inside a Hansel and Gretel place like this.

Ten minutes and an epic conversation about the endlessly festive and fascinating flavours of said fudge later (plus a couple of lip-smackingly delicious taste tests) and River was back in the taxi at last.

"What took you so long? My stomach is rumbling," Hayley complained, wasting no time at all wolfing down a chunk of her beloved salted caramel as they continued on their way.

"You don't know what you're missing," she goaded River.

Oh, but maybe he did. He pulled out a sneaky bag of his own from his pocket and nibbled on a soft cube of buttery cranberry and gingerbread flavour fudge.

"Hey, share the wealth! And that'll be extra on the tab. I do believe that was my twenty pound note that I handed over... and for which I am yet to receive the change."

"Here, have it back."

"What? You mean you treated me?"

River deposited the twenty pound note in the drinks holder, passed Hayley a cube of his current taste sensation, and threw in a mouth-watering piece of white chocolate and peppermint candy cane fudge.

"Well, you have perked up. Meanwhile, I think I've died and gone to heaven. Oh, my days!" Hayley's eyes bulged at these treasures and River reminded her to keep them firmly on the road. He hoped she didn't behave like this with all her clients.

"I guess I have perked up." River allowed himself half a smile. He was starting to get that warm fuzzy feeling inside that said he was onto something. It was an inner knowing that was impossible to explain to others; on a par with his 'chance' meeting with Mercedes. One more coincidence, and maybe he'd start to act on it.

Ten minutes later they passed the sign for the village of Wookey Hole, which got River contemplating things all over again. He guessed the sugar high also helped. "Tell me, Hayley: do you believe in signs?"

"Road signs? Well, most of the time they're pretty accurate, I guess, although I always think those falling rock signs around Cheddar Gorge are a bit overly dramatic. And as for the deer signs they put up around Exmoor, ha, you've got more chance of spotting the Loch Ness fricking Monster."

"Actually I was thinking of less obvious signs. Messages really. You know, like when you feel as if you're in the right place at the right time because you just happen to catch a snatch of conversation and it reveals a life clue… or, I dunno, you see something that you wouldn't have seen, if you'd taken just a couple of seconds longer getting off a train?"

"Can't say I do, Riv. Sounds a bit airy fairy to me."

River granted himself a full beam of a smile. It didn't matter. He didn't need anyone else's approval or opinion to know when he was on the right track.

"Here we are at last," Hayley declared. "Charming Caves Campsite and Caravan Park."

"Blimey. And I thought my aunt's caravan park had an uninspired name." River handed a bundle of notes to Hayley to cover his gargantuan fare.

"Be nice to the owners, River." Hayley warned. "We can't all be as worldly-wise, well-travelled and cultured as you. Besides, nobody can argue that there aren't caves to be found in this charming village. Who are you to talk? You named your cocktail bar 'the Cocktail Bar'.

Once again, Hayley was dead right.

"I'm gonna stay with you until I know you can start the VW up. You might be in need of my mechanics skills – or my trusty jump leads in the boot."

"Nah. It'll be fine, Hayley." River brushed away her help with his hand. "I'm sure they check on the vans here regularly and turn the engines over. It would be part and parcel of what Aunt Sheba was paying for."

"Okaaaay then," said Hayley doubtfully. "I'll turn around and walk back to the taxi slowly, in case you change your mind."

"You've done more than enough to help me today. The van and I will be grand." Frankly he just wanted to get the VW back to his mum and Terry's for an impromptu supper –

which would also be the perfect excuse to check Heather was eating properly. "I know the basics, in the highly unlikely event that she won't start." He really didn't. "Don't worry about it. Go home to Bob. Eat, watch EastEnders, have wild sex, sleep. It's been a long day."

"Yes to all of those, except I'm ecstatic to say I'll be trading the doom and gloom of the soaps for a spot of *Bridgerton* and a certain duke on Netflix." Hayley shouted back over her shoulder with a wink. "Makes it hard not to imagine Bob morphing into Regé-Jean Page when we're at it later… but what can a girl do?"

"Sounds great." River turned to peg it for the safety of the campsite's office.

"What about diesel, River? What if there's only a trickle of fuel in the tank?" Hayley shouted after him again, before getting back to the taxi and her dwindling fudge supplies. She wound down the window to hear River's reply.

"Knowing Aunt Sheba, she'd already thought to refuel it with unicorn juice." He reassured her. "It'll be fine. Now go."

River waved Hayley off, utterly relieved to be on his own, to be able to think, to be able to breathe. He marched across to the office, only just catching the guy on duty by the skin of his teeth before he clocked off. Well, River guessed that was par for the course in the winter. There was likely as little business here as in Glastonbury. He pointed River to the VW which was parked right at the end of the field (typical), and left him to it.

River felt a buzz as he wheeled his small case toward his racing-green and cream heritage, despite the dark closing in on him already. There didn't seem to be another soul on the campsite. That would make it all the more tranquil when he was pottering about inside the camper van, he decided. He smiled at the idea of a peaceful couple of hours before he headed to his mum's place.

Although he couldn't see very well in the fading light (note to self: damn, why hadn't he brought a torch?), the VW appeared to gleam brighter with every step he took. It might be old but it had evidently been given a glossy new coat of paint and that fresh lease of life radiated throughout it – from the engine, which River could imagine was probably reconditioned and reliable, through to the furnishings.

This was going to be so much fun.

He reached the door and emptied the key from the envelope into his hand. It turned with ease and, after locating the light switch, he and his suitcase surveyed their new surroundings. Very impressive. In a cosy Scandinavian way, admittedly. But it was less rustic than River had been expecting. Sure, the space was smaller than small, yet everything fitted perfectly. The stove, the sink, the cupboards, the plush-looking seating area, the table, the loo (he hoped that had been cleaned, thankfully it didn't smell offensive).

Then there was the roof bed, which opened manually. River craned his head to take a peek inside the little cocoon. It was definitely the epitome of snug. He fervently hoped he'd get to experience some blissful nights camping beneath the planets and the stars with Alice at his side – with a very naked Alice at his side.

He shook the thought from his head for a moment. It was just too depressing to contemplate life in this van, life in the world, without her…

The more closely he inspected the minimalist interior, the faster the cogs turned in his brain. And it was a stroke of genius that his aunt Sheba had got this place refurbed so thoughtfully; the sliding doors on the side of the van had shelving built into their backs, housing rows of quaint mismatched red and green mugs. The bottom shelves even held a tangle of star-shaped fairy lights. Cute. Then there was the bunting. That part threw River completely and his limbs began to tingle. Why hadn't he noticed straightaway? It was Christmas bunting. And every other triangular piece of fabric featured a *gingerbread* house.

He rubbed his hands and decided to have a quick ferret about in the cupboards before he sat at the wheel. There wasn't exactly a whole lot of storage space but his aunt seemed to be all about the hot drinks. A large caddy of rather ancient-looking cocoa, myriad herbal teas and tubs of coffee sat on the top shelf of the left cupboard. At the bottom sat a cafetiere, a kettle that looked as if it whistled, and a collection of mini whisks.

Now River moved on to the righthand cupboard to see what his aunt had hiding in there. He was greeted with a stack of red and green paper plates, which sort of went with the mismatched mugs, a cooling rack (random), bags of flour, currants, mixed spice, cinnamon, ginger, and a steel ring that looked like an oversized charm bracelet. Tentatively, he pulled it out. Which was silly. Even with the doors of the VW wide open, there was nobody around him who would be disturbed by the jingle jangle.

That was when River let out an almighty: "Fuck!"

Like Alice, he wasn't one for dishing out expletives à la

Gordon Ramsay, but in this case, needs must. This was no trinket bracelet. It was a ring full of biscuit cutters: gingerbread people; a token star, moon, bell, and a little house besides.

What the heck was going on?

This was beyond freaky! It was like he and his aunt were telepathic or something. Except she was dead and River didn't 'do' ouija boards or channelling spirits or mediums. As unconventionally Glastonbury as he was, those were things he preferred never to meddle with.

He needed to get out of here. He needed to talk this through with his mum. He relegated the cookie cutters to the cupboard, wondering if they would ping straight back into his hands. Mercifully, they stayed put. He slammed the cupboard door shut.

"Okay, River. Stay calm. Don't over-analyse things. It's just a coincidence."

Hmm… like the incessant chocolate and gingerbread signs you keep getting, his inner voice replied to his outer one.

River ignored them both, pulling the VW's sliding doors back together, lugging his small case to the footwell by the passenger seat where he lodged it as securely as possible, before jumping into the driver's seat, determined to get himself to his mum's house as quickly as he could.

He turned the chunky key in the ignition and mentally crossed his fingers that his earlier nonchalance wouldn't now decide to bite him on the backside.

Splutter, splutter, splutter.

Yeah, but that was only his first attempt. She was an old VW, despite her *probably* reconditioned and reliable engine.

River needed to stay level-headed and patient. Slowly did it.

And so River tried again, and again, and again. Each time giving himself a three-minute break between attempts. He crossed his fingers. He took deep breaths. He visualised the beautiful purr of the engine. He added some throttle. He added a lot of throttle.

SPLUTTER

"Oh, bugger!" he shouted, cradling his head in his hands, on the verge of tears.

Just as Hayley had predicted. He was an idiot.

That was it, then. He was stuck here for the night, until the park opened again tomorrow. The witch who was rumoured to haunt the village's caves had better flipping well stay put in them. Unless…

River pulled his case up onto the seat and flung it open, scrabbling around for his phone.

Well, wasn't that typical? He hadn't packed it in his pocket *or* his luggage!

There was only one more thing he could try. River knew Wookey Hole had a pub somewhere around these parts. If he turned right out of the caravan park and followed the B road into the village proper, he'd be sure to see it. He could use their phone.

He set off, looking all around him in case some random winter tourists should happen to appear in their static caravan or motorhome windows as he passed; as if his presence should trigger their electricity supply and reveal the neighbours who'd been willing and able to help him all along. Sensible people who travelled with technology.

Alas, it was wishful thinking. He passed the main office,

doubling back on himself in the realisation that it must have emergency contact details plastered to its door for such events as spontaneous fools forgetting their mobile phones (and not taking advantage of friends and their jump leads). River's heart sank when he thought of Hayley's offer. How quick and easy it would have been to remedy this!

Alas, here was another case of wishful thinking. Evidently the caravan park workers had no desire to be disturbed after 5:00 p.m. and were probably now enjoying several pints at the pub he was walking to.

Despite the chilly air, thankfully and unusually it was a titchy bit balmier in Somerset than Cornwall of an evening, River reached the pub in fifteen minutes. The decidedly dark and boarded up pub; its sole illumination that of the street lights – okay, and the keenos who had gone all out with their flickering garden reindeer, Santas, snowmen, and stacks of presents topped with elves, despite the fact it was still only November.

It was just like he'd read in the papers. No, not the glow to rival Blackpool – the death knell of the pubs. Talk about soul destroying. In both senses of the word, because now he definitely would have to stay on site for the night, shivering in his coat since he hadn't spotted any blankets back in the VW. Either that or hope for a passer-by who wouldn't think he was a conman.

He turned his back on the sad and sorry place, quickened his step and headed back to the caravan park. And yet, as he did so, something as magical as the festive embellishment in the backdrop behind him cemented his earlier brainwave firmly into his psyche. With a fervour that he knew would be too stubborn to loosen its grip.

No way could he continue to turn the other cheek to the devastating loss of community life. He may not be able to do great things, but he could do River-sized things with great love.

AFTER A SURPRISINGLY comfortable night in the camper van (River had piled all the clothes in his suitcase on the bed, along with a stack of tea towels from a cupboard. He'd even made a makeshift pillow with one tea towel, stuffing it with boxers and socks) he woke to a loud banging noise.

"Holy crap!" he exclaimed, heart thudding as he remembered where he was. He must be outstaying his welcome and eating into a day's rental, which someone was here to collect.

River jumped down a little too enthusiastically from the bunk and landed in an inelegant heap on the floor. The banging persisted. He took a deep breath, hoisted himself up with the help of the 'kitchen table' and opened up the doors, rubbing the sleep from his eyes to see Hayley wearing a classic *I-told-you-so* expression and holding a bunch of cables.

"Come in," he said with an eye roll that was directed at himself and himself only this time.

"You are a plonker."

"That's one way of putting it."

"I bumped into Terry late last night in Tesco. He said you hadn't visited them as half-expected. I gather it wouldn't start, then?"

"You gather right." River flopped onto the table with a

weary expression.

"Put the kettle on and I'll get this baby running in no time."

River jumped immediately to his feet, spurred on by Hayley's positivity.

Twenty minutes later, after Hayley had worked her magic so the camper van now emitted the most delicious purr, the two friends sat nursing their second mugs of steaming tea. River had even managed to find a few milk sachets and shop-bought biscuits to accompany it. Things were looking up.

"It's a shame you didn't get a chance to catch up with your mum last night."

"Tell me about it. I'm concerned about her, Hayley. She seems to have lost a ton of weight."

"Well, of course she has," said Hayley casually. "It's blatantly obvious what's going on. I spend many hours ferrying crew to and from the various fancy-pants houses my Bob and her Terry work at – she's feeling a tad insecure. That's all. She'll snap out of it."

"What do you mean?" River screwed up his features.

"The make-up artists, the designers, the runners. They're all pretty young things, skinny as you like. Keen to get a foot on the ladder of a blossoming TV career."

"So you mean to tell me my mum's incessant dieting is because she's petrified Terry will run off with one of them? No way. If that was the case then why aren't you worried that Bob…"

How River wished he could take back every last one of those ugly words.

"I… I wasn't implying anything, I'm so…"

"If I wasn't with Bob I could have my pick of any number of male admirers, I'll have you know. Those little twentysomethings with their tight arses, skinny jeans, and waterfall hairdos don't faze me one bit, and they wouldn't be a patch on me in the bedroom either." River didn't doubt it. "I'll tell you what: you leave it to me. I'll have a word with your mum… probably over a fish and chip takeaway. I'll call in on her this week to arrange it. We'll soon turn this silly phase on its head."

"Aw, thanks, Hayley." As far as humans went she was one of the best. "Do you want another tea for the road?"

"Are you kidding me? I'll be needing to use your loo if you make another brew." River tried not to wince. "I'd best be on my way. I'll follow you this time. And I won't take no for an answer. My next job's down at the college, near the motorway junction, so I'll see you safely off to Cornwall."

"You're on." He offered his hand for a shake. "There's no way I'm turning that offer down."

"Just one last thing: what *are* you going to do with this contraption, beautiful though she is?"

Inevitably River spilled his heart out to Hayley, revealing his recently imagined plans. Inevitably River's kettle did whistle cheerfully once more, providing him and Hayley with yet another mug of tea.

Hayley shook her head, a smile pasting itself to her lips. For one so blunt and proud of her perennial neutral expression-stroke-scowl, this was a rarity indeed and he'd have loved to have captured it in a snapshot. It suited her.

"I can't tell whether you're about to laugh or cry at my idea."

"It's bloody brilliant." Hayley took a sip of her tea, returning to it promptly with her bourbon biscuit, which she treated to a proper soaking. "I can see the headlines now across all the local papers."

"Which makes me sound like I'm doing it to get back in the limelight again." River shook his head. "I swear that's not the case, Hayley. I just want to bring the community together after the depressing scene I saw last night. This little brainwave is hardly going to set the sky alight but hopefully it will replace some of the seasonal good cheer that's missing in the villages, whilst getting me, *us*," River corrected himself, trying in vain to stay positive about his relationship status, "Back home where we belong. Away from that failure of a Cornish cocktail bar…"

"You needed a new project. Sheba clearly knew it too. And this one doesn't take anything away from Lee and Jonie. It's perfect." Hayley paused. "But the real question is…"

"What will Alice think?"

CHAPTER EIGHT
Alice

AGAINST ALL THE odds, Alice's soul-searching had her patiently waiting for River in the kitchen when he returned.

"Oh my God, it's you," he cried as he burst through the door with such vigour and joy that she was sure he was going to take it off its hinges.

Like two magnets unable to resist the pull of home, they flew at each other, Alice almost knocking over the ruby-red poinsettia plant taking pride of place on the kitchen table. But she didn't care. She never wanted to let her imperfectly perfect River go.

"I'm sorry I ran off, I just needed time out, I…"

"I can't believe what a numpty I've been, I should have told you immediately about both of those notes, it will never happen ag…"

They burst out laughing at their bizarre fusion of relief, relishing every precious moment as it enveloped them. After days in limbo, finding themselves in one another's arms again was bliss.

"What are we like?" said Alice, lifting her head from River's chest to look into his eyes. "If I'm not packing my bags to work at a fruit farm in Bath," which was where she'd randomly found herself last time they'd had a bust up, "I'm headed for a shepherd's hut in the Tamar Valley."

"Say that again?" River's eyes bulged.

"Oh, it was delightful... for all of a day, anyway... and then I got bored. Too much time to think, no internet, not even a radio."

"Al, that sounds a bit too remote. What if some axe murderer on a rampage knew of your whereabouts?"

Alice shrugged. "I guess. I never really think about these things. When I get the impulse to go, I *go*. Maybe that's what all the travelling in the band has done to me, screwed me up, made me run fast without turning back whenever I encounter a bump in the road."

River looked stressed. "We have to find a better tactic next time. Not that I intend for there to be a next time."

He leant in to kiss her gently, but she knew he was resisting the primeval urge to lift her into his arms and through to the bedroom. She felt the same way but this afternoon was about talking, making plans. Reluctantly, she pulled away from his embrace.

"So, what next? Where do we start?"

This time River insisted he went first. "I'd like to put my cards on the table. If I may?" He looked at her adorably and she tried not to baulk at the C-word. "But first of all, just to make sure you truly hear it: *I apologise. I'm wholeheartedly sorry*. I was a complete and utter twit not to be open with you. That might be one of my least endearing traits, and some may say it's inbuilt and inevitable, but it was inexcusable. You had every right to react the way you did."

River widened the gap between them and motioned for

Alice to sit down.

"Drink?" she asked intuitively.

"Yes, please. I'm gasping for a cuppa, even though what I'm going to say next marks another hopefully momentous life occasion, so champagne would probably be more appropriate."

Goosebumps flecked Alice's arms and her breath hitched in her throat. Surely he wasn't about to propose? It was funny. She'd always assumed River would get down on one knee in a super-romantic location, but home, as they said, was where the heart was... even if they were soon to be exchanging this home for another.

River's face was a fusion of serious and excited all in one go. Something Alice hadn't even realised was humanly possible.

"I... erm... had a slightly hare-brained idea while I was away," he began. "Ever since my aunt passed away – which has coincided with me accepting the sad fate of the business venture beneath us." River paused to look at the floor, in case Alice was in any doubt that he was referring to his Cornish bar. "I've been feeling this inexplicable cosy community pull. Think hot drinks and biscuits. Oh, all right." River held his palms aloft in surrender. "Think hot cocoa and gingerbread. With a Christmassy twist. And all served from a green Volkswagen camper van. Not here, obviously. Back in Somerset."

River reached across the table to clasp Alice's hands then, toppling the poinsettia all over again. "They need our help, Alice."

"Wh...who?" Alice squinted, wondering what on earth

was going on inside her boyfriend's head. Besides which, this did not sound one iota like a proposal, so she'd best park her expectations about her rustically beautiful hay barn wedding and accept it wasn't a necessity in this day and age. They loved one another, were committed to one another, and that was all that truly mattered.

"The village communities surrounding Glastonbury," said River, pure seriousness written all over his face now. "The pubs really are fighting to stay open. The papers weren't lying. Some of them are even boarded up. I've seen it with my own two eyes." He paused to reflect before carrying on. "It was weird. Like I was at a crossroads. I was actually standing in the middle of a B road at the time. On my right side was a derelict pub and all the hollow and haunting memories of what might have been, of folk toasting each other and revelling in merry community spirit. On the left side of me was one of those houses that looked like it had fallen into Santa's grotto: garish lights and crazy ornamentation everywhere. And yet… the owners were undoubtedly inside it, unable to actually see it, snuggled up in front of the TV, as antisocial as could be, although I understand they're doing it for the benefit of passers-by in the outside world. Somehow it just felt like something was missing. I stood there in the middle and realised I had the answer to it all. That was the moment."

"I'm sort of struggling to follow. Can you be a bit more specific?"

"We'll go back to Somerset – if you're still up for the move, of course – and have a winter sabbatical, travelling to all the small and undiscovered parts of our home county that we never got to know; we'll unite the locals, serve them mouth-watering gingerbread biccies and steaming hot chocolate. Lure them out of their houses, to interact with their neighbours. What do you think? I mean, obviously we'd need to get the homemade gingerbread sourced. Oh, and we'd want the best quality cocoa, of course. Then I'd need to work on the alcoholic and non-alcoholic infusions going into that. The van is pretty minimalist, but that's kind of a bonus, when we have so much to think about in terms of where exactly to lay our roots. There would be no distractions."

Alice bit her lip in contemplation. She couldn't deny that the idea was appealing. It certainly would buy them the decision-making time they needed.

"I'll admit, all this talk of food and drink is making me drool. And yes, it would be rather cool… I mean warm, cosy and toasty – at least, I'm assuming the VW has some kind of possibility for heating – to pootle around the villages, getting to know parts of Somerset better."

The right kind of travel. Blimey with jingle bells on. It would take them away from the frustration of the failure that was currently beneath their feet, as River said. Yes, a short break in the VW would sort everything out and bring them fresh perspective. Maybe, after that, River would get down on bended knee. And then Alice inwardly reprimanded herself for dreaming of confetti all over again.

"Okay. I'm in!"

Alice high-fived an ecstatic and slightly surprised, but relieved, River. She stood to fix them both that well-deserved drink.

"All we have up here is that bottle of caramel Baileys Rio and Justin gifted us last time we hosted supper – well, and the ice." Alice pulled open the freezer with one hand, flicking the door fully open with her foot (the landlord refused to upgrade it) whilst stretching across to the shelf and pulling down two crystal tumblers. She plopped in giant ice cubes and poured a respectable glug of the liquor into each glass, her heart gladdening at the delicious crackle of the ice as it melted into the pale beige cream. Alice couldn't wait to take a sip of hers, and belatedly handed River his. He wasn't the biggest fan of the 'mainstream and predictable' Baileys and its plethora of infusions. Ever the discerning bartender! Something told her all of that was about to change very, *very* soon.

She watched him with baited breath as he tasted his first drop, all curiosity.

"Oh, I've just had a thought," said River, a tiny smile tugging at his lips, his eyes flitting this way and that. "This might work in a hot chocolate."

Alice didn't have the heart to tell him his Eureka moment wasn't the most original in the history of hot cocoa recipes. But he was right, Baileys hot chocolates (in all of their guises from caramel to red velvet apple pie – depending on availability in the shops) would have to be a staple of their menu.

"Now it's my turn," said Alice, quickly draining her glass and going in for a refill already – in her defence, she flipping well needed it… "I haven't quite come clean with you." She took in a sharp breath and blurted out her admission. "I called your aunt Sheba the day she died, well, it was just a few hours before her passing, obviously. I needed a card reading."

"Wow. Okay." River emptied his own glass in one go, coming up for air and blinking rapidly. "That's a bit belated.

Why didn't you mention it sooner? Not that I can talk."

"I know. And I hope you'll let me explain. I certainly don't want us keeping anything from one another anymore. No matter how big or small."

"I'm listening."

River took her hand and stroked it gently, putting Alice immediately at ease to unburden herself of the similar doubts she'd long had about Cornwall; the bar, the horses, the hopes for the future, the burning desire to move back to Glastonbury – but not knowing how and where they'd fit in… and finally, the verdict of Sheba's shuffling.

There was no point in cluttering that long list with her new worry: would her boyfriend *ever* propose?

"I think the only words left are, 'To Aunt Sheba, to us, and to a festive and fun fresh start'," said River. He stretched out his tumbler and they toasted their new adventure.

DESPITE THE FACT River's avant-garde beverages had barely made an impression on the inhabitants of Pasty, Alice decided to organise a little surprise the evening before their departure.

Whilst River said his official farewell to the bar, scrubbing and cleaning the surfaces ready to drop the keys off at Money-Grabbing Mr Twiggs's office in the morning, Alice snuck a few friends in via the back garden and up the stairs. Rio, Justin, Jimmy and a couple of the book club members squashed together under the kitchen table – the only place to hide in their small kitchen – and jumped out on cue as River opened the kitchen door and switched on the light. Each of them was bearing streamers and party hats, and making a right ruckus. River gasped. This was clearly the last thing he'd expected and the emotion had him fighting back the tears.

It was the perfect send-off. Small and intimate, everyone chatting animatedly and feasting on tiny triangle sandwiches, cheese and pineapple on sticks, Kettle crisps and Jaffa Cakes. Which was a great way to munch through the kitchen cupboard leftovers, all washed down with a few bottles of red wine. Alice hadn't even thought about providing background music. Well, the sound system was packed away and she'd cringe if any of their guests insisted upon boogying the night away to Avalonia tracks. But their guests had other ideas anyway.

The book club took it in turns to read out a chapter from its current choice, a psychological thriller. It made for a production to rival anything you'd watch at Cornwall's Minack theatre. Then Rio and Justin asked for permission to clear the floor so they could give an exclusive rendition of their festive break dance, 'incorporating pots and pans'. Alice wasn't sure this was the best of ideas, but apparently the boys performed for Justin's well-established acting family every Boxing Day eve. They'd been working on this unique routine all year and needed some honest feedback so they could make any necessary tweaks and finally stop ranking last in the annual family competition.

It had certainly been different, and mercifully, none of Grumpy-Guts Twiggs's measly saucepans and containers, lurking at the back of the cupboards, had been destroyed in the process.

And then Jimmy pulled out a pair of spoons.

"You can actually play them?" asked Alice incredulously. She noted River's pained expression – and briskly ignored it.

Jimmy settled himself on the cushions of the kitchen windowsill, making for a wistful portrait. He put the spoons in position on his knee and deftly started to play them, singing alongside his captivating rhythm in a mournful melody. Goosebumps covered Alice's arms.

When he finally stopped the room fell silent, despite the vast amounts of alcohol that had been circulating. Rio and Justin clapped enthusiastically, followed by the whooping and cheering of the bookworms, followed by an ardent round of applause from Alice, followed by the lame pitter patter of a clap from River.

"That was incredible, Jimmy!"

"What a talent!"

"Were you self-taught?"

"Far better than anything on the big stage of any Simon Cowell talent show!"

The acclaim fell at Jimmy's feet like precision-thrown roses.

"Why thank you, good folk of Pasty. I learnt from my grandfather. It was a tradition when he used to come in off the fishing boat over in Penzance. The men would go to the harbour pub. They practised their sea shanties and spoon playing as they sailed back to land. I suppose it helped them forget about the dangers of the sea. Well, then once they'd had a pint or two, they'd share what they'd been practicing with the locals. There wasn't a stage as such, but the landlord would give them some space at the back of the inn. I was a young lad back then but I worked in Penzance harbour, where

I tended to boat repairs and the like."

Jimmy stopped to catch his breath, smiling as he reminisced. "I'd often nip into the pub at lunchtime, once I came of age, of course. I guess you could say my fascination for the spoons and the sea songs started then. I tried them out at home in my bedroom, and soon I was confident enough to join the fishermen, though they did mock my attempts at first, until I got faster and they could no longer deny that I held a tune better than the lot of them put together." Jimmy chuckled.

"Real folk, real community spirit. I love it. Warms the cockles. Did they catch any cockles while they were out in the boat?" asked Rio.

"Oh, yes… and a few mussels," said Jimmy.

"I'll bet," added Justin, arching a brow and flexing his biceps.

River just stood there in stunned silence. Maybe, just maybe, taking in everybody else's genuine applause, River was finally appreciating the rustic beauty of Jimmy's musical talents with his own two eyes (and ears)?

"Jimmy," River spoke at last. "If I were to give you a call in approximately two weeks' time – and foot the hotel and travel bill – would you do me the great honour of gracing us with your presence for a couple of days in Somerset? I've had an idea."

"Eek!" Alice couldn't help herself. "Please say this means you want Jimmy to open up the talent contest for our winter wonderland sabbatical on wheels?"

CHAPTER NINE
Zara

IT WAS REALLY lovely of Alice to mentally erase the not-so-distant past and make convivial chat. Zara wasn't sure she could have been as non-judgemental. Yes, they'd hooked up over cocktails at Sheba's funeral (Zara used to do a good bit of trade in the summer with the clients at Sheba's caravan park, where her gluten-free afternoon tea picnics had once been a hit), but when one considered the bizarre state of affairs the last time she and Alice Goldsmith had been in the same room, it was a miracle the woman hadn't slapped her.

For Zara had unwittingly let herself be befriended by Georgina. The girl who had got her claws into River before Alice had left the band and returned to Glastonbury.

Awkward. And all the more potentially tricky when one considered Zara had given Georgina, and Blake (Zara's then boyfriend, and Georgina's brother) access to the back of her rental property, not to mention permission to drill a hole through the wall into River's cocktail bar – well, the former skittle alley part of it – to hunt down that blessed bottle.

What had she been thinking? Well, like Zara had already said, she'd found herself embroiled in one too many shitty relationships; the kind where she'd do almost anything to impress. She supposed it was just another facet of her life.

Now here she was, about to temper a batch of chocolate, without knowing if she'd even get to sell the cute star and holly-shaped creations she intended to make with it. But what choice did she have? December's heating bill in her flat upstairs was not going to pay itself, and she still needed to send her parents, her sisters and their various and 'discerning' offspring, a bunch of swoon-worthy gifts that kept up the charade that she had a successful alternative lifestyle.

Zara had long ago chosen to walk away from the glitz and glamour of her parents' mansion in West London. A decision many a family member (and hanger on) had racked their brains to try to understand. Because Zara had everything most people's hearts could desire, back in Chelsea: an exceedingly stylish and comfortable bedroom with en suite and in-built gym in a £12 million pound town house, an endless academic budget, any number of back-scratching contacts who could secure her a dream career wherever she pointed her pinky, and more upper-crust suitors than you could shake a baguette at.

But the first summer she visited Glastonbury festival had changed all of that. Her pretty, rich, aristocratic and catwalk model friends had put on a damn good show of being in it for the weekend. There had been a sprinkling of mud, a spot of cannabis and hash cakes, wild sex on tap with randoms in tents, Radiohead and Coldplay, and non-negotiable pictures of their cute selves in cut-off denim shorts, olive wellies, white flowing tent-style shirts, sunnies and oversized floppy sunhats, which would appear in next week's edition of *Hello!* But Zara had been truly, madly, deeply and instantly smitten with her new surroundings. Like, authentically so.

Gone were the airs and graces, the pretences. Glastonbury felt like home. A pair of the most comfortable slippers one could dream of. Perhaps that was because of its links to Lemuria and Atlantis? Zara had always felt an inexplicable connection to these lost worlds, since she'd followed her ancient history degree off at tangents; the kind of hare-brained notion her politician father would titter at over his tumbler of whisky. Whatever. She just knew she'd lived in both worlds in her former incarnations.

In many ways, it was a wonder she'd ever got to Glastonbury at all. Daddy used to switch 'that nonsense' off whenever he caught her watching the festival on TV in her early teens. Just as deftly as he had switched off her revelation that one of his Westminster cronies had pinned her against the fridge for a fumble, when he'd chanced upon Zara in the kitchen alone at a family dinner party…

From that hideous, defining moment, she had known she had to escape Chelsea, the opulent home and the wealth that had been passed down through the generations. Despite their shared DNA, she wasn't cut from the same cloth as any of those people. And don't get her started on her sisters. Grace got paid essentially to loaf about, freeloading her wasp's waist from one trendy eatery to the next (barely digesting a morsel) and writing up her weekly experiences for one of the broadsheets. Apparently she was the It Girl of London fine-dining, nowadays. Meanwhile, Milly had full-on embraced her role of Yummy Mumma. Baby number six was on its way. Zara didn't know how she managed to procreate so continuously, especially with her billionaire husband frequently hopping away on a plane to conduct his business deals. Mils was sweet enough. Her heart was in the right place. But she thought Zara was bananas not to want the same pampered lifestyle. Milly's brother-in-law, James, had long carried a torch for Zara. She could so easily have stepped into the same ballet flats as her sister, spending her days flicking through the MORI catalogue to add yet more luxurious and super-soft cotton togs to her toddlers' wardrobes, booking up ski trips, bookmarking bang-on-trend organic meal ideas for the cook to experiment with later, and pondering over updates to the Devonshire holiday home.

None of her family came to Glastonbury to visit her. Why would they? It was a different world and they were not of it. Even her 'friends' had abandoned her. Sure, they still went to the festival, but why would they choose to slum it in Zara's modest, rented two-bed apartment, when they had free access to a luxury glamping tent in return for yet more snaps making their merry way into the magazines?

Zara didn't need to economise the way she did. She had an untouched trust fund. For thirteen years, she had chosen to ignore it. Not out of obstinacy or foolishness. Rather, Zara wanted to prove to herself that she could make it on her own. Every year of her life, from nappies to twenty-two, money had opened doors for her. All right, she'd assumed by the age of thirty-three that she'd be doing a little better, off the back of her life skills and talents, getting more than a foot in a door (any old door) by herself. But there was still time. She wasn't quite middle-aged yet, for goodness sake.

Her love life was another matter entirely. Things in that department were the epitome of barren. Door firmly shut, and Zara had no intention of opening it! At least not with the locals.

From her earliest dates in Glastonbury with the jugglers, musicians, fire eaters, poets, and artists who converged on the town in search of deeper meaning, through to her slightly more mainstream experiences with guys like Blake, whose families had lived in this part of the world forever, Zara was thoroughly disillusioned. If her love interests didn't turn out to be too unconventional to handle, then they came with a luggage carousel full of baggage.

Zara brought a gloved hand to her weary brow and examined the state of her chocolate. Well, at least that was perfect. She acknowledged the deep glossy bowl of molten liquid glinting back at her. Its colour was practically the shade of her own silky hair. Now she needed to act fast to fill her moulds and tap the chocolate into a settled position. She bit down on her lip in concentration. Once the delicate moulds were level, she had a couple of hours to jot down some ideas to drum up a bit of social media custom.

Ooh, perhaps she could punch some holes through the ends of her creations once they'd cooled, add some of the sparkly, festive yarn she had in the cupboard, and market them as Christmas tree decorations? Perhaps she could also persuade the Glastonbury councillors to buy enough to cover the behemoth tree standing proudly in the Market Square? Pfft, that would never happen. And even if it did, she had visions of her holier than thou exes (the eco-warrior ones), nabbing the treasures from the pine's branches, every time they unicycled past in defence of the tree's minimalistic rights.

Social media sales ideas wouldn't take up the whole two hours required for chocolate setting time though, would they?

No.

Zara knew the other thing she'd been procrastinating over forever had to be faced at last. An old school friend had tracked her down weeks ago, making contact with her on Messenger. Lucy was settled in Tuscany and looking for an English artisan baker to give her growing business a twist by inventing, sourcing and providing a whole new list of products. She doubted Zara would need the life change, since business looked to be booming in Glasto, but if she felt like a new challenge, could Zara let her know by the beginning of December? If she didn't hear from her, she'd start hunting for somebody locally…

Zara was still in two minds. And that was despite the fact she'd already given in her notice on her property. Part of her knew she needed a fresh start. Her folks and old friends might even come to visit her in Tuscany, it was much more up their street. Her mother and father had property in the region. Well, of course.

She rather liked the idea of trading robed wizards for Roman Lotharios. Maybe a stint in Bella Italia would prove that romance wasn't dead after all? Although she wasn't completely bowled over by the idea of meddling with the moreish Mediterranean bread and cake menu. It had the distinct ring of fish and chip shops in Benidorm. Did that wheel really need reinventing? *Pane Toscano* and *castagnaccio* were pretty damned perfect as they were. What was she supposed to do, add mincemeat and Bakewell tart batter to their fillings?

The other part of her felt like someone had ripped her heart out. What if she gave herself another couple of years in the mystical town she so loved to call home? Sure, she'd spontaneously handed in her notice on her flat and shop, but that needn't stop her from staying in the area. Thirty-five felt like a jolly good benchmark and barometer for success. If she hadn't turned things around in Glastonbury in another couple of years then she could jack it all in, put it down to experience, and move on to somewhere far, far away.

But Lucy's benevolence would have moved on then too, wouldn't it?

And Zara was damned if she was giving her parents the satisfaction of touching that trust fund.

CHAPTER TEN
River

THERE WAS SO much to do and so little time. Especially when you were in a dream-like state because things with your lover, BFF, and wife-to-be (if River could ever find the right moment to propose), were absolute perfection.

Since River had returned to Cornwall with the VW, he felt as if cloud nine was his new official residence. Alice seemed to be in full bloom too – even if it wasn't yet spring. Life was perpetual change and it felt like they'd hotfooted to another circuit of their relationship's evolution. Things had been seesaws for them at times, and yet here they were, on the brink of a brand new escapade. River couldn't have been more excited for what the future held, and he had a renewed determination to savour the days. Life in the van would be cramped and difficult at times, for sure. But he knew it was where the pair of them were meant to be right now, and he knew it would reveal the answers to the way ahead. There was one slight snag. Okay, make that two: they didn't have any supplies.

Oh, they could go to the cash and carry and buy giant tins of cocoa in bulk, and they could load up the van with uninspired boxes of factory-produced biscuits, too. But that was not what he'd had in mind when he'd started this. Authenticity, heart and soul were everything. They were the missing ingredients in so many of these Somerset villages that'd had their community spirit pulled apart like a Christmas cracker. Cadbury and McVitie's simply wouldn't do.

"I can't believe I didn't see it sooner," said Alice. "The answer to our prayers is pretty obvious."

"It is?"

"Zara," Alice stated coolly.

River fell silent. "Oh, I dunno." His mouth twisted. "I mean, I think she's a lovely enough girl on the surface, but just look at the way Blake and ahem, the G-word, wrapped her around their little fingers – and then broke into my property."

Alice narrowed her eyes.

"My, er, *former property*... from which they stole a certain bottle of elixir while they were at it. No." River shook his head. "I'm not sure we could trust her. *How could she have let them do that?* Not to mention the fact she gave the go-ahead to all that DIY work, when she's merely a," River broke off to make quotation marks in the air, "'tenant.'" Alice was practically squinting now at his double standards and uncharacteristic snobbery. "Much as I'm in favour of a little rebellion when it comes to landlords and landladies," he added with a light chuckle, "That was taking things a bit too far. I think she's a tad naive, Al. We need suppliers we can rely on."

"And I think everyone deserves the benefit of the doubt. Okay, Zara definitely was a little on the gullible side letting them do what they did back then. On the other hand, it sounds like the past few years have been mighty stressful for her trying to keep her business afloat. We'd be doing her a favour. You heard her the other night. She's struggling. I'm sure if she's mainly working with us then it won't be an issue. I have every faith in her chocolate skills, if her delicious organic pastries were anything to go by. I may not have sampled all of them. But the vanilla *millefeuilles* and raspberry tarts I did treat myself to, when I occasionally popped in after helping you at the bar, have lasted long in the memory."

Alice licked her lips and River tried to ignore the hunger pang her foodie descriptions had ignited.

"Okay." River decided he'd have to concede to Alice's wishes. It wasn't like they had a host of other alternatives. "Let's say she can magically supply us with chocolate melts, cocoa powder mixes and the like… how does she get them to us?"

"For goodness sake, I'm sure she has transport," said Alice, rolling her eyes.

"I s'pose. What if it snows, though?"

"Come on, that rarely happens here. Stop inventing excuses. Give the girl a chance! Everyone deserves that at Christmas. It's a decent enough solution until we decide if we're going to continue with this little venture beyond the new year. By which time Zara may well have left Glastonbury, just as she hinted she might."

River chewed on his lip.

"Well, what do you say?"

"Fine. Do you want to call her? Oh, and I'm thinking our first VW pitstop needs to be symbolic. Let's start in Wookey Hole: the village where Aunt Sheba last parked this baby.

We'll move on to a different village every night. Make it fair. Get everybody's peckers up."

"Great." Alice agreed. "I'll make the call before you change your mind. Let's hope Zara's not inundated with Christmas orders. Although I kind of hope she will be, so she can pay the rent. So, that's the hot drinks side of things sorted. It's a pity she's not kitted out for baking anymore. How are we going to tackle the all-important gingerbread?"

"Erm," said River. "Yeah, on that score I think we'll need a little divine intervention. For once, I have no idea."

CHAPTER ELEVEN
Zara

ZARA COULDN'T REMEMBER the last time she'd experienced as much promising activity in one day. Lucy was thrilled, her excitement travelling down the line from Italy. Zara knew this had to be a good sign. She ignored the tiny kernel of doubt that had lodged in her stomach. She'd made her mind up and she was going for it. The offer was too good to refuse. Now all she needed to do was raise enough funds to book her one-way flight (oh, and settle her pile of final warning bills).

As if in answer to that very prayer, Alice had sought her out on Messenger. Zara wasn't the biggest fan of Facebook, other than using it for business purposes. Quite possibly because her family liked to hop on it a little too frequently to show the fakest side of their lives: Milly and the munchkins watching hubby and Grandpapa playing polo, Grace licking her chops after sampling Alain Ducasse's trilogy of fish on an impromptu Eurostar day trip to Paris. And so on and so forth.

'Hey, Zara! Hope you're doing well? I've been thinking about our chat at the cocktail bar the other day, and well... if you're still at a loose end over the Christmas season, Riv and I have a little business proposition for you. Call me...'

Alice had left her number and Zara had phoned her immediately to find out what they had in mind.

Could she supply a travelling Volkswagen camper van hot chocolate (and gingerbread) bar with a selection of the following:

Cocoa powder mixes in dark, milk and white varieties (some plain, some infused), and chocolate melts with a variety of flavours and fillings?

Yes and yes.

She could even throw in some complimentary artisan chocolate coins and mini-Christmas trees for decoration. And she had a fold-up serving bar they could borrow for the duration. Tick, tick, tick.

It wasn't a project that would make her rich. But then, she never wanted to be swaddled in vast sums of money ever again. Money soured people.

It was a sweet project befitting her finale in this eccentric little town – a great opportunity to escape to Glastonbury's outskirts to experience something else besides mandalas, crystal pendulums and stinky incense. 'Twas (almost) the season of goodwill to all men (and former rock stars) – and Zara Hamilton-Asquith was in.

CHAPTER TWELVE
Alice

WELL, THAT WAS easy. One box ticked, another gazillion to go.

Actually, no. Everything was coming along nicely. A bit too nicely... Jimmy had turned up with his flexi-fare train ticket a whole two days early. He didn't drive anymore so Hayley was enlisted to collect him from Taunton station for another long journey in her taxi to Wookey Hole.

"What the?" River, crouching down at the rear of the camper van, blinked rapidly as Jimmy strolled onto the campsite, whilst Hayley and the smoke from her tyres faded into the distance as if knowing her early 'delivery' was a surprise best avoided. "I'm pleased to see you, sir, but I thought I'd booked you into a hotel in Wells... as of precisely two evenings' time?"

"Aright, my 'ansum?" said Jimmy in Cornish. Shoot. Alice hoped he wouldn't carry on like this for the duration. She didn't quite predict a riot but she did predict Riv would get mightily pissed off. "Giss on!" Jimmy continued, pacing toward them determinedly with his battered and very ancient-looking case, which appeared to be covered in actual cobwebs. "You told me I was booked in there as of tonight."

"I'lltellywot... I kent membr," River gave him tit for tat and Alice tried not to crack up at the two of them. For someone who'd fallen out of love with England's southernmost county, her boyfriend had picked up Cornish lingo rather well.

The conversation continued to bat to and fro until Alice raised her hand, as if that might physically shut the pair of them up. Then she weighed in. "Enough! Jimmy, I seriously do hope the only leg-pulling going on here is you yanking ours. There's no room at the inn." She pointed at the gorgeous but undeniably titchy VW camper van, whose makeshift, foldable stage was currently being fitted to the back end of its trailer.

"Of course I'm joking," said Jimmy, suddenly sounding like a whole different version of himself. "I've paid for the extra nights' stay myself. Fancied a longer break. But there are only so many breadcrumbs I can feed the swans around the moat of the Bishop's Palace in Wells." Alice didn't dare get them off track again by enlightening Jimmy that actually, baked goods were strictly off the menu for those majestic birds, who were only to be given grain, lettuce and potatoes nowadays. "So I thought I'd come here and lend you a hand. I'll call Hayley later for a ride back to the hotel, or else I can catch the bus."

"Fair enough," said River, standing now and finally giving Jimmy a back pat. "It's good to see you and I'd far rather you turned up early than late. Actually, it's perfect timing. We've got soup on the portable stove and you're in luck – the campsite has just received its bi-weekly delivery of fresh bread."

Alice rubbed her fingerless cashmere-gloved hands together. She couldn't wait. This morning's al fresco porridge felt like a lifetime ago.

"So what's the deal here?" asked Jimmy. "I know the part you want me to play but what I can't understand is how you've put everything together so quickly."

"Once I decide to do something I'm a bit of a loose cannon." River laughed.

"River has his contacts. Bruno's worked miracles helping us get our licence to sell from the van pushed through super quickly *and* sorting out our gingerbread dilemma. You'll meet him," Alice stopped to look at her watch, "in about an hour or so."

"It's not what you know, it's who you know, hey," said Jimmy, arching a bushy white brow.

Never a truer word spoken, thought Alice. She shuddered when she recalled their rude awakening the other evening. How had she and River never thought of any of this important legal stuff? Especially when he'd run two bars! As usual, they'd got carried away and wrapped up in the sentiment of things. Which was why their serendipitous *rendez-vous* with Bruno at the motorway service station on the way here had been a godsend. Bruno's company had landed a contract to cater for a number of UK bands touring Europe several years ago – Avalonia being one of them – and Alice and River were very fond of him. He always went the extra mile to ensure every dietary whim was not only considered but delivered with a bow on top.

Bruno had been on his way back to Somerset from a culinary course he'd been teaching in Cornwall (it sounded suspiciously like the one Rio and Justin's friends had signed up for) and he'd had half an hour to spare. He'd invited Alice and River for a coffee (and a hot chocolate) at the service station's Starbucks so they could tell him all about their intrepid new adventure. Not only had he made a couple of urgent calls there and then to work his magic and secure them a licence but, notepad at the ready, he'd also made a list of their specific gingerbread requirements so he could forward them a formal proposal and quotation the very next day.

"But you're too big for all this twee bakery malarkey," River had jested, unable to believe the gift horse before them.

"You're never too big to get back to your roots, Mr J." Bruno put him straight. He shook his head in *whatever-are-we-going-to-do-with-you* style and his jet-black, textured quiff barely moved a millimetre. A realisation that fascinated Alice.

"I s'pose. Look at us two," River glanced at Alice. "But that was a conscious choice. Surely you have bigger fish to fry than supplying a nostalgic old van with some reindeer and robin shaped biscuits."

"I wouldn't have offered if I didn't want to get involved. I'm at a bit of a loose end over the festive period." Bruno took a giant swig of his coffee. "Shit! That was hotter than expected!"

Alice stifled a giggle. River failed miserably.

Bruno exhaled deeply. His brow furrowed in a way that suggested hot coffee wasn't his only problem. It was clear to Alice that there was a little more to his kindness than met the eye.

"All right. Maybe I wouldn't put myself forward in normal times. But it's the first Christmas since my divorce."

"Oh, mate. I'm so sorry, I had no idea," said River.

"Me neither," Alice added, only just noting the lack of a wedding ring.

From what she remembered, Bruno had been involved with a hair and makeup artist, having met her while the pair of them were at the beck and call of some mega-musician or other. They'd got on like a house on fire and married shortly after. How devastating was that? On the scale of golden relationships, she'd have put them right up there with Pierce Brosnan and Keely Shaye Smith. They just seemed so made for each other.

"I've moved on emotionally. Honest I have," Bruno replied. He looked them both in the eyes with his own deep chocolate pools, and although Alice was well and truly in love with River, whose denim blue orbs she wouldn't trade for anybody's, she couldn't understand how a woman would walk away from the catch sitting before her. "Pandora met somebody else. A woman, actually."

Alice wanted to gasp but that would have been deeply inappropriate. Bruno's revelation served to remind her how often she subconsciously and unintentionally stereotyped. Why shouldn't Pandora have met another woman? Why did it always have to be a man who turned a woman's head?

"I'm sorry," said River again, rather unimaginatively.

"Don't be. I'd suspected something for a while and it's far better this way than if we had brought kids into the mix. Although sadly, Pandora took custody of the pugs." He frowned. "I've thrown myself into work this year and it's been a tonic. I'm ready to date again actually. Tentatively, but all the same. It's high time I dusted myself down. So, on that note… if you ahem… know of anybody who can put up with the ebbing and flowing work patterns of a chef, well… you have my permission to try to matchmake. I trust your judgment over Tinder's… *I think*!"

The three of them chuckled in unison.

"Hmm." Alice laced her fingers and flexed her arms out, as if that might help her come up with a name. "Nobody springs immediately to mind, but we'll have a think all the same," she reassured him.

"So, you're based in Somerset permanently, or what?" asked River. "Last time we saw you, you were positively an East End of London lad, as I recall."

"True." Bruno replied with half a grin. "Hackney was my haven for a while. I know it sounds obvious, but I loved its hip appeal." He sipped a little more cautiously at his coffee now before explaining. "We sold the flat, made a pretty penny each, and I moved back to Somerset. A little village not far from Wells." Bruno closed his eyes and sighed deeply. "Oh, okay, you've got me: I've moved back in with my folks. Only temporarily. All the travelling meant I hadn't seen them for yonks and I needed to get back to the fresh country air – and make some decisions before I shelled out on a new pad, wherever that might be. Initially it was a win-win situation, but now, I think I've outstayed my welcome. It might be a farmhouse but Mum's not too impressed with me taking over her beloved kitchen."

"Near Wells, you say?" River was intrigued.

"Yes. I'm guessing you might have heard of it, but we never did get a chance to talk about our mutual Somerset roots when you were in the band." Bruno went in for another gulp of coffee. "It's called West Pennard."

"Are you kidding? I went to primary school there!" River's eyes lit up at the mention of the cute village sandwiched between Pilton – the true location of the famous Glastonbury music festival – and Glastonbury proper. What a small world.

And that had been that. Once each of them had fully digested their auspiciously unscripted get-together on the side of the M5 – and the remainder of their hot drinks – there was no question that all of this was somehow meant to be.

By the time Alice had recounted the tale to Jimmy in the present, and by the time they'd lined their stomachs with leek and potato soup and hot crusty buttered bread, a bobble-hatted Bruno was striding over to greet them with a gargantuan picnic basket and a smile to match. River had been about to remove the stage from its trailer hooked to the back of the camper van – another favour from another friend: a small-time musician on this occasion – but then the vision of Bruno had caught his eye and he'd dropped everything, jumping up and down like an over-excited puppy.

"Woah, boy! You haven't even sampled it yet," said Bruno as he approached Alice, River and Jimmy.

"Jump right inside and be my guest." River opened up the sliding doors of the VW and invited everybody in. "If we're going to do a taste test, we're going to do it in style."

Everybody quickly took a seat, which was just a little cramped, since the camper's scant seating area was the first thing one stumbled upon to the left; its postage stamp-sized table hugging the L-shape of the relaxation facilities. Bruno, standing, tried to remain deeply serious as he arranged his paraphernalia, and finally removed his bobble hat to reveal his trademark hairstyle, but Alice spotted the joy in his eyes, the way he was swallowing back his grin. His cheeks were positively glowing, compared to their lacklustre hue when they'd bumped into him the other day. And she didn't think this could just be due to the weather. Evidently, he was genuinely enjoying himself and couldn't wait to see the expressions on their faces when they took their first bites.

He expertly removed a box of samples, placed it on the table, and a collective 'ooh' ensued.

Alice didn't know where to look first. This was way beyond her expectations. Which begged the question: how could he possibly produce such a festive feast for such a brilliant price? But she wasn't going to argue about that.

"Wow," Jimmy was the first to speak. "These are definitely worth breaking a tooth over!"

"Thanks. I'll take that as a compliment," said Bruno.

"I'm speechless," said River. "And we haven't even tried them yet."

"What he said," chirruped Alice.

Like a box of decadent chocolates with each ambrosial variety screaming for attention, she hadn't a clue where to begin.

"I guess I'll give you a rundown then," said Bruno proudly, pointing to each of the gingerbread samples he'd lovingly baked. "First off, we have the classic gingerbread man. Now I can do these with skirts on too – which isn't to insinuate the gingerbread woman can't wear trousers and vice versa."

Jimmy looked seriously stunned at that. Bruno moved swiftly on.

"Next we have these." Bruno carefully picked up the little

iced 3D gingerbread house, amidst a collective gasp. "Oh, they're quite sturdy. Don't worry. You might have seen them on Pinterest."

"*Pin what?*" asked Jimmy, predictably.

Alice passed Bruno a mug to demonstrate. She knew exactly what Bruno meant. When she wasn't 'pinning' wedding ideas on the social media site, she'd spotted the cute cottages popping up in her newsfeed. He anchored the dinky edible house on the mug's rim using its little doorway.

"Cor, that's really summit." Jimmy shook his head in wonder.

"Love, love, love it." River licked his lips like the fox in the Ladybird book *The Gingerbread Man* that Alice used to read as a kid. "That and a hot chocolate equals a match made in heaven, at any time of the year."

Alice giggled. The guy was plain obsessed. And who'd have predicted this transition from bartender to biscuit fiend? Then again, Bruno's intricate piping skills were worthy of an art gallery. Those roofs looked like they were coated in layers of real snow, and even at such a miniature scale, the attention to detail was phenomenal: stained glass window panes (she guessed those were made from melted down boiled sweets), gables, letterboxes and even door knockers.

"Moving on to the Christmas wildlife selection." Bruno pointed to the next batch of creations and another group groan of delight broke out. The menagerie of red-nosed reindeer, red-breasted robins, polar bears, penguins and turtle doves was a sight to behold. Some of these gingerbread creations were iced with crisp white royal icing, some boasted pillar box-red adornments, some were the proud owners of chocolate chip eyes, and some sported flaked almond embellishments. How the guy had put this lot together at such short notice, Alice had no idea. He was a culinary wizard, who surely couldn't have been working alone.

After that came gingerbread Christmas trees, neatly piped with pistachio, rose, and white chocolate. Then there were iced gingerbread snowflakes, Santas, presents, sleighs and mittens.

The array was breath-taking, and still Bruno continued to pull things out of the hamper as if he were Santa himself.

"I thought it might be cool for you to sell some of those build-your-own-gingerbread-house kits too. But not the pre-packaged ones that end up looking a million times worse than the picture on the box. These will be authentically rustic. Freshly baked and utterly delicious. I can provide you with piping bags and foodie ornamentation, decoration stations too… if you're interested, that is? *River?*"

River's jaw had dropped to the floor. In a good way, Alice could tell. But it was not his most becoming look. She elbowed him in the ribs.

"Oh, my God. Yes! We can use the fold-up stage area for kids to make those… before the performances start."

"Performances?" quizzed Bruno.

"I forgot to mention those." River raised his brows as if to challenge Bruno, as he had a surprise of his own.

"I'll give you a demo in a moment, lad." Jimmy winked.

"It may not have crossed your minds, but there does also exist a smattering of curious human beings who aren't so enamoured with the beloved spice that is ginger." Bruno had already moved on to the next performance of his own.

And oh, heck. Another point they'd omitted to consider. What were they like?

"Never fear." As if reading Alice's mind, Bruno produced a smaller box from his picnic basket, which was starting to resemble Mary Poppins' bottomless bag. "For such choosy customers, I can offer melted snowman biscuits." Alice, River, and Jimmy were the audience at a magic show now. Bruno delicately laid the shortcake-based biscuit before them; its topping a marshmallow-headed snowman whose body was a pool of glossy royal icing. Again, the detailing was incredible: the coal eyes, the tiny carrot nose, the scarf and the buttons. Everything had been thought of.

"Next we have Christmas pudding biscuits. These are made of chocolate." Bruno placed a perfect, chunky sphere in front of them. Its curvaceous snow-white frosting, and bright green and red sprig of holly made Alice's mouth water.

"And finally, how about a plain vanilla biscuit base studded with cranberry, orange and white chocolate?" Bruno revealed a rather delectable-looking stocking.

"Jeez." That was River.

Alice and Jimmy were gobsmacked.

"Now, I know you said you wanted gingerbread of the biscuit kind, but I couldn't resist seeing what you thought of my gingerbread muffins and my gingerbread, mascarpone and molasses cake. Some people prefer a bit more stodge, what with it being winter."

From yet another box, Bruno lifted a spectacularly golden and cream multi-layered sponge.

"Formidable," said Jimmy. "Now there's a word I haven't dusted down for a decade or more."

Unperturbed, Bruno emptied the hamper of his final creation: a simple but very moreish-looking muffin.

"If it's too plain I can supply you with cupcakes instead… a generous dollop of buttercream or milk chocolate frosting to finish them off, all nicely swirled, of course… and then perhaps a small gingerbread person on top? I can't claim that idea was mine either. Good old Pinterest is awash with biscuit people leaning out at a jaunty angle on top of cakes and willing everybody to chomp their heads off. So, what do you think, lady and gents? Will this be enough variety for your discerning village clientele?"

"A resounding YES to everything that comes out of your kitchen, you bloody genius!" River gasped before biting down on his lip.

"Never mind the customers, let's dig in!" cried Jimmy.

"Well, well, well," came two familiar voices, causing everyone to jump literally an inch. "Looks like we arrived at just the right time."

River and Alice did a synchronized double take. It couldn't be. *But it flipping well was!* Rio and Justin bumbled up to the camper van in tandem, shed their massive hiker-style rucksacks at the open door as if checking in to a hotel, and flung themselves at the gathering with the kind of excitement that needed tamping down lest it tip up the vehicle and all who sat in her.

CHAPTER THIRTEEN
Zara

AFTER PUTTING THE final touches to her cornucopia of chocolate offerings, Zara drove to the campsite in her ancient but trusty Ford Ka. Sure, she'd done the touristy things in Wells: visited the cathedral and had a picnic on its verdant spread of a lawn, drooled over the displays in the fudge shop on the corner of the high street, admired the elegant swans gliding around the moat of the Bishop's Palace, and spent more money than she should have at the weekend market, but she didn't think she'd ever ventured deep into a village like this, on the farthest side of the England's smallest city. Which was crazy, what with Wookey Hole and her caves being one of Somerset's biggest sightseeing draws – complete with a legendary witch who could give even the most unconventional of Glastonians a run for their money.

The journey to the village was picturesque. Somerset's patchwork quilt of fields looked particularly idyllic today; the low winter sun leaving welcome flecks of light all over the vista, differentiating the shades of green, which ranged from shamrock to seafoam. Cosy cottages, sprawling farms, and tasteful modern houses nestled in amongst it all. Some of them were what could only be described as 'readier' for

Christmas than others! What a quaint little place, though Zara could see why River wanted to liven things up. She may have been biased, coming from Glastonbury's vivacious high street, but it was all really rather sleepy here – or it would be, until the unlit bulbs festooned across some of the house facades were illuminated come evening.

A gleaming green tractor rounded the bed in front of her, and from behind that there was a whizz, as an even shinier red Mercedes overtook the sluggish vehicle from seemingly *nowhere*, rudely jolting Zara from her thoughts and forcing her to slam her foot on the brakes and hope for the best; her precious cargo flinging itself into the back of her seat with considerable force.

"Shit!" Zara's heart raced. A bolt of dread lurched through her body. The guy speeding along, now mercifully back in the right lane, put his hand up as if to apologise. A bit late now!

"Idiot!" she screamed in delayed reaction, her pulse ratcheting up even more as she found herself pummelling furiously at her horn. It probably sounded like a mouse compared to his Merc's roar. And that made her even more wound up.

Whilst she'd certainly glared at him, all she'd clocked in that split-second as he passed was a quiff of a hair-do. Like some dark-haired and blurry version of Tintin.

All right, hands up, she probably was bombing along a little too quickly herself, considering the narrowness of the road. But what a bellend, overtaking like that when he must have been able to see her. Sure, her own red car – her little ladybug without spots – was nowhere near as buffed up as his, but it hardly blended into the hedgerows either.

Zara tugged on her left plait in a bid to regain her composure. She dreaded thinking about the state of her goodies in the backseat. She really should have wrapped the seatbelt around them, or lodged them properly in the boot. But that was hardly the point!

She drove on slowly. She hadn't quite expected to see the campsite sign so soon. She decided to keep going until she could find a layby or a quiet turning where she would give everything a quick once-over. It didn't take long. The carpark of one of Wookey Hole's pubs, sadly boarded up, made an ideal pitstop.

Gingerly, she stepped out of the car and brushed herself down, as if removing all of the stressful energy that pompous git had unnecessarily created. Zara folded down her driver seat, her car being a so-called three door (which always made her laugh, for how could a boot be described as a legitimate passenger entry point?), inhaled sharply, and peeped inside the first cardboard box. So far so good: the hot chocolate powder combos in their tall mason jars were all intact. She took a deeper breath and looked inside the box sitting next to it. She'd packaged *most* items in bubble wrap, they should be OK.

A mosaic of chocolate pieces stared back at her in defiance.

"Oh, bugger!" she cried, pushing away her fringe in disbelief, tears pricking at her eyes.

It had taken her hours to painstakingly make those top two layers of chocolate melts and tree decorations. These weren't your bog standard melts either, but milk chocolate bombs surrounding luxury marshmallows (whose casing was now cracked and about as appealing as a plate of old Brussels sprouts); they were Cointreau and orange zest-infused Nutcracker soldiers (all of that diligent piping of their moustaches and uniforms in smithereens), and there were several dozen hot chocolate stirrers in every flavour from praline to mocha, raspberry and dark chocolate to milk chocolate honeycomb – the only part of them that hadn't been crushed to pieces was their wooden sticks.

Typically, she'd run out of bubble wrap at the eleventh hour this morning… and hadn't accounted for meeting Lewis Hamilton on a race track this afternoon.

"YOU JUST MISSED Bruno," Alice greeted Zara, who was tentatively pulling her boxes behind her on a little metal frame with wheels.

"But you've hit the jackpot with us instead!" chorused a couple of guys. One lanky and custard-blonde. The other squat, muscular and red-headed.

Zara remained mute, proffering a smile that she hoped wouldn't look strained. She couldn't help but raise her eyebrows at the bizarre welcome, though she was sure it would go unnoticed. The current length of her fringe would give Rapunzel some serious competition. She hoped their baking supplier, whom Alice had already mentioned in one of her recent messages, wasn't the twit in the red car she'd just lambasted. Nah. He couldn't possibly be. He'd looked more like a city trader than a country baker in that poser-mobile.

"Are those the samples and stock?" River beamed.

"Hey, don't even think about eating your bodyweight in

sugar all over again," Alice reprimanded him. "This will be a much more refined taste testing, as is befitting artisan chocolate."

"We, on the other hand, are ready and waiting after our host, Mr Jackson, rudely locked his guests out of the camper van and forgot every single rule of etiquette." The redhead rubbed his hands together and winked at the blond guy standing next to him.

"Where are my manners?" said Alice. "Zara, meet Rio and Justin." Alice gestured to the two males so quickly that Zara couldn't work out who was who. "You already know River and me, of course." She did. She still felt a little sheepish around River but he didn't appear to hold a grudge towards her for her misguided friendship with Georgina. How could he, when he'd been equally duped by the woman? "And then we have Jimmy... at least, he was around here the last time I looked."

"None of the entourage should be here today," piped up River, who was fiddling about with an outdoor cooking stove. "Jimmy decided to descend on us two days earlier than his invite. And as for this pair." He pointed at Rio and Justin. "Well, they've pretty much gate-crashed."

"You'll soon be eating your words once you've seen our new and improved breakdance act," quipped the tallest guy. Zara thought he was Justin. "Besides, as I keep reassuring you, we're booked into the village Airbnb, so you can stop stressing that we're going to be cramping your romantic style and kipping alongside you and Alice in the van."

"You didn't honestly think you'd get away with inviting Jimmy for the inauguration of your talent contest, and leaving us out," sniped the male Zara presumed to be Rio.

"I didn't want things to get out of hand." River held up his own then, in defeat. "The next thing you know, the flipping book club brigade will descend on us."

"Surely that would be a good thing," said Rio. "When we threw that surprise leaving party back in your kitchen, you chose Jimmy to kick things off here in Somerset precisely because his act is so different and it might encourage all kinds of latent talent to emerge from the prim and proper village cottages. Those book club narrations were pretty impressive, although I can't deny my penchant for a bit of spooning." Justin chortled at that. Zara felt her cheeks flaming, images of her last steamy spooning session with her ex-boyfriend, Blake, popping into her head most unwelcomely. "But answer me this: how many of these villagers will be breakdancing with household props?" He slanted a victory brow at his declaration.

"They make an excellent point, Riv," Alice cut in, not before pivoting to Zara with a *bear-with-me-all-will-become-clearer-soon-I-promise* expression. "The boys' rather *distinct* act sets the tone for what you're trying to achieve. In just the same way as Jimmy's. The last thing we want is to end up with a roadshow re-enactment of *Britain's Got Talent* meets *The X Factor*. Which is fine if you like that sort of thing. But it's also a format that's been done to high kingdom come. If you want something different, you have to set things off with far more of a bang, so the direction is obvious for those thinking of taking part."

"Okay, okay," River conceded. "Jimmy can kick the performances off for the first two nights, Rio and Justin the second two. But that's it. Then they go home. That'll be enough of a hint to the villagers and the local media that we're encouraging one-off artistry. No One Direction. No Celine Dion. No dog duets or ventriloquists. And definitely no eighties cabaret."

Everyone sighed collectively in relief, Zara included.

"I… erm." She finally found her voice. "I brought most of the samples and stock with me." Zara didn't know if it was better to come across as a tad forgetful, or the world's clumsiest driver. She plumped for the former. "The rest I can drop off tomorrow evening, if that suits?" Bloody hell. Now she'd have her work cut out. Why did she have to go and let herself in for such a crazy amount of toil, in such a short space of time?

"As long as we have most of the cocoa powder mixes and a few of the melts and stirrers to get us started, I'm sure that will be fine," said Alice. "Don't stress." Zara let out an even larger sigh of relief.

"Right then. Let's hop inside the van again for pudding!" said River.

Jimmy was already seated at the tiny camper van's table, sleeves rolled up, knife and fork poised at the ready in a comic move that had everybody in hysterics and put Zara immediately at ease. She knew she'd created cocoa bean excellence and couldn't wait to see everybody's reactions. Blimey, it was a bit of a sardine tin though. As if he could read her mind, Rio relegated himself to the swivelling driver's seat, and Justin took to a kneeling position on the floor, an act which made him look like a praying mantis.

"I'll go and boil up some milk for the drinks," said Alice,

side-stepping Justin, who, despite Alice's own model-like height, was almost up to her shoulders. She opened the fridge for a large bottle and headed outside to heat its contents on the stove.

Zara briskly laid out her wares for her eager audience and tried to keep a straight face as Rio almost uprooted the driver's seat with his incessant spinning and clapping at the imminent liquid chocolate fest.

"Excuse them. They don't get out much," said River.

"How can you expect us to keep a lid on it when you, Alice and Jimmy gobbled all of that fit and phwoar Bruno's goods up, before we as much as got a look in?" Justin set him straight. "Damn right we're champing at the bit."

"I can assure you that most of us," River looked pointedly at Jimmy, who Zara suspected was the exception, "Nibbled politely in the manner of a judging panel… that's to say, with discernment and in moderation, knowing we needed to save room for dessert."

"Okay," said Zara, trying to compose herself once the mason jars were lined up, looking like the epitome of rustic kitchen chic. "Everything is labelled, as you can see. But I'll just give you a quick run-through so you know what's what."

"Sounds great," River encouraged her, while Alice called for a queue of mugs so she could fill them with hot milk for the first part of the taste test.

"Obviously I've catered for the basics. So the first three jars are milk, dark and white chocolate. But then I thought it would be fun to spice things up in keeping with the season. So I've labelled each of those special jars ref their dry ingredients; the spices, orange zest, choc chip chunks, mini marshmallows and such… and written the additional ingredients to be added just beneath." Zara demonstrated this with a wooden spoon. "I've packed all of those extra bits and pieces at the bottom of the box that I'll be leaving here with you – Cointreau, cinnamon sticks, coffee liquor and so on, so we can run through any questions you might have about those in a bit. Given your mixologist background, though, River, you're probably more than acquainted with these steps of the recipes."

River nodded enthusiastically.

"Basically…" Zara hated starting a sentence with that word. It was up there with 'at the end of day' and 'nice', but heck, she was tired. She wanted nothing more than to get this drill over, so she could return to her shop kitchen to salvage as much of the damaged order as possible. "The mason jars you see before you contain the base mixes for eggnog hot cocoa, choc orange with a kick, peppermint, gingerbread, and a mince pie special."

"Cor!"

"Yum!"

"Flip me!"

Jimmy, Rio and Justin's eyes bulged at the prospect.

"Zara, you have well and truly excelled yourself," said River. "This is exactly what I dreamt of … but not once did I think this sheer variety of lip-smacking deliciousness would be viable… and at such short notice, too. *Thank you!*"

"Well, you've got to try it first." Zara motioned to Alice, who was holding a tray of steaming hot milk. "This," she waved a hand at the camper's gorgeously homely interior, "is definitely a magical place to serve gingerbread and hot chocolate at Christmas. Like Alice was saying earlier, if you're going to do something new, you have to go all out and do it in style. Give your customers something to remember."

"We won't know how successful things are going to be until we've toured a few villages," said Alice. "But I get a wonderful, heart-warming feeling about this."

"Now then." Zara helped her unload the piping hot mugs from the tray. "Who wants what?"

Excitement buzzed around the camper van, but eventually she managed to translate everybody's orders. Then all became silent, taking their responsibilities as beverage critics dead seriously, until they were exchanging a flurry of praise and gratification.

The chocolate melts, stirrers and tree decorations that had made it in one piece were unveiled next, and before long everybody was blissed out in post-serotonin wonder. Job most definitely done!

It would have been rude to peel herself away immediately, so Zara helped Jimmy, Justin and Alice clear up whilst Rio discussed the days ahead and River showed him a map of the route options for the little bar on wheels around the Somerset villages.

"Bruno insisted we stop at West Pennard, Pilton and North Wootton," said River.

"Well, of course he would," answered Alice as she left Justin to stack the plates to dry and gestured for Jimmy and Zara to deposit the boxes near the cupboards. "That's his original neck of the woods so he's getting all nostalgic about it. But if we're not careful, we'll spend too much time in one part of the county. We need to spread things out a bit. There are hundreds of villages in need of some festive cheer… and only so many days before Christmas."

Hmm. Zara also sensed it was a little too close to Alice's parents' sprawling property in the nearby village of Butleigh. No wonder she was trying to throw one of the VW's spanners into the works. If Zara's relationship with her own parents was a benchmark to measure such things against, then she couldn't blame Alice.

"Which are your favourite Somerset villages, Zara? Any recommendations?" asked River, snapping her out of her pondering.

"I'm deeply ashamed to say that I haven't really left Glastonbury all that much, except for visits to Somerset's bigger touristy places like Bristol, Bath, Wells and Weston-Super-Mare." Zara shrugged. The latter had been the longest day trip with Blake, due to his incessant whining because he hadn't managed to suss out the workings of the grab-a-teddy-bear arcade machines, not to mention the-waste-of-time-and-money tuppence coin games. Zara kept trying to explain to him these were either glued to the shelves, or held in place with super magnets.

"I… er… well, I did a lot of travelling in the past before I moved here, stayed in some amazing places, and all in such a short space of time. Christmas was usually spent in Barbados or the British Virgin Islands, February half-terms were Dubai or Oman, Easter was split between Florence and Provence. As for summer… that was a haze of holidaying in hotspots across the Med… which we'd usually reach via yacht. A little bit like you being on the road in the band, I guess. I became a bit blasé about it."

Shit. Where had all that lot come from? But it was too late to take back the secrets of her wealthy past, now she'd laid them on the table for everyone's perusal. Just like she'd unloaded the chocolate. Evidently she felt so at home here with this little cluster of people that she could spill her life story out to them. "And then, ever since I moved here, it's been just me and the business. No staff to fall back on, so I can't really take a holiday." Zara quickly finished up.

"Gosh," said Alice. "Some of those destinations are certainly ringing some childhood bells. I can't help but think our paths must have previously crossed at a cocktail party or a polo match!"

"And I can't help but think ours definitely didn't." Rio snorted. "Blackpool was about as good as it got in my childhood. Jammy cows."

"I'm sorry, I… I'm not sure what came over me."

Zara quickly stood to gather her things, ashamed of herself for blurting all that out. The last thing she'd wanted to do was offend anyone. She could only blame that uncharacteristic outpouring on the Quiff. Ever since he'd practically smacked into her earlier, she'd been feeling off kilter.

"No, I'm sorry, Zara," said River. "I shouldn't have assumed you knew the area so well, when you're working all the hours God sends."

"Ignore Rio," said Justin. "He's always had a chip on his shoulder. We've actually been to most of those places now. Well, except Oman. We honeymooned at the Sandals resort in Barbs, though. Ohemgee. Outta this world luxury. That was the time we got chatting to Simon Cowell at the airport."

River did something Elvis Presley with his lip then. Zara,

sensing it was a scowl gone wrong, was cringing inwardly at Justin's abbreviation for the Caribbean island where her father undoubtedly still owned his plantation. The locals truly loathed it when visitors did that.

"Want me to do another rendition on my spoons for the lady before she goes?" asked Jimmy.

Zara's curiosity couldn't help but be piqued, despite the fact she had a mountain of work to do. She'd come across every kind of musical instrument in Glastonbury – from the all-too-common didgeridoo to the bagpipes, and the ukulele to the svelte Martin Backpacker acoustic guitar. But never had a past musician boyfriend, and never had a past eccentric customer, treated her to a performance on, well… cutlery.

"No, you're all right, Jimmy. I think we ought to be calling Hayley to get you back to the hotel now," River interjected.

"And how about we ask the lady herself?" Alice coughed loudly, as if to remind her boyfriend that he wasn't Zara's spokesperson.

"I'd like that, Jimmy," Zara answered decidedly. "Then I could run you wherever you're staying, if it's a local stop."

"Or I'll be going back that way too," said a brand new male voice coming from directly (and a little too intimately) behind Zara, delivering with it hints of exquisite, less-is-more cologne. "Promise I'm not eavesdropping," the rich, smooth voice continued over her shoulder now. "I left my trusty piping bag behind when I was demo-ing the gingerbread icing."

Zara swivelled to take stock of the face behind the confident words, then was quite unable to process the vision standing far too close for comfort in front of her. Then again, it was a small camper van, especially considering the number of people that were currently bunched together inside it.

"*You?*" she thundered so loudly that the audience did a collective intake of breath.

The Quiff, who she'd quickly deduced was bloody Bruno – Rio's earlier description was infuriatingly right; he was, indeed, sex on legs – toppled backwards off the step, landing less than gracefully on the well-trodden grass outside the van.

CHAPTER FOURTEEN
River

"HEY, IT'S YOU!" River heard Bruno declare, his voice tinged with a mix of surprise and excitement.

"Hey, it's me! *Hey, it's me?* I'm sorry, do I know you from somewhere, other than behind the wheel of a car you really need to retake your driving test in?" Zara spat. "And more to the point... why am I the one apologising after you almost made me swerve into a fricking hedgerow... and... *and beyond*, nearly ploughing straight through that and onto somebody's cabbage patch, finishing up in their kitchen window?"

Oh, dear. River looked at Alice, but she was as clueless as he was. What on earth could Zara mean, when she and Bruno didn't know one another from Adam?

River's two suppliers (aka the two most important people in his life, after Alice, at this current moment in time), did not appear to have hit it off. At all. Although the greeting Zara had given poor Bruno had certainly *knocked* him off. Clean off the steps of the camper van by the sounds of things. Bugger. Loath as he was to stick his beak in, River couldn't let Zara's frosty reception put paid to any of his intricate plans for the next few weeks. Too much was resting on them.

"Hey, what's going on guys?"

River stood behind Zara, keen to restore conviviality in the camp, worry etched across his forehead, one hand planted on his hip, which was a new piece of body language for him, and made him feel like a teapot.

Predictably, Rio, Justin and Jimmy appeared behind him, crowding the doorway quite unnecessarily like a bunch of rubberneckers at a car crash site. Which was kind of apt, River supposed, given that Zara seemed to be hinting she'd almost driven her own car into one of the village houses.

"Just what is it with you males today?" Alice cut in, adding several tuts. "Mind your own business. Every one of you. And that most definitely includes you, Jackson!"

Reluctantly, River let Alice drag him back inside, while Zara – and Bruno, who was now at least standing – remained locked in a strange pre-battle of wills.

CHAPTER FIFTEEN
Zara

THE MAN STANDING before Zara was terribly easy on the eye. His own were dark: onyx, brooding and striking; perfectly complementing skin with an enviably olive hue. And he was just about the only man on the planet to wear a quiff so well. Unless you counted James Dean. Come to think of it, he looked exactly like the kind of man she was hoping to discover in Tuscany.

"*It's me. Bruno.* We were on the same course at uni, remember? Well, only for the first couple of months. I had to drop out when my brother went missing and my parents couldn't cope. But then I enrolled on another course down in Southampton the following year and caught up."

The gorgeous creature waved a hand as if to dismiss his history and Zara gulped down her compassion over his sibling. She didn't gel with her own sisters. The eldest, Grace (whose behaviour was nothing like her name) had certainly indulged in one too many nights out in her teens – the kind that had kept her parents up until daybreak, wondering if they should call the police. But nothing on a par with this. What a tragedy!

"Excuse me... I'm waffling," Bruno apologised. "Obviously, I've now moved to the West Country, after a few stints on the road catering for River, Alice and co, and well, here I am. River needed a major favour and I just so happened to have time to step in. I'm guessing you're my foodie counterpart... that would be, on the erm, chocolate side of things."

Zara didn't know what to say.

"Oh, and we found Nolan in the end, by the way. So all good."

"Right," was all she found she could manage, quite startled at the way the guy had manipulated the conversation so that it was now her showering him with sympathies. She had to find a way to get back on track (and out of the proverbial hedgerow) with her own matters. Yet, once again, words failed her.

It was the funniest thing, and about as untimely as lulls in conversation got, but in that moment, Zara's synapses sparked. It all came flooding back to her. Of course. She *did* remember Bruno now. She'd long forgotten his name, but memories flashed back loud and clear. He was the absolute stud who had reduced the girls, and some of the guys (huh, not forgetting the teacher) to rabbits caught in headlights the day he'd waltzed into their cookery class at the National Bakery School of London's Southbank University. And he was a stud that had matured not so much in the manner of a muffin, but a rich Christmas cake.

Shit. Now where was she?

Oh, yes. Zara inhaled deeply and composed herself. She wasn't prepared to let the guy talk his way out of his appalling behaviour so easily. He'd not even said he was sorry! Besides, she'd been surrounded by cherubic male models throughout her teenage years and early twenties, as she'd been dragged around London's soiree, launch and publicity stunt circuits. Glastonbury's males might not quite compare, but Zara'd had more than enough practice at remaining impervious to good looks.

She flicked her plaits behind her shoulders, made an awkward stretch across the VW to retrieve her boxes and trolley wheels, batted her errant braids back into position again, and made for her car, brushing Bruno's shoulder in a move she'd hoped to pull off as a warning, but unfortunately she'd chickened out on using too much brute force at the last minute, so it had watered itself down to a delicate frisson instead.

"One piping bag," she heard Alice say behind her, presumably passing it to Bruno. Which meant Zara needed to quicken her steps. The idiot had got what he'd returned for and could already be in hot pursuit.

But then she realised she'd forgotten something too. Damn. She couldn't be so cruel as to continue this determined flight, as she'd offered Jimmy a lift. Leaving him behind would hardly make her look true to her word. Especially when River and Alice were expecting the remnants of a broken order from her. She needed the money too much for them to pull the plug now. And no way would she give Bruno the satisfaction of thinking his offer of a lift in a swankier vehicle was the no-brainer. So now the only thing she could do to turn things around was to make it look as if she'd simply been heading back to the car to pack her things before returning for the old man. And that should give Bruno enough time to take his piping bag and shove it up his cute arse, striding back to his mahoosive Merc so he could speed off into the sunset, their paths never to cross again.

She took a deep breath, an action which seemed to be the theme of the day, and walked purposefully back to the camper van, intent on making this quick.

"Shall we?" Zara held out her arm for Jimmy to hook onto, ignoring Bruno's curious stare. Jimmy stood to attention and started to shuffle out of the van.

"Zara? *Is everything okay?* Are we still on for the missing chocolate bits and pieces?" Alice questioned.

"Of course. Why shouldn't we be on? I'll message you to arrange the best time to drop them off." Zara fired out her words as rapidly as possible, hardly daring to look at anyone's face except Jimmy's. Although she could see from the corner of her eye that Rio and Justin were trying like mad to suppress giggles.

She hated it when she got all worked up like this. It wasn't as if Bruno was the first to trigger the uncontrollable fight or flight behaviour in her that loved to rear its head when least expected. But this claustrophobic camper van was not the place to analyse any of that. Zara needed to accomplish her mission. Rescue the elderly dude, drop him off safely, and get herself back to the solace of her beloved kitchen to make up for lost time (and inconsiderate male drivers).

"Right, it's just you seem a bit…" But Alice didn't finish her sentence.

"I thought you wanted to watch me playing the spoons," said Jimmy with a distinctly downturned mouth and droopy, glistening blue eyes.

"You really should see him," Bruno added. "He's pretty

amazing. I was treated to a demo earlier."

Zara bit her lip. How she wanted to let rip at the guy for his lack of etiquette. Bruno owed her a behemoth apology, for goodness sake, and here he was hanging about like a very bad smell. Except he wasn't. He smelt luscious. Woody, aromatic, spicy and citrus. Which was seriously grrr, when you were an artisan foodie who adored fragrance. Grrr in both bloody senses of the word. It was enough to make her want to pounce on him.

"Pfft," quipped Rio. "And you haven't seen mine and Just's talents yet!"

"Oh, erm, yes," Zara conceded, momentarily glad to have been brought back down to earth.

And oh, erm, bugger. Well, she had sort of promised earlier. Before that ghastly surprise. For a split second, Zara thought she could let Jimmy play for her in the car. But within moments she could see exactly where this bizarre afternoon was headed. Rio and Justin would only find a way onto the Ka's backseat too, hell bent on not missing out. Best she feigned delight at watching all the entertainment here and now, and nip it in the bud.

"Excellent!" cried River. "The stage is up. No time like the present for an encore."

Zara shuffled uncertainly back out of the camper van, waiting for everything to begin. She caught sight of her flustered and messy reflection in the VW's window and grimaced, an action which wasn't lost on Bruno.

"You carry them off well… the um… the pigtails."

"They're plaits, *braids*. Pigtails would just have a bobble at the top. Like a ponytail, but two of them."

"Oh, okay." Bruno cocked a brow. "I... I seem to have unintentionally put my foot in it again. It's just, not many women your, *our* age can carry them off but on you they look—"

"Are you for real? First you almost derail me and seriously injure me... or worse. An act you've still not apologised for, by the way. And now you're trying to tell me I look cute for a middle-aged woman. Christ, I'm only thirty-three!"

"No, no. That's not what I was implying at all. And I swear I said I was sorry. Anyway, you were hardly driving within the speed limit yourself. You couldn't have been, else you'd have had time to pull over."

Could this man get any more annoying?

Zara strode over to the stage, fuming at Bruno's macho attitude. Now he pegged himself as Jeremy Sodding Clarkson. *Pull over in-bloody-deed!* Jimmy settled himself into another chair and dug a pair of spoons out of his pocket, placing them back to back, lifting his leg to create a 'double tap'.

Once he got into full throttle and began to hum along to his rendition of The Beatles' 'Penny Lane', she felt herself relaxing again. He was really rather good and it wasn't difficult to give him a standing ovation (overlooking the fact everyone was already on their feet in their small audience).

Then it was Rio and Justin's turn.

"For the love of God, please tell me you've brought your own props with you for today's theatrics," shouted River. "We can only fit the bare bones of pots and pans in the VW and I'm not volunteering for any of them to get broken."

"Take a chill pill, Riv. We've got that side of things covered," chirruped Rio.

"Yeah," added Justin. "And in keeping with all things baking, we'll be performing today's break dance with rolling pins, cookie cutters and a sieve."

Just when Zara thought she had seen it all in Glastonbury. These guys were something else.

Alice cranked up the stereo to the song of their choice – a Chaka Khan and Rufus number from way back when – and the boys began to windmill, headspin and jackhammer; a strange, but decidedly impressive game of catch going on between them all the while, as kitchenalia was lobbed from one dancer to the other. Only once did they let a rolling pin fall.

Clapping at their finale was heartfelt too… especially as it meant Zara and Jimmy could now make their swift exit, and she could soon forget all about the less pleasant moments of this goofball day.

"It's certainly improved since the version you treated us to in Cornwall." River summarised their act. "But I can't help thinking a festive song would work better."

Rio pouted. Justin slumped into Jimmy's discarded deckchair, trying to get his breath back.

"You're right, River," Bruno the smart arse replied. "Jingle bells would work a treat! I believe there are some funked up versions of it available in CD form. I'll pop into the music shop in Wells for you and see what they've got."

"Awesome!" River applauded.

"Trite," snapped Justin.

"Christmas," said Alice, adding a shrug.

"Speaking of which… aren't you going to name the bar?" quizzed Bruno.

"Do we need to?" That was River, brows knitted. Quite rightly too. Zara knew that he and Alice were up against the clock to get the show on the road, they didn't need the Quiffmeister adding to their workload.

"Of course you do," said Jimmy. "And since we're on the subject of yuletide songs, there's only one thing for it." He got his spoons back out of his pocket, in the absence of a drum roll, and tapped them furiously against the back of Justin's wilting form in the chair. "*Twinkle, Twinkle, Little Bar!*"

CHAPTER SIXTEEN
Alice

"I DIDN'T REALISE Zara was so aloof," stated River.

He and Alice were climbing the narrow and ropey bunk ladder into the overhead 'bedroom'. It was their last night on the Wookey Hole campsite before they unleashed their festive roadshow on the world – well, the serene villages of Somerset. Fitting, since tomorrow was the 1st of December.

"I wouldn't call her aloof. I think she's had a catalogue of dodgy relationships, that's all."

"No need to take it out on the good guys though." River held out a hand to help Alice up the last step.

"True, but we weren't there on the road when whatever happened, happened, Riv. It sounds like both of them were driving like maniacs… one slightly more than the other."

Alice crawled onto the mattress. It had been the longest of days, although unfortunately, as she attempted to fully stretch her limbs, she remembered that her new sleeping quarters weren't exactly able to accommodate her bedtime yoga moves.

"I can't help feeling bad about that." River faffed about with his pillows. "If only we'd built more time into the set up to accommodate…"

"What?" Alice stopped flexing her feet. "No way is it our

fault! If anything, your bright idea has given both Zara and Bruno an opportunity they otherwise wouldn't have had. You can't take responsibility for your suppliers' crappy motoring skills. They're grown adults."

"I know," River sighed. "But now I'm fretting we're going to be putting them under too much pressure to deliver fresh supplies wherever we're stationed; my heart will be in my mouth that they arrive in one piece."

"One day at a time." Alice patted his duvet-covered thigh. "Rio and Justin's breakdancing might frighten the crowds away before we've even got started, in any case."

River laughed and Alice cuddled into the perfect crook of his neck. The window above them offered an equally perfect view of the star-spangled sky. The West Country villages got such little light pollution (with the exception of the bold reindeer and Santa bedecked houses and gardens) that this had become a wonderful ritual already... followed up most evenings with some rather restricted – in the movement stakes – sex. To call this space cosy was being economical with the truth. Alice loathed the expression 'not enough room to swing a cat', but the fact could not be denied; it would be impossible.

Twinkle, Twinkle, Little Bar. Jimmy's Eureka moment from earlier was another kind of perfect. Puntastic in fact, Alice acknowledged as she gazed at what she thought was the North star, illuminating the journey they were about to embark on in the van.

They lay there in companionable silence for a while, only punctuated by River playing dot to dot with the constellations overhead, and then doubting himself, mobile phone at the ready so he could double check his verdict against the wisdom of his astrological App.

"Is it wickedly naughty of me to say I have plans for Zara and Bruno?" Alice tittered. She could no longer keep the rebellious thoughts windmilling in her mind to herself.

"What do you mean?" River propped himself up on one arm to study her, the beginnings of a curious grin working its way across his lips.

"The sparks between those two are brighter than Hailey's comet. Surely you can see that?"

"All I can see is you." He did something dreamy with his eyes. "You light up the VW too much for me to notice anything or anyone else."

"Ew, that's so cheesy… and wholly un-rock star. But I'll take it."

Alice giggled as River dived in for a kiss. She reciprocated, his soft lips feeling like home. She more than felt the same but she didn't need to echo that sentiment back to him. They both knew that.

"It's true." He lifted a brow. "But seriously… Bruno and Zara?"

"Zara and Bruno. Yep. There's chemistry there, all right. The kind you could bottle and sell for millions. Now to work out how to pair them up."

"On the subject of bottles," said River, completely redirecting the tangent Alice had them galloping off at. "Do you think Mercedes would have included a hot chocolate and gingerbread bar in her visions for the mission?"

"No," said Alice, firmly.

"Why not?" Curiosity grazed his face.

"Because Christmas doesn't need us to meddle with it. There's a reason it's called the most wonderful time of the year. Communities produce their own brand of magic, too. All we have to do is encourage them to tap into it, then we'll have a double whammy of alchemy just waiting to pour out of this little van – wherever we decide to park her up."

"But I can't help but wonder if …"

Alice shook her head fervently.

"Not this time, Riv. Let it go. You played your part. You turned three people's lives around. The ripples from that alone have enfolded most of Glastonbury in one way or another. This is a whole new chapter in your life. The mission with that bottle was beyond stressful. It didn't take off again in Cornwall like you'd hoped, and maybe with good reason. Besides, a cocoa bar is infused with another kind of Mexican magic – that of the bean."

"Oh, yes. I guess you're right," River agreed. "I never saw it before."

I'm right about many things, thought Alice as she surrendered to sleep.

River's focus on this brand new shiny adventure might be pinning itself on the *joie de vivre* of the community wrapping itself in a giant hug of chocolate and ginger. But Alice had honed in on a spot of most satisfactory matchmaking.

THE MONUMENTAL DAY of location and show number one had arrived at last. River and Alice trundled along in the camper van to a designated spot in the heart of Wookey Hole, which had been offered to them complete with a generator. The campsite owner's farmer friend had agreed they could base themselves in a field that was walking distance for the villagers. In fact, his benevolence had turned into something to rival one of Santa's elves, and he'd littered the village with candy cane-striped arrow signs, pointing locals in the direction of the revelry. All of which neatly proved Alice's point: people produced their own magic once the promise of the Christmas cocoa bean (and something seriously yummy to dunk in its warm pool of bliss) captured their senses.

Meanwhile, Bruno had arrived with another kind of sign; one for the VW.

"Fetch us a ladder, mate!" he greeted River.

Alice swiftly unhooked the portable inside ladder and propped it up against the sliding doors outside the van ready for Bruno, who wasted no time in scaling it to work his own wizardry, putting the finishing touches securely into place.

"Woah! That is absolutely splendid," said River, stepping back into the field and admiring the welcoming twinkly lights that spelled out the bar's name. The naked bulbs emitted a carnival feel of warmth, well-being, and welcome.

"How did you get it made so fast?" Alice was totally spellbound. The camper van had been transformed into something straight out of a winter wonderland. The kind of foodie station that would look at home in any London Christmas market.

"The perks of currently living down the road from a sign maker who supplies the length and breadth of the UK with illuminations." Bruno shrugged as if this was quite normal.

"It's incredible." River drew Alice and Bruno in for a

group hug. "Say you'll stay around for a bit," he motioned to Bruno. "Jimmy's getting the bus here at five. Rio and Justin will wander down from their rental in the village at around the same time. But we've no idea how things will pan out in terms of the locals' curiosity being piqued. We've got to hope like mad there's nothing good on TV tonight!"

"In other words, you want me to play village do-gooder, giving everybody a hearty round of applause so things don't look like a complete flop."

"Without wishing to sound desperate, yes!" said Alice, swallowing a nervous giggle.

"Did you... erm... hear anything from Zara yesterday, by any chance?" Bruno turned to her, eyes like a puppy.

See. Alice knew her instincts were right.

"Who, Zara?" She let a real giggle slip. *Uh, oh. Alice needed to act more* au naturel *than this...* especially when she was trying to coax the deer-like Zara Bruno's way. "She's fine, yes." Alice quickly composed herself. "I think she was just a bit stressed yesterday. After dropping Jimmy off she had a few things to tend to in the kitchen and, as far as I know, she'll be back here tomorrow to drop off the rest of her order."

"Excellent. I mean that's... erm, it's good to hear."

"Isn't it just?" Alice sucked in her cheeks to hide the smile that was begging to beam its delight.

Damn, she was letting down her guard already. But did it really matter? Bruno had already given her carte blanche to play Cupid when they'd met up at Starbucks in the service station that day.

"Do you have a rough idea of her ETA?"

"Three o'clock. More or less."

"Great. I'll add it to my virtual diary."

Alice couldn't help but wink. Zara might not appear to be enamoured with the guy yet, but Alice had X-ray vision through the icy barrier her friend had put up. Not that she'd be so uncouth as to force one friend upon the other. Some gentle nudging, on the other hand…

"Hang on," Bruno backtracked, "I thought you were only spending one night in each village?"

Alice shook her head. "That's the general plan but Wookey Hole's already turned into the exception to that rule. We need forty-eight hours to sort ourselves out, suss out supply versus demand, then book ourselves into a field or a yard or whatever at the next few stops, so we're not completely flying by the seat of our pants."

"Makes sense. So where *is* the next stop?"

"Good question." Alice shrugged before panning the vista for her long-lost boyfriend, who she finally spotted at the back of the trailer unhooking the stage for what felt like the millionth time. "Riv? *River?* Did you and the guys finally reach a decision on the route when you were poring over that map yesterday?"

"Yeah," shouted River. "We'll try our luck at North Wootton next. Ralf" – that was the farmer whose field they were currently parked in – "is owed a favour by the bloke who runs the vineyard there."

"*Voilà*," said Alice, hands outstretched. "Don't ask me where we'll be after that. We'll keep you informed as we go, though."

"Surely West Pennard would make sense after North Wootton? The two are sort of neighbours… and Ma and Pa have ample acreage and facilities. *A fuck-off gert generator."*

Alice winced. It was the first time she'd heard the cool, calm and polite Bruno swear. She was also keen to head as far away from Butleigh as possible… and fast.

"Sorry, the expletive was unnecessary. But it is pretty big." Bruno seemed to intuit half of her thoughts. Aw, what a gentleman. "And you'll be making my life easier too when it comes to delivering the bakes," he added. "Not to mention Zara's. It's a hop and a skip from Glastonbury." Alice's heart nipped at that.

"Fabulous." She struck out her hand to shake Bruno's. "Let's break the good news to River, make a brew and sort out the rest of the logistics for the month. If we leave it to my better half and his friends, we'll be on the road to nowhere."

CHAPTER SEVENTEEN
River

SPONTANEITY WAS RIVER'S middle name. Yes, really. Hands on heart-style honestly. School register time had been the most cringeworthy affair. Fortunately, teachers only ploughed through the middle name rigamarole at the beginning of term when they were getting to grips with their new pupils – and accidentally read out their entire appellation. By which time it was too late. The damage had been done and everybody knew you had the world's most unconventional mother, so they would rib you incessantly, the fever pitch cruelly dying down the day before you had a substitute teacher… only for them to unnecessarily resurrect the fun and games all over again.

"It's a badge of honour, son." Heather had frowned in exasperation whenever River had come home in a sulk at the start of each fresh term. "You could have been a plain Jane like me."

He couldn't even begin to tell his mum how much he'd have preferred that.

"I'll change it by deed poll the second I can!"

He'd tramp up the stairs, taking the thunder cloud above his head with him, and slamming his bedroom door firmly shut.

But then one day River had decided he kind of liked his middle name. Spontaneity was sort of in keeping with the band. And it was very much in keeping with everything he'd set out to achieve post-stardom.

Unfortunately, spontaneity didn't help one iota, when you were trying to write up your menus and sort out your foodie and drinkie provisions for your winter wonderland on wheels. Nor did it help sort out quality control issues with the flimsy stage, which seemed to have constant ideas of its own and was forever buckling in the middle, depending on weight distribution.

River was glad that Alice and Bruno had taken the travel itinerary off his hands. Bruno's parents' farm sounded idyllic, too. And from West Pennard, they really ought to amble on to Butleigh; a subject he knew would prove thorny with Alice since her family lived there, but it was the season of goodwill to all men (and all households). If a permanent move back to the area was happening, then Alice was sure to bump into her parents from time to time. It was important she made the first move... even if she had done it so many times it felt like doing the hokey cokey. He'd have a quiet word with Bruno in a bit and make sure he touched on the idea.

ONCE RIVER HAD checked and double-checked his menus versus his ingredients; once he'd re-inspected the stage, time-tested Alice on her milk-heating skills, sent Bruno onto the village streets to chat with locals and get word out, briefed Rio and Justin for the umpteenth time ref the sound system and its diesel generator, and re-lined all his cocoa powder mix jars up in alphabetical order after Jimmy had snuck into the VW undetected and muddled them up whilst making himself a hot brew, it was show time.

Jimmy, now clad in a jaunty reindeer headband and a flashing nose, cut the red ribbon, officially opening the 'bar' amidst a modest round of applause. But River wouldn't let that deter him. It was only day one and it was a weekday. The Christmas spirit was sure to grow incrementally every twenty-four hours as they edged ever closer to December 25th.

It made a change to see his friend with another kitchen implement in his hands besides cutlery, although River hoped Jimmy wouldn't start trying to play the scissors. Ralf, the farmer, had also rounded up a small cluster of his family and friends. River bit back the urge to shake every one of them like a snow-globe. Everybody was hanging back annoyingly, shying away from being the first one to place an order. Until suddenly they weren't: out of nowhere a flurry of colour appeared on the horizon; first a succession of bobble hats and scarves flashed over the top of the hedge… and then a mob of very hungry and thirsty looking humans appeared!

The shit had just got real. And whilst River couldn't hide his delighted grin, he was also slightly alarmed at the sheer volume of villagers. He'd really rather expected more of a moderate trickle. Had Bruno taken a loudspeaker on his rounds? But it was too late for second thoughts. River bristled up to the wooden serving table, kindly donated by Zara. It fit in front of the VW's sliding doors snugly so that he had a makeshift counter from which to greet his customers and make jazz hands at his carefully curated chalk calligraphy menus – complete with artfully arranged polaroid snaps showcasing the hot beverages and mouth-watering morsels awaiting customers. The photos looked a touch like the kind of thing you'd find in a badly-in-need-of-an-update Mediterranean holiday restaurant, admittedly, but somehow the kitsch vibe worked.

A strikingly attractive female in a matching green scarf and woolly hat was the first to assess his wares, her eyes dancing from snapshot to snapshot, and back to River's meticulously penned list of treats.

"Ooh." She rubbed her hands together in glee. "I think I'll have a hot chocolate with coconut milk, and an iced gingerbread house on the side, please."

River froze on the spot. Stars temporarily circled his head as if he'd been clubbed over the head like a cartoon character.

"Er, would you mind repeating that?" He panicked, unable to process the words his very first customer had uttered.

"Okay," said the female, looking just as startled as him. "That will be one solitary hot chocolate... made with *coconut milk*... with one of those cute gingerbread houses attached to it. *Purrrlease.*"

"No, I, erm... I think you're mistaken." River attempted to chortle away his nerves, and inwardly berated himself for sounding freaky. He straightened himself up in a bid to sound more convincing. "We don't do coconut milk... or almond, rice, spirulina nor wheatgerm." He'd no idea if said varieties of milk existed as he counted them off on his fingers, but he might as well cover the rainbow of weird and wonderful lactose alternatives. "This is a plain old cow's milk gig."

River narrowed his eyes at the outlandish demand. The

first customer had only been and ordered something well awkward, that wasn't even listed on the menu! Did they look like a sleek Waitrose operation that stocked every culinary creation under the sun?

He rolled his eyes at Alice in a way that was meant to translate as *there's-always-one*. But Alice was a *customer-is-always-right* kind of patron – aka River's complete and utter opposite. Both here in this rudimentary van, and back in the finery of his cocktail bars.

It was crazy that they'd never worked together behind a counter until now, but Alice had always had her own career interests when it came to his Glastonbury and Cornwall drinking dens. *Horses, and horses.* Sure, she'd helped out now and then with a bit of token waitressing in manic times, but he'd never seen her in action when it came to customer service. And River was quickly regretting not having trained her up with a series of potential client scenarios. That would have to wait until later tonight.

"My apologies." Alice elbowed River out of the way to take over. "And we are so eternally grateful you've flagged up our forgetfulness." She slapped her forehead for quite unnecessary (in River's opinion) effect.

"No worries," the brunette woman replied with a smile.

"I didn't catch your name," Alice continued, "but you've come along at the best possible moment. Now we have a chance to make amends and refine our menus, to include what sounds to me like the most delicious liquid and lactose-free version of a Bounty chocolate bar… in a mug. Hopefully you can hang around for a while so I can get my team on it?"

River gulped at the very thought. And then he gulped

again at the growing queue, praying the rest of his customers didn't have similarly eccentric ideas. Although, as a former mixologist, he knew that chocolate and coconut did pair beautifully. Even a dairy-free version.

"It's Fiona. Fiona Jenkins," she said. "I'm actually a food and travel blogger, although I'm officially off duty today. I've just been visiting the caves in the village with my friends." Fiona gestured to the trio of women standing behind her, each colour co-ordinated with their cosy accessories, as she was. "We're on a short break doing some Christmas shopping in Bath but we fancied a change of scene today. When we saw the festive signs around the village, we became instantly besotted with the idea of a choccy and gingerbread fix… so here we are, and well, I guess this has just turned into a buswoman's holiday."

Indeed they flipping were here. River tried not to pout like a spoiled brat. And okay, he tried not to frown over yet another important matter he and the aforementioned 'team' had collectively managed to overlook: food allergies and intolerances. Not even the previously gluten-free-devoted Zara had as much as hinted at the possibility. Then again, he hadn't exactly asked her to.

Nope. This was his failing. All of it. And now he hated his middle name all over again. Spontaneity – and generally running before you could walk, let alone crawl – had delivered him a disaster. Knowing River's luck, this Fiona had probably been trained by Jay Rayner in culinary journo critique, as well. Heck, she could also write a column for one of the national newspapers, for all he knew. Great. What a first impression he'd given her!

Well, if things were going to get chaotically out of hand already, they might as well do it in style. River removed his apron, whispered to Alice that he felt his services would be put to better use elsewhere tonight, beckoned Bruno to help her out in the 'kitchen', and turned his attention to the entertainment instead, getting Jimmy set up for his stage debut.

It came to something when he was willingly volunteering to spend time with a spoon player and a rolling pin and cookie cutter dancing double act, over convivial chatter with customers enjoying his beloved chocolate and gingerbread. River could only hope Jimmy, Rio and Justin's performances would lead to them finding some hidden gem Houdinis, harpists and hula-hoopers…

CHAPTER EIGHTEEN
Zara

ZARA MIGHT HAVE been a little younger than Alice, but she hadn't been born yesterday. She'd known exactly what the woman was up to, the moment she'd picked up her phone to listen to Alice's voicemail.

"*Calamity and panic stations! Zara, listen, I know it's the tallest of orders... especially as you're clearly snowed under because you haven't answered any of my calls, but we've completely overlooked the non-dairy thing. I can't believe it. Such an obvious box to have ticked, but there you go. We were all in a rush. Anyway, we desperately need some cartons of coconut milk, almond milk, and rice milk. I suppose it wouldn't hurt to add goat's milk to that list... plus any other milk alternatives that the massive health food shop in Glastonbury stocks. Can you get some across to us ASAP? We've got actual customers waiting. One of whom is a foodie blogger. I only wish I was joking... but believe me, they refuse to go anywhere until this is fixed. Thanks a gazillion!*"

Zara had seen it in Alice's eyes yesterday: the look. Or more precisely the *I'm-going-to-pair-you-up-whatever-it-takes* look. As if a blogger would wait around for a lactose-free hot chocolate. This was a blatant ruse – a sneakily clever one, admittedly – to get Zara and Bruno together. And even if said blogger existed, there must be somebody else on hand to sort this out? Somebody like Rio or Justin, who was milling about with nothing to do. But it was no use complaining. Zara needed this job and that was all there was to it. Thankfully, she'd somehow worked like Wonder Woman to compensate for the damaged chocolate supplies, whipping up fresh batches of melts and stirrers. She might as well drive them over today and sort the drinks quandary out while she was at it.

By the time she'd pulled into the farm's lane, where Alice had explained she could park, it was properly dark but the farmhouse's lights showcased a rustic trail of festively-striped arrows that were very much pointing to a field, accessible via what looked to be a large gateway up ahead. Once Zara was out of the car and about to load her goodies onto her little trolley again, she could make out the quirky VW over the hedge. Give River and Alice their due, it looked amazing. Who wouldn't be reeled in by the sight of those brightly lit bulbs and the smell of hot gingerbread that was already starting to waft her way?

How had they managed to pull it all off? Bruno had only delivered everything for the first couple of days yesterday, and River hardly had room inside the van to be adding his own freshly-baked reinforcements to the mix…

Zara picked her way with great care over the stony driveway and through the open gate into the field. A couple of token revellers had already started to head home from the festivities, passing her with giant grins plastered across their faces, clutching mouth-watering biscuits in their gloved hands. The rest evidently couldn't tear themselves away, and Zara could see why just as soon as she reached the field's entrance.

This was incredible. Like something out of a Hallmark film, and then some. Zara wasn't really a fan of that type of movie. Historical fiction, both on the big screen and between the pages of a book, was much more her bag. But even the staunchest of Scrooges couldn't fail to be impressed with the delivery of River and Alice's vision. The clusters of people standing around their camper van radiated utter joy. Blimey, though. If folk were this excitable now, how would they contain themselves as they got even closer to Christmas?

Zara smiled semi-triumphantly, realising she was playing a not-so-little part in all of this. Soon she'd spotted Alice standing behind the counter she'd loaned them. There was no sign of River, though. She guessed he was beavering away in the van prepping drinks. Deciding not to disturb Alice, since she was engrossed in small-talk with a customer, whilst simultaneously slicing off a chunk of the most decadent looking golden and cream-hued layer cake, Zara sneaked around the rear of the counter and climbed backwards into the VW, humping her trolley carefully up and into the van. She'd drop off the all-important non-dairy supplies first. Some of her chocolate melts were carefully stacked on top of those in another box, and the rest she'd need to go back to the car for.

But before she could think about where to offload her stuff, she took another step back, only to feel her Wellington boot connect with a very definite foot.

"Oh, shit! I'm so sorry, River!"

A mini catastrophe played out behind her, the crash of a pan, the splash of liquid.

"You've scalded me. Quick! I need to get my top off. I can feel it burning my skin!"

Zara sucked in her cheeks. That was not River's voice. It was another man. And she wasn't talking Rio, Justin or Jimmy. Goddammit. What was that infuriating guy doing here *again*? Didn't he have piles of baking to keep on top of? And failing that, something, *anything* better to do with his time, than constantly get in her way causing sodding mayhem at every twist and turn?

"I might have known it was you," she snapped. "And you could have put up an 'enter with caution' sign on the door… either that, or Alice really should have told me that dropping off this lot in the camper would be akin to a bull trying to enter a china shop."

"Are you always this charming? Or is it just when I'm around?"

Zara turned to clock Bruno's strange mix of a face: one part satisfied that he'd batted her back such a quick quip, under the circumstances, and two parts thoroughly pissed off that his festive jumper was now sporting a gigantic chocolate mark just south of the rear end of the reindeer emblazoned upon it. Zara couldn't help but snort at that. He probably hadn't noticed the stain's precise coordinates from his vantage point, either. Served him right. Literally. And it would go some way to make up for the fact he had highly inconvenienced her, courtesy of his dreadful motoring skills, keeping her in the kitchen until all hours last night. Ha! Well, now he could have *his* night ruined. He'd be stuck in that jumper for the evening.

"Lift it up, then." Zara couldn't believe the sassy words

that were flying out of her mouth unchecked. "Let's inspect my good work. Not that I'm remotely interested in studying your naked chest, but according to that outburst, I've burnt you so badly you'll need a trip to A&E *and* a skin graft."

Bruno appeared only too happy to obey Zara's command, as she rested her trolley securely against the low cupboard adjoining the sink. His eyes twinkled, flirting with mischief and challenge. She was not falling for this. And then she realised it was she who was the fool. For she *had* fallen for it: hook, line and sinker. *What had she thought to herself earlier, about Alice's 'calamity SOS' message?* Strangely, Zara had quickly forgotten all about her suspicions, once she'd seen today's trip as an opportunity to spare herself the bother of delivering her chocolate tomorrow. Now she could see that Alice really had been trying to set the pair of them up all along. Because *surely* it was River who should be standing alongside his girlfriend behind the counter serving the villagers? Where in the heck was he, then?

But Zara couldn't wonder for a moment longer, once she'd laid eyes on that magnificent torso... and the smattering of dark hair that started rather suggestively at its owner's navel. Thankfully, Bruno's upper half wasn't remotely pink, the thick knit of his hideous Christmas jumper (which made even Colin Firth's in *Bridget Jones's Diary* look good), having soaked up the cocoa assault admirably. Rather, his chest was bronzed and ripped. The latter decidedly so.

Oh, dear God. How could the universe pull this little stunt on Zara, when she'd sworn off men for life? Well, okay, men with the exception of the little queue she was hoping would be waiting in Tuscany. And at Christmas too! What was this? Some kind of early Yuletide gift? Zara tore her eyes away.

"Don't you want to give me a medical? Just to be sure that I'm completely intact?"

And at those very words, Zara's hand had shamefully taken on a life of its own; an identity quite separate from her brain, as she raised it in response, palm willingly outstretched, fingers eager to investigate. Bruno took this mindless manoeuvre as carte blanche to slide her slender hand into his incredibly sexy and incredibly warm palm (Zara had always had a thing for hands) before common sense – on either of their parts – could get a look in. He pressed her hand tenderly to his equally toasty chest, never letting his gaze leave her face. Zara suppressed a gulp, holding her breath. Talk about being plugged into an electric socket… especially when he began to move her hand about sensually. Talk about a strong, thumping, hot-blooded heartbeat too.

"I d… don't have health and safety training. You'll have to find someone else."

Zara (reluctantly) tugged her hand away, and tried with all her might to extinguish the searing flash of lust in the pit of her belly; the one that was rapidly in danger of travelling somewhere else within seconds.

Mercifully, a house remix of Mariah Carey's infamous Christmas song blasted into the December night then (the first and the last time in her life that Zara would ever experience gratitude for the popstar and her high-pitched lyrics). It doused the intensity of the moment most welcomely – as did Alice's head and shoulders, which suddenly appeared at the door, looking somewhat shocked at both the half-naked Bruno and the culinary debris strewn across the floor.

"Slight mishap, don't worry." Bruno sing-songed smoothly at Alice's startled face. "We've got this... and those mince pie hot chocolate specials will be with you any minute now, boss. And, oh, if I'm not mistaken, it sounds like Rio and Justin are about to take to the stage. I'm so glad I was able to find them a better CD!"

Zara couldn't help but be impressed at Bruno's capacity to remain this level of calm in a crisis. Evidently he'd worked for a few Gordon Ramsay types in the kitchen. Not to put Alice in that bracket, of course.

And then Zara quickly berated herself for so gratuitously doling out brownie points. The man was an idiot. Smug, charming, gorgeous... But an idiot, nonetheless.

Wordlessly, she ripped off some sheets of nearby kitchen roll to deal with the spillage on the floor, and she put the pan in the sink, relishing the chance to compose herself. Bruno would have to take care of the rest, and it appeared that he already was; Alice's intrusion a wake-up call to his duties. Zara removed the 'milk' cartons from her trolley, squeezing them into one of the kitchen cupboards. Then she carefully placed one half of the chocolate supplies on the small table and went to give Alice a quick rundown of events, before the now-dressed Bruno got carried away again. All she had to do next was deftly speed back to the car with her trolley, collect box number two, and be on her merry way.

A hand gripped the top of her trolley on wheels just as she was about to pull it away.

"Allow me to do the honours and accompany you. I

insist."

Zara sighed deeply at Bruno, who had already, somehow, *miraculously*, restored the intricate drinks order *and* tidied up. Well, overlooking his tragic pullover. There wasn't much that could be done about that. Time seemed to slow itself down as she mulled over her options: 1) indulge the guy and get it over with, politely turning him down the minute he tried to dive in for a kiss in the farm lane (as inevitably he would) or 2) play ice maiden, and have everyone think she was a mean bitch. The bog-standard options that seemed to present themselves to every female in her precise predicament.

But today those stalled seconds gave Zara a brainwave and she realised she had an option three. Heck, there had always been a third choice. Since she was lumbered with him until the twenty-fourth of December, she was going to damn well outsmart him. Bruno was a mere Wile E Coyote, whilst Zara was Road Runner. *Meep meep.* She swallowed down a giggle. It was Christmas, after all. If she had to put up with the annoying antics of this twerp then she might as well enjoy herself, constantly ensuring she stayed several steps ahead of his game.

"So kind of you. Thank you," she said, studying Bruno intently. "Here are my car keys to go with it." She nodded at the trolley, that stood between them now, pressed the keys into Bruno's other hand and manoeuvred him towards the camper's door. "There's one more box on the back seat of my car... I don't need to tell you what model I drive... we've already become thoroughly acquainted in that department." She threw in a wink. "Bring the rest of my supplies back to the van – *carefully*, and as if you're wearing a pair of the finest kid gloves. Meanwhile, I do believe it's my job to find Fiona the Coconut Milk Fiend, so I can whip her up my very best hot chocolate coconut liquid elixir and bathe in the limelight of it being featured in her blog."

Oh, Bruno wasn't quite expecting that. "Right. O-okay."

As if she'd cast a spell on him, he put her instructions into immediate action, and Zara also set to it, concocting Fiona's drink before the enchantment wore off. Apparently the poor woman had been waiting for almost two hours now. Timing-wise, Zara's planning couldn't have been more perfect. Victorious, she craned her neck around the sliding door to motion for Alice to call for a jubilant Fiona to be rewarded for her incredible patience. Zara's heart went out to her. Having to watch all her friends guzzle down their warm, dairy versions of cocoa goodness must have been torture… especially when you added Mariah's warbling and Rio and Justin's questionable dance moves to the experience.

"May I take a few piccies for Instagram and my blog?" Zara could have burst with pride at Fiona's unexpected request (she didn't think she'd ever been featured in a blog, and despite her parting words to Bruno, she'd only been joking!). She nodded her head in fervent agreement, especially as Bruno would have a bird's eye view of Fiona adoring the beautifully put-together beverage when he returned. Zara had expertly decorated it with grated dairy-free organic chocolate and coconut shards, too. The aroma was positively Caribbean.

"Perhaps we could add a piece of that impressive tower of cake to the montage?"

She posed it as a question but, since there was nobody currently queuing for cocoa or gingerbread, and since Zara couldn't find a valid reason to disagree (*why not use my beautiful chocolate Nutcracker soldiers?* only sprung to mind later), Fiona sliced off a behemoth wedge of cake, and now she was angling it this way and that beside the pine-green mug, her large Nikon camera at the ready to capture the perfect shot. In other words, within seconds Fiona had put a match to Zara's dreams. Typically, Bruno didn't miss a trick. His eyebrow arched in appreciation of the acknowledgement of his talents as he entered the VW with the last of Zara's boxes.

For fuck's sake. Zara wasn't sure that she'd ever met anyone in the culinary world who was quite so up themselves. Sure, she'd done her homework that morning and spent an hour with her coffee reading about Bruno's various accolades plastered all over the internet, but he was categorically not her cup (of tea, coffee, or hot cocoa). Too self-assured, too full of one-liners, and too good-looking to boot. As if sensing her annoyance, he hopped back out of the van and wormed his way into her conversation with Fiona, plying the girl with those twee gingerbread houses he was supplying the bar; the gingerbread houses that were supposed to be the supporting act to *Zara's* drink!

Enough was enough. Zara made her excuses to the snap-happy Fiona and stormed into the VW, pulling her bobble hat out of her pocket and stuffing it on top of her head. Then she flung herself at her trolley and trailed it behind her with a giant huff as she exited the field. She must have looked exactly like a furious granny with a little shopping bag on wheels, but she was beyond caring.

CHAPTER NINETEEN
Alice

"WHERE'S ZARA?" ALICE couldn't keep the puzzled expression from her face. She couldn't believe the girl had gone already. She'd not even thanked her properly for saving the day. She'd certainly not had time to process that rather racy scenario she'd stumbled upon when she'd peeped inside the camper van. There wasn't much wrong with Alice's female intuition, that was for sure! But get a room, guys. Much as she wanted to see this potential couple wrapped up in a Christmas bow, she'd rather they took their antics to a place of their own…

"Stormed off," said Bruno, looking more than a little sheepish.

"And why would that be? Erherm, aside from the obvious."

Bruno sighed as he wiped over the kitchen work tops, which already looked pretty sparkling from where Alice was standing.

"Okay. So here's the thing. I'm crap at flirting."

"Unless I was imagining one of you half-starkers earlier, I find that hard to believe, Mr Lombardi."

"No. I mean yes, I wish. But no. Oh, no, no, no!" Bruno

snow-ploughed a hand through his hair. Still the quiff didn't move. "Please don't get the wrong end of the candy cane there, Alice. Zara trod backwards and onto my foot with one of her huge wellies when she came into the camper van... I was carrying hot drinks... which consequently flew everywhere. A huge splatter ended up on my sweater." He pointed below his solar plexus area without looking. "And I panicked that it had scalded me, so I flung it off. As you do."

"Right," Alice replied, wholly unconvinced, but equally aware this was between Bruno and Zara.

"I mean it, Alice. I'm *really* crap at flirting. Either I come on espresso-style or I have a tendency to push the wrong buttons and annoy. I guess." He stopped to study the cloth in his hands again, as if it might care to offer him some advice. "I've become rusty. It's been so long since I've dated."

"Okay," said Alice, dismissing his worries. "Put that on the back burner for the moment. I've had a brainwave. If you're genuinely interested in Zara, that is?"

"Are you kidding? She's awesome. Quirkily beautiful in her own right, with her own inimitable style, which I just love. But I sense we'd be good together too. There's not much I can do about it, though, if the feeling's not mutual, is there?" He shrugged in defeat.

"There's plenty of time for things to turn around. A whole month of opportunity. You just need to be patient, take things slower."

"Maybe I'm being a fool. Who's to say she'd even be interested?"

"Erm... that would be her uber-dramatic reaction every time you're in range."

Plus the fact Alice was sure she'd seen Zara's hand pressed to Bruno's chest, and not just in an assessment of a hot chocolate burn kind of way.

"Hmm, surely I triggered that when I overtook the tractor that day. I think Zara's behaviour around me is anger rather than anything else."

He frowned and let out a large sigh.

"Nope. I think it runs a little deeper than that. Trust me."

And Alice *knew* that it did. What she didn't know was how she was going to manifest a civil conversation for the pair, let alone a kiss under the mistletoe or an actual date. Normally, she would leave things be, mind her own business. But Zara had just that day confided in her that she'd accepted a new life opportunity in Tuscany. Short of booking the flights, she was all set to go and would be leaving Glastonbury on the twelfth day of Christmas (or in modern day terms, January the fifth).

Well, it wasn't happening. Not if Alice Goldsmith had anything to do with it… Because if there was one thing she had learned, it was that home was where the heart was.

River interrupted her thoughts then, holding a hand aloft to high five Alice and Bruno as he wearily stepped into the VW.

"How'd it go?" he queried. "Judging by the queues and smiles, I'd say with a bang? I've been so busy sweet-talking all our wannabe performers who have, hands on their hearts, promised me they'll show up tomorrow night with an act or two, that I've not had a proper chance to catch up with you both."

Clearly River had been in his element in the wings. Perhaps it was best that he devoted himself to the entertainment, leaving the serving of the food and drink to Alice – just until they'd found their feet after a couple stops.

"Sounds great," she said, smiling encouragingly.

"Yeah," Bruno added. "What do they have in mind? I'm a sucker for anything Il Divo-esque. Helps me cook up a storm."

"Hmm… I don't think it'll quite be on a par with that." River bit his lip. "So far we've got three teens dressed as the Witches of Wookey Hole for a Florence and the Machine song. Then the ex-captain of the darts team from the former pub reckons he can organise some darts trick shots for old times' sake. And, although it feels a little uncouth when we're serving up hot chocolate, a couple of the farmers are on about a cider drinking competition."

"Oh, right. Well, all definitely unconventional!" Bruno's wide eyes said it all.

"Wow," said Alice. "I'd never have thought spoons and breakdancing would encourage such diversity, but the plan's clearly working."

"Something like that," said River. "Let's see if they go through with it tomorrow first."

"I trust Jimmy's back at the hotel?" Alice was awash with sudden guilt for not having given their elderly friend a second thought for hours.

"He's staying in the village tonight. Rio and Justin's Airbnb owner has a spare room going so he's given it to him for free."

"Aw, that's so sweet."

"In return for complimentary drinks and biscuits for his

entire family tomorrow night."

"I see." Alice rolled her eyes. "It's a good job we're mainly doing this benevolently, as an excuse to see a bit of the countryside, and not because we need to make a living."

"I'm sure there will only be a handful of them, don't worry, Al. On the other hand, Bruno, if you could get us some more gingerbread in, that would probably be a good idea."

"I'm on it!" Bruno saluted River with a grin. "And I'm thinking I ought to head home. It's been a long day and there's lots to do for tomorrow… not to mention squaring things with my parents, but I'm ninety-nine percent certain they'll be up for hosting you for a night or two after your North Wootton vineyard stop."

"Excellent. Thanks so much for your help today," said Alice. "And regarding the Zed word… it's early days, although perhaps you should rethink your erm… your wardrobe."

"But I thought I was getting into the spirit of things." Bruno held his palms out, looking puzzled. "It didn't do Mark Darcy any harm, and I would argue that this reindeer creation is infinitely more stylish."

"Ohhhh!" River covered his mouth, unable to disguise his giant guffaw. "Shit!"

"Indeed." Alice raised her brows as Bruno looked down on his body to appraise himself, eyes wide as he finally spotted the unfortunate location of the brown stain. "Once you've seen it, you can't unsee it!"

CHAPTER TWENTY
Zara

ZARA SAT BOLT upright in bed, blinking rapidly. She rubbed her eyes, she shook her (perpetually wavy from her daily braids) hair, she raked a hand through her fringe. But nothing could erase that hot and steamy dream... in which her hand hadn't just stopped at Bruno's chest, but travelled all the way down to the top button of his jeans and the *erherm* that lay within.

She couldn't risk falling asleep again and re-enacting any of that malarkey. It was high time for coffee, even if it was only seven o'clock on a weekend. Slowly, she acclimatised to the chilly apartment air, poking one bed-socked foot, then the other, out of the cocoon of her bed to feel about for her slippers. Her snug, warm duvet was still wrapped around her and her tartan pyjamas. Hibernation was a hard thing to relinquish in a dwelling with temperamental pipework, but the hot caffeine fix wouldn't brew itself. She took a deep breath, dropped the bedding and made a mad dash for the kitchen.

After the first sip or two of coffee, calmness was restored, only to be replaced by a burning and growing curiosity. Zara pulled Fiona's business card out of her purse and fired up her laptop to track down her blog, knowing it was highly unlikely that anything had been written up yet. She was bracing herself for Bruno's bloody showstopper of a cake (in all honesty, it could have rivalled anything in the finals on The Great British Bake Off). It was certain to be centre stage when the feature was published.

As the page loaded, Zara opened her mouth, speechless, staring at the arty image beneath yesterday's date, with the heading: *'Introducing Somerset's Hot Chocolate Hostess with the Mostess'*

Her snowy-topped, coconut-infused hot chocolate looked other-wordly, sparkling on the screen. It was making even its creator drool. *Wow.* Evidently, this Fiona was a bit of a legend with a lens. The write-up on River and Alice's travelling Christmas bar was equally spectacular, and was sure to attract foodies far and wide. Fiona had explained River's community spirit vision in great depth too. But what a puzzle that Bruno's cake had been granted mere postage stamp coverage, as a little PS at the end of the article. Zara gulped down the rest of her coffee and swallowed her guilt away. That was not her problem.

She threw two slices of bread in her desperately-in-need-of-an-upgrade toaster (if she hadn't been Italy bound, she'd have had to cave in and order a new one from Argos as a Christmas present to herself) and googled the budget flight price comparison website she'd been keeping her beady eye on whilst she waited for her toast to turn golden brown.

"No way!" she screamed.

The lowest price for Pisa on the day she needed to travel had gone up by a whopping £150. She'd just have to put off her booking until next week, hoping the same didn't happen again. It was stubborn of Zara not to tap into the trust fund, of course. She could easily replace it. But she viewed that exceedingly large pot of cash like a tube of Pringles. Once she took a pound from it, there would be no turning back. She wanted to feel like she had achieved this next life move by herself. It set the tone for everything going forward, so she refused to give in to temptation.

A beep on her phone snapped her out of her musing. Alice's name flashed up. Zara sighed. What now? Couldn't she even eat her breakfast in peace?

"Just wanted to thank you properly for coming to our rescue at such short notice yesterday. I've paid a chunk of money into your account," Zara read the message aloud to the four walls of her pokey kitchen. *"Would you mind doing the honours again and getting in some more of the 'milk'?"* Zara's stomach knotted. She really couldn't handle another Bruno *rendez-vous* so soon. *"You wouldn't believe the Mexican wave Fiona's request set off yesterday afternoon!"*

And now Zara was firmly back to viewing Fiona as Marmite. She hated her as much as she loved her!

In fact, Fiona's trumpeting over her coconut hot chocolate alchemy had already sealed Zara's fate and ensured that she'd be working non-stop to create and deliver chocolate – in all its guises – to the tummy-rumbling villagers of Somerset.

Bah Humbug.

Where was her own Christmas cheer? Zara felt about as festive as a piece of threadbare tinsel. She simply had to snap out of it and join the merry masquerade. Just for the month. These people were trying to help her. It was all well and good, thinking she could take on the world without her family's money, but without a support network, too? That was impossible. She wasn't sure she'd ever met anybody as paradoxical as herself. If she packed this antisocial attitude in her suitcase and took it to Italy, she could forget finding herself a hunky romeo. She might just as well get used to spinsterhood already.

None of which meant she was about to let her guard down with Bruno, by the way.

She tapped out a fake cheerful *absolutely, no bother at all* reply to Alice, who pinged her back to say she'd forgotten to mention that they probably had enough supplies to cover hot chocolate orders today in Wookey Hole and tomorrow at the vineyard in North Wootton, but the day after that they'd be in West Pennard… at yet another farm – a pin was added to the WhatsApp message and Zara let out a faint sigh that at least she didn't need to travel far. That made life a little easier.

A smell roused her from her thoughts. Great, the toast was burnt! She took it to the sink to scrape off the charcoaled bits, cursing herself for being so frugal and not updating her appliances. Then she quickly smothered it with butter and marmalade before it got cold and made her even more grumpy.

Biting into the bittersweet creamy comfort, she realised, perhaps for the first time, that this antipathy towards the opposite sex came down to one man and one man only: Blake *bloody* Hopkins.

Fair enough, it was Zara who had pulled the plug on their eighteen month relationship – and thank the Lord she had, since shortly after her decision, Blake had gone and signed himself up for that crazy Channel UK Today reality TV show filmed in King Arthur's Community school in Glastonbury: *Bubblegum and Blazers*. Well, the last thing Zara needed was the paps following her around and flashing pictures of her nothing-to-write-home-about foodie business to the nation. To her London family, more precisely. But Blake's words of retaliation, as he'd stood in the flat's doorway, had stung:

"I can't believe I didn't see it before. You're a loser, Zara. Super quick to think you're the big I AM, going against the grain, doing things differently from *your people* – but just look at how little you've achieved."

His eyes had bored into hers, as if willing her to take heed of his lecture. But Zara had turned her cheek. Red rage had then consumed Blake, and he hadn't held back. He might not have been a violent guy but this wordy outburst had been like a series of continual slaps, knocking her down one after another, before she could so much as formulate a justification.

"You make a mockery of the rest of us. You've got all this help and financial backing just lying in wait, courtesy of those stinking rich parents of yours, and you can't appreciate it," he'd crusaded on. "Plod, plod, plod. You're barely treading water, too arrogant to admit defeat. Meanwhile, some of us have never had those kinds of opportunities. Pfft. You could have gifted me with a few thousand to help me escape the supermarket and set myself on a new career path."

At this point he'd thrown his hands in the air in exasperation, as wildly and stereotypically as any man she might hope to find in Italy. "Yet you prefer the struggle! *For everyone.* Dragging us all down while you're at it. *What is wrong with you?* And how many times have I offered to help you out in the bakery? I've worked with food for years! Okay, maybe only the shop type. But I'm a fast learner. You could've paid for me to go on a course to learn to bake bread and cakes. I could have teamed up with you. We could have gone into business, been a force to be reckoned with, and waved off all of your high street competition in one fell swoop." Much as she hated to admit it, she knew it was true. Blake was a stickler for grafting, passionate about food in his own way. "You're an embarrassment to the ethics of this working class town! You'd just as well piss off back to London, love."

Zara could still feel the indent of that final punch to the gut, a couple of years down the line.

Blake's own behaviour and life situation had hardly been a bed of roses at the time, not to mention his questionable relationship history… although he'd certainly reinvented himself after winning the TV show. But his accuracy in that parting speech had been quite astonishing. And hurtful. And belittling. It marked the bitter end of Zara reacting to even an eye flutter from a good-looking male customer. She could barely bring herself to return their smiles.

At least that's what she'd thought, but then along came Bruno and now she was officially Glastonbury's hottest mess.

CHAPTER TWENTY-ONE
River

HOW RIDICULOUS THAT River hadn't set foot in the village where he'd gone to primary school since, well, since his primary school days! West Pennard was as suspended in countryside time as he'd fondly remembered, albeit with the addition of some thoroughly impressive large houses that seemed to have extended the boundaries of the village and inflated the local property market.

River couldn't resist a quick meander up Church Lane to see his old school playground and the adjoining church, whose small bell tower window he and his friends had perpetually squinted up at until they'd felt dizzy. It did make him laugh. All those precious and varied childhood memories flashing back at him: conker fights at the bottom of the field, stitch-laden cross country runs that doubled up as annual opportunities for two of the terrors in his year to run away and play 'hide and seek' from all the teachers, school fêtes and homemade cupcakes (Heather had packed River off to those with stem ginger creations, of course), the ear-splitting screech and flying spittle of recorder lessons, the literary adventures of Roger Red-hat, lurid orange maths textbooks that failed to make the subject any more appealing, Union Jack flag-making, for the day Princess Diana whizzed past them all in her posh car on the main road between Somerset engagements and River had just about caught a flash of her violet blue hat and its feathers, country dancing (hey, park that thought for a little talent show inspiration), and getting your calculator to spell the word 'BOOBS'.

Alice would have had an equally idyllic experience at the village primary of neighbouring Butleigh... a stop he fervently hoped she and Bruno had added to the itinerary. He'd not yet drummed up the courage to ask. Which was ludicrous, but he was always mindful of pushing his girlfriend, particularly after her reaction to the secret letter fiasco that had seen her skitter off into hiding in deepest, darkest Cornwall.

"Well, North Wootton was certainly on the quiet side," said Alice, interrupting his thoughts.

"That's one way of putting it, but after the mayhem of that second evening in Wookey Hole, I was secretly glad of the respite." River shuddered. "Just imagine if the vineyard inspired another drink-your-parents-under-the-table style competition!"

"Hmm... yeah, that cider performance did get a little out of hand. Hardly helped by a certain duo egging everyone on."

"I could have knocked Rio and Justin's heads together by the end of the evening! Thank goodness most of the elderly had shuffled back home by that point," said River, shaking his head. "It was the greatest feeling in the world to get the mission back on track in a new place last night, but gawd, was it ever tedious towards the end, attempting to coax the villagers onto the stage."

"Well, I guess a vineyard brings out the refined in everyone."

"True, but all we sold were run-of-the-mill hot chocolates!"

"I did try to drop hints at what people were missing out on, by seductively sucking on a candy cane before dipping it into my white peppermint hot chocolate. I guess I should have polished up my Marks and Spencer ad voiceover while I was at it."

"You'd have cast me under your spell *and* the drink's. How did I miss this?" River's pupils dilated. Alice play-slapped him on the bottom and he scooped his light-as-a-feather girlfriend up, twirling her around until she begged him to stop. But he refused to put Alice down… not before taking advantage of the very large bunch of mistletoe hanging on the front door of the cottage directly across the road. He zigzagged the pair of them over to it, laughing recklessly since Alice had no clue what was going on, until he finally stopped beneath it and planted a kiss on her lips. A kiss which not even the honking from passing cars and, 'Get a room and get off my porch,' from the outraged owner of the property could pull apart. The avalanche of black olives was a slightly different matter. And it begged the question, who in the heck had a supply of those ready to pelt from the bedroom window?

"Put me down, Riv and let's get back to the camper van! Maybe the mistletoe is for the exclusive use of their household visitors… and I kind of feel like we've kind of outstayed our welcome."

"That's hardly the point, and this is a public road!" River yelled the latter at the bearded and spectacled old man, daring him to carry on scolding.

"Tell us where you got the mistletoe from and we'll go," said Alice, attempting a little festive peace-making. River sensed she had not so much themselves in mind, but Bruno and a certain female.

"The Lombardi farm on the edge of the village." The man showed his face fully now for a couple of seconds. "Now do bugger off and stop being an eyesore!"

"Mr. Fry? I... is that you?"

The little grey-haired man lost his nerve immediately, retreating behind the curtains once more.

"Blimey, Al. That was only my old teacher," River whispered as they scarpered back across the road. "And he's still got the same attitude. Nothing's changed since the day one of the boys in my class said one of the B-words during a French cricket lesson and he punished the lot of us with a thousand lines."

"Why did teachers always do that in the eighties and nineties? Use the rest of the class for scapegoats when it must have been clear who the perpetrator was?" Alice tutted.

"Beats me." River shrugged as they hurried to the VW. His former teacher could still have the sports car he'd so loved to flaunt outside the school gates – and he could decide to mow the pair of them down.

Bruno's parents' farm was a few roads away, backing onto fields that spilled into an endless vista of lush green; a giant jigsaw of countryside in every shade of the colour imaginable. From here you also had the perfect vantage point to the famous Glastonbury Tor, which *almost* negated the need ever to beg for a ticket to Sir Michael Eavis's Glastonbury music festival, which was actually in Pilton. River had always felt awkward around Sir Michael, now an octogenarian, since Avalonia had never been invited to play at the festival – unlike Reef, whose front man, Gary Stringer, also hailed from Glastonbury. He really shouldn't let it annoy him anymore, not now he'd moved on from music to mixology (or to being a mobile merrymaker), but the rejection still left a taste in his mouth quite as bitter as any Negroni.

"So, I have a proposition for you," he said to Alice as they climbed back into the camper van to locate Bruno's folks' place. "If I confront my demons in Pilton and suck it up, asking the big Mr E if he'll agree to put us up for a night, will you embrace Butleigh… and the possibility that your parents might show up for a refreshment and/or a performance?"

"Pilton has been sorted by Bruno. He used to cater for the festival team, and some of the A-list performers, don't forget. Michael is more than happy for us to pitch ourselves at the festival site for a night… as long as we tidy up properly afterwards."

Alice didn't quite fire her reply back to River but it was certainly lacking her trademark warmth, for some reason.

River gritted his teeth at Michael's insinuation he and his customers were litterbugs; they always cleaned up after themselves, thank you very much. And he gritted his teeth twice at his friend's ever impressive networking skills: Bruno was hardly up there with Nigella in the culinary fame stakes, but apparently that didn't matter. His contacts could rival Wikipedia, his know-how the Encyclopedia Brittanica. So much so, River was beginning to get a complex. Maybe it would be easier to admit defeat now and let Bruno project-manage the whole thing?

"As for the second part of your proposition." Alice broke off to sigh, answering him belatedly. "Yeah, okay. I'll suck it up in Butleigh. But just for one night… and then we're out of there."

"Great," said River, allowing himself to relax. Perhaps Bruno's brilliance had only made his own life easier. It wasn't that River thought a relationship with Alice's parents was fundamental to her welfare, but if they were to move back to the area permanently, civility was a must. There would be nothing worse than his girlfriend constantly looking over her shoulder for fear of bumping into her mother and father.

"Zara's due to call in later with supplies, isn't she? And Bruno will be on site the whole time, thank goodness. On the entertainment front, Jimmy went back to Cornwall yesterday, but Rio and Justin are here for a couple more days. That will help us get the party started, by which time word of mouth will cross villages and people will know we are looking for diversity, if they're planning on coming along to grace the stage and entertain the customers," he continued.

"Erm, I'm not sure you're hearing the same version of events as me, Riv. The boys have told me they plan to follow the camper around for the entire month."

"*They what?*"

River couldn't believe it. He loved his friends to bits, but the last thing he wanted was for this to turn into the Rio and Justin Show.

"I know what you're thinking." Alice batted back his concerns. "We'll just have to set them up with a continuous challenge if they want to participate regularly in the talent contest: a different performance each week."

"I guess so." River conceded. "We can hardly refuse them that. They've been a great support to us, both here and in Cornwall."

He pressed his lips together and wrinkled his eyebrows. Not the best look, but what was a boy to do when a groundbreaking thought struck him from the ether? "*Eureka!*" River's beam grew slowly until it was a megawatt smile that stretched from ear to ear. "Oh, Alice, you *are* amazing." His eyes flashed in sudden awareness of how brilliant this could be… if only he could pull it off.

"Was it something I said?"

"Perhaps." He winked. "I think I've found an awesome opportunity for them."

River probably shouldn't have revealed that much. This was the most preposterous plan he'd ever thought up out of nowhere – and there had been *more than a few* on a similar scale of bananas-ness in his thirty-seven years on Planet Earth. But this brand spanking new idea was going nowhere until it was acted upon. Now he'd have to sneak about with the stealth of a fox, for as many furtive conversations with Rio and Justin as possible.

Thankfully, Alice already seemed far more interested in admiring the horses fringing the neighbouring fields as they motored slowly down the lane to Bruno's farm. Before River could turn off the ignition, the chap himself had appeared, wide eyed as if River'd telepathically transmitted his brainwave, and as bushy tailed as the aforementioned fox, eager for them to follow his hand signals to park up in the designated space in the farm's yard.

River jumped straight out of the van and hugged his

friend, who plied River and Alice with a flurry of facts and fiction about the farm:

"Three years ago Mum had to give up her bedroom for one of the Cold Play dudes whose luxury yurt had been double booked down at the Glastonbury festival site. She forgets which one, but I think it's safe to say it wouldn't have been Chris Martin."

"Remember my brother Nolan who went missing several years ago? He'd been living in the shed at the bottom of the orchard for three days." Bruno pointed into the distance where River could make out a stand of bare apple trees behind a hedgerow. "This is a fairly common thing with kids on the autistic spectrum, and Noles had been pilfering items from the house and stashing them away for days before he took off." Bruno made quotation marks in the air at the last bit. "Still, it shook my parents up big time, as you can imagine, and well, then it just didn't feel right that I carried on with uni that year. So I came home and Nolan literally helped me sketch out my future business plans. Somehow this seemed to help him process the changes that would take place when I did return to education, and I'm pleased to say he's done more than fantastically himself. He's a computer programmer nowadays. Sorts out all of my techie stuff."

"That *is* cool," said River. "And wow to all of these stories."

"Oh, I didn't tell you about the time the herd of cows bolted the field, destroyed the washing, and trailed it into the kitchen while my mum was hosting a VIP—"

"I sincerely hope my son's not making you glaze over," said a short rotund woman, with an elegant salt and pepper bun balanced high atop her head.

River, Alice and Bruno jumped on the spot. How had she crept up on them so silently? Bruno did a round of brief introductions, and soon his mother, Christine, was joined by a man who was so much her double in the looks department that they could have passed as brother and sister – although River had already surmised that Bruno's mum wore the trousers. He quelled the sudden instinct to laugh as Arlo, who was even shorter than his wife, stood to attention next to her, offering his hand for a shake. Quite where Bruno got his average height from was anybody's guess, and it was all River could do to suppress the milkman-style theories circling his brain.

The distant sound of tyres on gravel snapped River out of his pondering. The noise grew until a little red Ford Ka pulled up behind the camper van and Zara slowly stepped out, offering everyone a shy wave as she peeped through her mass of fringe.

"God bless that woman and her ability to constantly magic up the serotonin-loaded supplies in a jiffy," exclaimed Alice.

But Zara couldn't extricate herself from the farm (and the potential for long and leisurely group conversation) quickly enough. In fact, today's disappearance might well have beaten all of her previous records. River didn't know much about the preliminary signs of romance but one couldn't deny the rosehip glow of Bruno's normally olive cheeks as the woman did a brisk U-turn and sped off into the sunset.

✧ ✧ ✧

"Mum? What a surprise!" River ran over to greet Heather, his decidedly – and happily – fuller in the face mum. It was wonderful to be reunited with her. And at a much happier occasion than the last time they'd met.

"Nice to see you too," Hayley chirped, piling herself on top of their hug.

"Room for a little one?" Terry joked as he nudged himself into the action, until the mix of pungent and questionable aftershave versus sickly-sweet perfume got a bit too much and River playfully pushed everybody out of the intimate rugby scrum.

"Hayley was keen as anything to try out some of the gingerbread and hot chocolate we've all been hearing about. When we said we were heading this way to see how things were going, she offered us a lift and it seemed silly to bring two vehicles. It's better for the planet this way."

Heather had tears in her eyes as she walked over to the camper van, linking arms with River. Hayley had vanished already and Terry ambled along behind them with Alice. "My, oh, my. You've done your aunt Sheba so proud, darling. She'd always intended for us to ship this girl," Heather patted at the side of the VW, "over to America so we could make a pilgrimage to Sedona. Well, that wasn't to be." Heather sniffed. "But this has clearly always been on the cards."

River jolted as he recalled Alice's card reading revelation. "Sedona's nice." It really was, River had visited briefly. "But nothing beats the villages around Glastonbury. I'm sure Twinkle, Twinkle here has crossed, and will cross, many a leyline on our local travels."

River rubbed the van's door affectionately, and then

stopped in his tracks because he looked like he was massaging a Volkswagen camper van, and even for him that was a bit weird.

The VW would never have survived a wild cross country trip from a Western US seaport over to Arizona, though. What had his aunt and mother been thinking?

"On the subject of Aunt Sheba," said Heather, resting a gloved hand on River's forearm. "The will is due to be read next week. I know you're flat out with this wonderful venture but I really get a hunch you should be there. You and Alice."

"One for you." Hayley had reappeared, to hand out some gingerbread mittens to Heather and a hovering Terry, before River could as much as form a reply. *What? Where did she get them from?* The 'kitchen' wasn't even officially open yet. "Three for me." Hayley held her own stash of spiced biscuits – a gingerbread Santa, a reindeer, and a snowflake – out like a flamenco fan.

Heather and Terry took giant bites of their iced gems and couldn't have looked more like care-free kids as they wandered over to Bruno and his parents, who had now beckoned them for a non-negotiable farm tour.

Finally, River let out the giant sigh of relief lodged in his chest. "Oh, Hayley. I cannot tell you how good it is to see Mum tucking in like that. I'm guessing you've taken her out for fish, chips and all the trimmings, then? She's looking loads healthier."

"We've had one or two get-togethers, yep. Between me and Terry, we've worked around the clock to make sure she's been eating properly. I think it helped that I suggested your mum and I were invited on set to watch the DIY show behind the scenes. Once she saw all of the young runners and production assistants in action, and Terry not batting an eyelid, she realised she'd been a bit judgemental of the poor guy... not to mention silly."

"I'll say. Thank you doesn't seem enough. You nipped it right in the bud, before things spiralled out of control. I owe you one."

Before anyone knew it, it was opening time. Bruno's parents had sent word out into the village and it was a decent turnout who greeted the VW's inaugural evening in West Pennard. Unlike the folk of Wookey Hole – and perhaps it was owing to today's location being closer to a certain music festival – most people turned up in Wellington boots, as well as coats, bobble hats, mittens and scarves, to sample the sweet treats... and dance! Even before Rio and Justin had taken to the stage with that damned break dance to plant the seed of diversity in earnest, the twinkle of the bar had produced its own kind of jollity. Couples twirled one another around, children held hands and jigged about in circles, and lone performers found their own patch in the grass to get their groove on. It was enough to make River wonder if Bruno hadn't spiced up the gingerbread, or if Zara hadn't spiked the drink powders.

Even Conrad Fry put in an appearance. River gulped, loitering behind the camper in case he got struck by another olive. Neither Alice nor his old school teacher seemed to recognise one another from the day's earlier antics, thank goodness. She served him his drink and gingerbread and River dared to peep around the corner, surveying the forlorn-looking man; a shadow of his former self who appeared to have lost something.

"It's Elsie," said Christine. Bruno's mum had sneaked up on River again out of the blue. "She broke up with him a month ago down at the bingo hall in front of the entire village and ran off with the young number caller. Conrad's been visiting the farm ever since for fresh mistletoe. As if a new bough a day will bring that tart back!"

"Gosh, poor bloke."

Now River could totally appreciate the telling-off the old man had given him. It was probably best to keep him away from the stage, though. The last thing anyone needed to hear in the first week of Christmas was a sad love ballad.

On the subject of the aforementioned Rio and Justin, River was desperate to speak to them. But it seemed they'd taken on something of that 'waiting for a bus' phenomenon. They were always there when you'd reached your limit with their company, and nowhere to be flipping found when you needed them. Finally, River was rewarded with a glimpse of the lanky Justin's blonde tufts, spotlighted by the humongous combine harvester in the field, whose giant LED roof lights had been switched on especially for the occasion, giving the tableau set out before them all a surprisingly cosy glow.

"Three things," said River, when he'd finally reeled the boys in. "First off, there are two different stories circulating about how long you're intending to stay with us. Which is the truth?"

"We'll er… we'll be with you until Christmas Eve." Justin confirmed, nose tipped self-righteously in the air. "We're enjoying ourselves too much. There's no rush to get back to any kind of work as we're still waiting for the Beeb to commission our next TV project, and we don't need to go to the in-laws until Boxing Day. So yep, you're pretty much stuck with us, I'm afraid." He folded his arms in defiance.

"Good," said River.

Rio giggled nervously. "We thought you'd be furious, mate?" He arched a brow, his body language questioning.

"Not at all. I know none of the Wookey Hole performers would have been brave enough to hop on stage if it wasn't for you two getting the party started. You've really helped us get the vision of the performances across to audiences. That said, it's time to come back to the remaining two things on my list. Number one: I really need you to freshen up your act. Like yesterday."

Rio pursed his lips at the news. Justin planted his hands on his hips. Evidently they weren't expecting this.

"Do it for me, Alice, Zara and Bruno, and do it for yourselves, guys. This break dancing malarkey is all well and good, but we'll be climbing the walls if we have to listen to Mariah every night from now until Christmas. Your routine might be *different*, but those high notes, and those lyrics are as mainstream as it gets… aka everything this show on the road is supposed not to be. I need you to challenge yourselves with a new and unique performance every week. And keep it clean."

The boys side-eyed River, mouths downturned. Rio sniffed. Somehow River thought he could interpret this as acceptance, and he ploughed on.

"Look, forget me saying 'like yesterday'. You can carry on until the end of the week. Oh, and as for the last thing… follow me into the van." River gestured to them both, relieved to see a new and immediate spring in their steps. "I can't risk anybody eavesdropping."

CHAPTER TWENTY-TWO
Alice

"BUTLEIGH-BOUND TODAY!" RIVER announced keenly. Frankly, all Alice wanted to do was go back to sleep. It was too early for this level of enthusiasm over a potential family reunion, and her stomach churned at the implications.

"Yes, I know," she said with a muffled sigh.

"So, how do you rate our performance of the past two nights?" River's eyes gleamed expectantly and she was thankful for the change of subject.

"I'm still a bit speechless at how well it went."

Alice loved the way they'd embraced the continental Christmas market thing. The air had definitely been redolent of all things Alpine, and it was magical to see that recreated on a village farm. Speaking of which, she'd spotted that olive-throwing teacher of River's arm in arm with Cassandra. It looked suspiciously like lurve was in the air for them too. She mentioned her sighting of the couple to her boyfriend.

River almost hyperventilated.

"N… not *Jane Austen* Cassandra?"

"How many other Cassandras do *you* know?" Alice grilled him.

"Well none, obviously. I just… That's a bit freaky."

Alice supposed it was. Cassandra, in her long and lacy Georgian-inspired frocks, bore more than a little resemblance to a character plucked out of a Jane Austen novel. She'd been ever-so-slightly smitten with River when he'd opened the Glastonbury cocktail bar. The memory of her spidery violet lashes and spindly fingers splayed across his counter still made him shiver. "River Jackson, I'm sure the sixty-something lady is well over her brief infatuation with you," she replied. "I expect she was in the village doing the rounds with her mobile library. Or did you forget she felt inspired to start one of those up, after you'd opened her cat sanctuary for her?"

"Blimey. So she did. I'd forgotten how far those ripples of joy had spread." River stopped to reflect. "The three chosen ones who'd stumbled across the Magical Mañana not only had their lives turned around, but they really did wave their own magic wands over the lives of countless others."

"And the same will happen with this venture. Without the help of a bottle. If that utter Grinch of a teacher hasn't proven it to you already, nothing will. Christmas is imbued in magic. From dusk until dawn. There's not a moment throughout December when the impossible can't become reality."

"Cassie and Conrad, though?"

"No reason why they shouldn't make the perfect couple." Alice shrugged.

And if this mini Christmas market on wheels had already cast a snowglobe of romance over those two, then there was no way it could fail to make a couple of Zara and Bruno...

"Sales-wise we did good," Alice continued to assess their performance. "Better than good, in fact. If the whole village of West Pennard didn't show up the first night, they certainly did by the second. But I never thought I'd see the day that a farmer's rap and a Cheddar cheese grating demo, complete with token confetti-sprinkling over the crowd, would win a talent contest."

Alice thought that the customers had taken the latter rather well. If it had been her she would not have been enthralled at the idea of picking strands of stinky farmhouse cheese out of her curls.

"If there's one thing I'm learning already, it's that imagination runs riot in these villages!" River's eyes twinkled as brightly as his bar had last night. "Arlo and Christine were the best hosts. Nothing was too much trouble. I'm not so sure I'd have that same level of generosity with a bunch of people eating, drinking and bopping all over my land. It was great to see Nolan too, although I should imagine the noise level got a bit much for him at times."

"It was so lovely to put a face to the name after hearing all those stories, just wonderful to see the two brothers together. Nolan adores Bruno," Alice added.

"Almost as much as he adores his gingerbread reindeer."

"You've definitely met your gingerbread-fiend match with Nolan." Alice chuckled.

"So, anyway…" said River. Alice could tell from his inflexion that he was steering them toward a conversation she'd rather not have; a conversation she hoped she'd avoided with the many tangents of their chatter. "How are you going to play it, in the event your parents do meander along tonight?"

Yet again Alice channelled her inner resolve not to sigh dramatically or bite back. She knew it was for the greater good; a milestone that needed to be reached in order for her to feel completely comfortable about moving back to the area permanently.

"Oh, I honestly don't think they will come. I mean this is hardly their cup of tea – or hot cocoa." She failed to mask the nervousness in her voice. "They'll curtain-twitch to see who's out and about, for sure. But in any case, the village green is right down the other end of Butleigh from them – and that's where we'll be parked up tonight, by the way: right in the heart of the village."

It was crazy that she hadn't yet had a chance to relay all the finer details of their route and stops to River. Perhaps both of them were enjoying the opportunity to kick back and relax a bit on that score after so many years of (mostly) meticulously planned world tours on the Avalonia band bus. "I doubt what we're doing will distract my father from his armchair and stinky pipe in the library. Meanwhile Mummy will undoubtedly be hosting some festive ladies' evening or other, with her cronies. And I'd be astounded if Tamara's about."

"Gawd, let's hope not." River's face was a picture at the mention of Alice's sister.

"Yes, let's!"

Tamara had been the one to fund the DIY operation that had knocked a hole through Zara's then-bakery, straight into the skittle alley of River's cocktail bar, so that Georgina and co could get their hands on that damned bottle of Mexican elixir. It seemed Tamara wasn't content simply to be showered with the family money or toe the line of 'suitable' suitors (or husbands) and careers (doing sweet FA since said husband earned so much). The truth was, and Alice knew it made her sound shallow to acknowledge it, even the youngest of children would immediately distinguish between the two siblings, looks-wise. They were fairy tale princess versus ugly sister: Alice had been blessed in the beauty department; Tamara, not so much.

✧ ✧ ✧

HOURS LATER, AFTER a quick detour to Somerset's much-loved Clarks Village retail outlet in nearby Street, where River had stocked up on a panoply of discounted shoes, Twinkle, Twinkle, River and Alice pulled up on the still frost-bitten village green of Butleigh. Once again, Bruno's handy list of contacts had come good and he'd secured them the necessary permissions to park on the land.

The late afternoon passed peacefully and Alice was glad of the lull, and relieved none of her parents' pals had wandered onto the green to quell their curiosity. It seemed most people were otherwise engaged. Mince pie baking, carol service organising, and jolly holly church decorating were some of the quintessential village pastimes that came to mind. But more than likely folk were simply at work, and kids at after school clubs.

Rio and Justin looked properly miffed at their meagre performance prospects when they first pulled up in their iridescent blue Alfa Romeo Spider, making for quite the picture. Halfway through clipping their cabriolet's roof back on, they perked up:

"We saw you with that sexy shoe measuring man in the Clarks factory shop, River! How did you keep a lid on it?"

"Shut up and come and help us get organised," River

sniped.

Alice wondered what was so dazzling about said male shop worker. She also wondered how their friends could fit any shopping in their car, let alone a month's worth of suitcases for this sojourn.

Something magical happened at five o'clock. Streams of elves bustled onto the green from every point on the compass. At second glance, they were children in bright green and red hats; the little village school's winter uniform. Alice began to panic. And not just because they appeared to be without parents or guardians. Something about this scene felt like it had the potential to set off large scale mayhem, with the entire village – her parents included – having finally woken from a deep Sleeping Beauty slumber to smell the hot cocoa and gingerbread, following its trail until they descended hungrily upon the camper van like a gang of zombies.

But there was no time to be alarmed. Their first customers had arrived. A bevy of teachers rounded the corner, marching purposefully toward the VW, purses and wallets at the ready. Oh, heck. Now Alice remembered why this was happening. Bruno had said he'd print posters and leave them on the notice boards in the village shop and outside the school gates. The guy was getting a bit too efficient.

Gingerbread people in all shapes and sizes flew off Alice's counter, and River could barely keep up with the incessant demand for specialty hot cocoas, warm milk infused with chocolate melts, and mini gingerbread houses. Rio and Justin played waiters, running up and down the snake of a queue, prepping River as far in advance as they could with the approaching orders. They even handed out free tree chocolate decorations for the littlest kids, who were stomping icy feet and jogging on the spot to keep warm.

But the glowing faces, wide smiles, sparkling eyes and festive cheer made every second of stress that accompanied the mad onslaught worth the while.

A couple of men appeared with a tall ladder to decorate the trees clustered on the edge of the village green with twinkly Christmas fairy lights and large candy canes. Now the children couldn't contain their excitement. So much so that Alice felt sorry for their parents on Christmas Eve, and wondered if she was really ready to raise a brood of her own.

Naturally, Bruno seemed to have second-guessed the snowstorm of kids, and turned up, as if by magic himself, with not only the prerequisite gingerbread stocks, but a mountain of DIY gingerbread house kits to keep the children further occupied. Rio and Justin selected four young volunteers at a time to sit on the stage and take pride of place whilst decorating their houses, and the rest of the youngsters had to sit on the frost-topped grass, hoping not to get wet bottoms through improvising with bin bags that had been deftly distributed by their teachers (surely Bruno hadn't been so organised as to prep them too?). He hung around to supervise and help the tiny ones with their edible creations. Once again, Alice couldn't help but feel the swell in her heart at his joy. It was infectious. Somehow she and River had inadvertently given him a renewed sense of purpose via this crazy idea, and he was rising to it admirably, all thoughts of divorce definitely long gone.

As six pm approached, the teens and adults arrived in high-spirited bunches. Rio and Justin belted out Mariah on the sound system, and Alice's ears retreated behind her furry earmuffs. It didn't make serving the customers easy, but they were more than happy to point at the gingerbread and hot chocolate their hearts desired.

And then, finally and mercifully, Mariah gave way to spur-of-the-moment entertainment. There was an over-enthusiastic duel between a couple of dads who'd rushed home to dress up as King Arthur and a Saxon; costumes and roleplay that had either quickly been dusted down in memoriam of an am dram stint from the past, or pointed to some quirky cosplay fandom. Staying on the Knights of the Round Table theme, next came a teen magician who fancied himself as a modern day Merlin, but really needed to polish up his smoke from the fingers trick so as not to set fire to his cloak on his next stage adventure. Bruno's health and safety skills had proven priceless, here, and he'd operated the portable fire extinguisher with ease amidst rambunctious applause. A group of mums re-enacted their playground French skipping days with a long piece of elastic – now this was more like it – and Alice had been tempted to join in to see if she could muster up her old moves. And a grandma marched onto the stage with her compact potter's wheel, crafting a Santa jug, a reindeer gravy boat and a baby Jesus figurine in under twenty minutes. How the audience cheered!

Meanwhile, Alice was getting desperately short of chocolate melts, with only a handful of the popular marshmallow ones left. What was keeping Zara?

"I did offer her a lift here today during the scant few seconds of time she granted us when she came to my parents' place two days ago," said Bruno, evidently sensing Alice's unease. He had, as reliably as ever, stuck around to help her deal with the food and drink demands whilst River oversaw the stage action.

Seven-thirty chimed from the church bells and finally Alice could make out Zara's outline trudging across the green with her melts, mixes, and a restock of various milks-that-weren't-milk. It was tempting to complain, but she was here now and that was all that mattered.

She was here… and so were a couple of other people, who were most definitely treading the fresh footprints Zara had created: the female of the pair sporting her trademark black Fedora hat, the male with his Balmoral tweed flat cap and walking stick. And both were kitted out in matching beige Burberry trench coats. Alice's parents!

Oh, shoot. Actually, no. Shoot wouldn't do. She meant shit, shit, SHIT. She'd lulled herself into a false sense of security, hoping they weren't going to be coming, hadn't she? And now she was totally, completely, and utterly under-prepared. Her heart hammered. *What to do?* Well, in such situations, Alice had learnt there was only one thing for it: to run away – at least to the inside of the camper van – refusing to emerge until the coast was one hundred percent clear. Free of fellow Goldsmiths.

"Hey, Zara!" She heard Bruno's greeting as she deftly hid behind the door, clutching her chest, desperate to slow down her breathing. "I was more than happy to come collect you and run you back home today. You've cut it a bit fine, you know. We're inundated."

No, Bruno, no!

Alice cringed at Bruno's lack of decorum. Well, he had

warned her he was rubbish at flirting, and he could definitely extend that to conversation. He was addressing his love interest as if she were his *commis chef*. Alice desperately needed Zara to feel at ease enough to stay put and take over the serving duties alongside him – at least until her parents had gone. No way was she setting foot outside of this little haven while her mother and father were in such close range. She dreaded to think about the conversation they would soon be having with River, once they recognised him, but she'd get Bruno to fill him in on her predicament and the two of them could spin a convincing yarn ref her non-appearance. It was all too weird to deal with, now the moment was upon her. River had worked so hard. If her parents saw her here and decided to rake up the past – which wasn't a possibility, but a given – it would ruin the entire pitstop, and in a spectacular style, rivalling even the antics of those festive-wrecking villains in the *Home Alone* movies.

Zara had blinked rapidly, her face a mix of horror and disbelief, upon entering the camper van ten minutes ago and being hit with Alice's bombshell. "What do you mean?"

"It'll probably only be for a couple of hours. I just can't face my folk. You know how it is." Alice had laughed nervously, wringing her hands. "It's a huge favour, I know. But I'm relying on you, Zara. As is Bruno. As is River. As is that ever-growing crowd of hungry and thirsty customers."

"But I can't just give up my evening like this. I… I've got stuff to do. My P… pilates class. I'm sorry but I've paid upfront for it and I won't get the money back."

"Zara, I'll pay you triple time *and* the cost of the class."

"It's not about the money."

"No, you're right. It's not. This is… it's about a friend rescuing another friend… and I would hope we're that by now? Oh, Zara." Alice exhaled deeply, hating herself for landing this on anyone, even if it did have the unplanned bonus of Zara and Bruno spending sweet time together. "Do you honestly think I would spring this on you if I weren't desperate? Please say you'll stay. I have nobody else to ask." She looked blankly around the VW as if to prove her point. "You're my only hope. I know I should face my mum and dad, but what can I say? My family is a nightmare and I'm not ready to see them again. I'm not sure that I'll ever be. They… I… Well, it's complicated but I'm the black sheep. I've never been able to do right for wrong. I'm continuously falling short of their standards. They went berserk when I joined the band. Can you imagine what they'll have to say about me working on a hot chocolate and gingerbread stall? No offence, when half of that is your creation. And God knows, they'll be happy enough to eat and drink what we're serving. Which only goes to show how hypocritical they are and, well… I'm just done with the drama, frankly."

Something about Zara's demeanour softened, then. Just for a moment. Friends helped one another out. That's just what they did. And Alice had sobbed her heart out to this one.

It wasn't as if Alice had planned this. In fact, she'd followed through on River's request to visit Butleigh full of goodwill and good intentions. But when it had come to it, she had no choice but to look after her mental health and take it slowly with her mum and dad.

Perhaps she'd known deep down she wouldn't be able to see them all along. Besides, River was hardly on speaking terms with his own father! This short, sharp, unexpected shock proved it was enough of a step forward just to see her parents again today at a distance, after so long. She honestly couldn't have predicted the way she'd flounder. The last encounter with her mum had seen her slam the door on Alice, for goodness sake. And the most recent *rendez-vous* with her dad had been nothing short of a farce; he'd fooled Alice and River into thinking he wanted to invest in a property in Cornwall with them and then mysteriously pulled out just as the contracts were meant to be signed. She still hadn't worked out whether this had been for genuine reasons, or some crafty and premeditated move of her mother's.

Alice's bottom stayed rooted to the small sofa. Gingerly, she reached for the curtains so she could fully stretch them over the length of the window – just in case a sudden gust of wind should manifest itself inside the VW and blow her cover.

Zara dumped her belongings and sighed as if she'd somehow been privy to Alice's innermost thoughts. "I understand more than you realise. I've chosen to conduct a very distant relationship with my own family, as it happens… which is why I'm agreeing to this. But let me make things clear. I am doing you a massive favour by working alongside that guy, and there will be no repeat performance. Bruno is the most infuriating male I have had the displeasure of meeting in a long time. And there have been more than a few candidates for that role. Indisputably he's a great chef, but indisputably he's a great tosspot, too."

Zara opened the camper door carefully and squeezed herself out sideways, so as not to draw any outside attention to Alice, who'd picked up her half-read novel and hidden behind it, refusing to let her eyes leave the fun and games of the cosy crime and its multiple red herrings. Not even to watch the rise and fall of Zara and Bruno's banter. Or was it bickering? Alice sighed. Because if one good thing could come from tonight, it was *both* of them realising they were made for each other.

As if on cue, the intro for the timeless country hit, *Islands in the Stream,* played softly across the airwaves. Heck, this was hardly the level of unconventional River was aiming for. Alice closed her eyes and allowed herself to catnap along with the melody of the gentle notes anyway. Well, it was pretty impossible to embroil herself in a small town whodunnit now that a duet was about to do their best Dolly and Kenny impersonations. She hoped they'd hit all the high notes.

Ah, make that she hoped *her mother* would hit all the high notes. A very definite Geoffrey Goldsmith belted out the first line of the song, sounding like a goat. Alice didn't know whether to laugh or cry. By her parents' standards, this was unconventional all right.

CHAPTER TWENTY-THREE
Zara

SO THE CURRENT pattern seemed to be that Alice would call upon Zara every other day. It sort of worked when she reminded herself this was only a short term thing. But once again, why hadn't Rio and Justin been put to better use? Especially that day when they'd ignored the closed sign on the door of Zara's chocolate shop, and breezed in to whisper top secrets to her feverishly. Which may have been a whole other story, but still it grated on her. Surely Rio and Justin could have got off their lazy arses to visit the health food supermarket and get the non-milk milks while they were at it? It made no sense at all that they weren't sorting this bit of supply out, now they'd decided to take a month's sabbatical with the sole purpose of touring the Somerset villages along with the camper van. Once again, it was Zara who was doing all the running around. Yes, she was getting paid for her time, but was that really the point? On top of the chocolate batches she was constantly supplying, the cartons of almond, coconut, and rice milk weighed a ton. And now cashew and hemp milk had been added to the list! She didn't have the muscles for this. And she would be suing Avalonia's ex-lead singer if she ended up pulling one.

She'd been so (prematurely) proud of herself for that quick exit from West Pennard… those alarming boughs of mistletoe with the honesty box positioned at the start of the lane! Zara should have won River's talent contest hands down, for nailing the necessary level of choreography to escape unscathed.

She was less proud of herself for the Butleigh blunder. That stupid idea of hers to flip her routine and turn up late so she could take advantage of everyone being busy, drifting in and back out of the revelry, had backfired big time. And talking of stages, Alice had staged such a carry-on, timing it precisely for Zara's arrival, so she just happened to need to hide away in the blessed camper van. That left Bruno with a massive queue of customers who couldn't exactly serve themselves. Zara would be lying if she said she didn't believe Alice, though. She'd definitely have felt the same at the prospect of her own parents putting in a random appearance. In fact, if Zara were in Alice's shoes, she wouldn't have entertained the notion of going within a hundred miles of their house in the first place.

Then there was Bruno. The guy might push all of the buttons Zara didn't know she had, but how could she leave him to fend for himself against that lot? No, instead she'd seen herself be guilt-tripped into playing doting assistant to him, scurrying about like a blue-arsed fly cutting, boiling, mixing, swirling, and doing last minute gingerbread piping too. All so Alice could lounge about reading a book at her leisure.

"You'll be paid triple time for this. You're an absolute star, Zara."

Zara had to admit she'd done well to swallow her pride

and get on with it, briskly filling Bruno in on the situation in code and, mindful of the fact Alice's parents could be in the queue, her antenna were pricked and she was on the constant look out for River so she could relay the delicate state of affairs to him too, staving off any unnecessary drama.

"I don't believe it," he'd whispered to Zara. "I thought she'd moved on and was up for this. It's such an important milestone so we can move back to the area." He pulled his beanie hat over his forehead and down to the tips of his eyelids as if this might totally disguise him from the dreaded Goldsmiths. Furtively, he looked left and right. "I don't believe it!" He repeated, eyes filled with unease. "They're only next in line for the stage. Why didn't I spot them sooner?"

"So leave them in the capable hands of Rio and Justin. That's what they're here for... to help. Once her folk have performed, you can sneak back over incognito. Their next port of call will be here for refreshments and there's no reason for them to suspect this has anything to do with you or Alice. As far as they know, you still live in Cornwall."

Zara watched River's Adam's apple as it reverberated in his throat.

"And... erm, River?" He turned to her. "It's smart to forgive but it's also smart not to forget. In fact, sometimes it's the most sensible course of action one can take. Much as we'd all love to live in a fairy-tale bubble, family life isn't always hunky dory. Take it from someone who knows. Alice is under no obligation to overlook her parents' behaviour. If they're toxic, if they're never likely to change, then forgiveness is enough... forgiveness is the most you can ask of her, actually."

She truly hoped River was processing all of this. Nothing

in life was ever perfect. Waiting for it to be would mean Alice would never be able to move back to Glastonbury. Zara chose to ignore the fact this trusty piece of advice could also be applied to herself.

"Zara's right," said Bruno, and her heart galloped at the way he spoke her name in his deep molten chocolate voice. "I mentioned no names in the posters and fliers I put about, I swear. I knew you wanted to do this based on your own merits, and not off the back of being members of a rock band. To all intents and purposes, anyone could be running this foodie event."

Zara scowled at Bruno, the push and pull of his annoying habits triggering her again.

"F... foodie *and drinkie* event," he corrected himself, smiling endearingly her way.

"Oh, my God." Zara slapped her forehead, realisation breaking the trance before it had its wicked way with her. "That write-up from Fiona. What if Alice's parents saw it and that's why they're here? Fiona's better connected than any of us realised."

"Let's assume and hope they're too busy with their upper crust pursuits to stumble across a food and travel blog," said River. "Although you're right. Alice showed me Fiona's website and I clicked on her various social media buttons at the bottom of the feature. Woah. That lady has a following and a half." Bruno's eyes seemed to twinkle at this specific piece of trivia. "How I wish I could rewind time so I didn't greet her like a total twit."

River left them to it then, hovering at the camper's edge until that unforgettable (and not in a good way) rendition of

Islands in the Stream came to its conclusion amidst a surprisingly tone deaf crowd, who clapped enthusiastically... or perhaps it was because their suffering was finally over?

Meanwhile, somehow a mutual understanding had quickly developed between Zara and Bruno and they'd worked almost telepathically to whittle down the queue, all whilst providing outstanding customer service, animated chatter, and festive smiles.

But then, of course, it had to happen: cockiness reared its ugly head.

"I did see the blog, you know," he enlightened her.

"Right." Zara tried to hide her self-satisfied grin. Evidently, Bruno was hinting at her hot chocolate creation in all its crowning glory.

"You do realise it was me who persuaded Fiona that ladies should go first; that my baking adventures have had more than their fair share of press coverage... hence the cake appearing in a smaller shot at the end of the feature."

"I do hope you're joking."

"Of course not. You made a little thing of beauty and nobody can deny it. But mine was undeniably grander."

Zara's toes curled into her boots. She would not rise to this. That's what he wanted.

"You're just jealous. Not everything in this world is about size being best – cake, car or anatomical credentials."

"Touché." Bruno raised an eyebrow, and Zara realised who he reminded her of: the beautiful, late Nick Kamen, star of the Levis ads, pop singer, and Madonna's protégé. "My God, I've met my match with you," he added.

Zara busied herself carefully packing away the unsold

'melted' snowman biscuits, cursing inwardly at the sudden shakiness of her hands. Finally, she managed to straighten herself up to let Bruno have it:

"In the career-driven sense of the word, yes. I think you'll find you have met your match in terms of ambition. In every other sense of the word, the answer there would be a resounding 'no' and some very wishful thinking on your part."

"I... I wasn't going to say anything, except I'm not sure if you read the papers... and certainly you wouldn't read the London ones." Geez, did the boy ever stop? "That *Hostess with the Mostess* piece about you was duplicated in many high end rags. Fiona's pretty well connected, you know."

"You don't say." Zara stopped to study his features. She'd already deduced Fiona had contacts via the conversation with River. What was Bruno playing at? And how dare he insinuate he'd given Zara a leg up with her career? "Why would anyone in the capital bat an eyelid at a chocolate coconut drink? It's hardly avant-garde enough for London foodies." Zara thought of her foodie reviewer sister, Grace, sipping it alongside a thesaurus so she could slate it *en vogue* and cringed.

"Because it's from Glastonbury. Because it has so much marketability, especially if you continue to source local ingredients." Right. And Glastonbury high street and the local farms were awash with coconut trees, weren't they? Zara shook her head. "Because you have the most fabulous business opportunity right under your nose but you're looking at the wrong place to sell it."

"Is that so? I'd say the customers have left here tonight with warm hearts and full bellies. Not all of it down to your bakes and cakes."

"Yes, they have. And all of that's down to you *and I*. You've got that bit right." Oh, a semi-compliment. "We work like a dream together, don't you think?" Bruno's eyes scorched her core in the scant microsecond she dared look into them. Dammit, her pulse was rocketing again. Why couldn't River, Rio or Justin come along and dilute things? Alice was as much use as a chocolate teapot, lounging about still with her book.

Zara stewed over her previous thoughts. Dammit again. They had partnered up well in the professional sense, but no way would she give Bruno the satisfaction.

"What I'm trying to find out," he continued, "is, have you thought about targeting a brand new customer base? Casting your net wider?"

"Go on."

She attempted to blink in a manner that would encourage him to make haste with his unsolicited professional advice, and briskly winced, knowing full well Bruno would have translated it as a full-on girlie eyelash flutter, thanks to her bloody fringe! She'd go home and chop it herself – even her long-overdue visit to the hairdressers had been postponed, to help fund her Italian trip.

"Come along to Pilton tomorrow and see if things become clearer of their own accord. Let's do this bit of service together again. Even if it's only for half an hour. In the presence of Glastonbury Tor, on that magical Glastonbury festival site where so many ideas have been set in motion, where music has changed the world, where rebirth happens." Bruno winked.

It scared Zara sideways. Not *his* body language, no. Rather it was the fact that she knew exactly what he was trying to impart. She saw it in that moment as if she were looking at a reflection in a mirror. And it was a great idea, a sound idea. But it was *his* idea. And she was not taking it. Once again, the universe wasn't listening!

She did not wish to be handed gifts on a plate: neither in monetary form, nor in brainwave form. At least not via other human beings. Her destiny came from her. Every bit of it. She wanted to scream at the inky black sky, to blast the stars with her disapproval. *Let me stand on my own two feet and prove myself for once!*

"I can't, Bruno. I… I've got yoga."

CHAPTER TWENTY-FOUR
River

RIVER HAD TAKEN to pacing. He'd spent the past couple of decades seeking approval from the institution that was Glastonbury festival. Now it'd been granted in a very roundabout way. Here he was, watching Bruno, Rio, Justin and Alice soak up the benevolence of Sir Michael Eavis's welcome instead. The four of them were sprawled out on a tartan picnic rug sunbathing in jumpers. The weather had turned unseasonably mild, negating the need for coats, and the winter sun wrapped the fields in a delicate glow; the kind that put him in mind of the happy-ever-after part of a fairy tale. He had finally been semi-noticed by the music mogul who ran the legendary annual festival, and he couldn't even enjoy it. Well, wasn't that always the way? Although in his case, there was a good reason for being on edge. Hopefully.

"Psst. Rio, Justin: can I just borrow you for a second, to erm… run through the new performance ideas for next week?"

River didn't need to wait for his words to take effect. The men sprang immediately to their feet and followed him to the camper, leaving a de-stressed Alice and a downcast Bruno behind them. River'd had time to mull over Zara's advice. She was, as Bruno had also confirmed, righter than right. So there'd be no more cajoling the love of his life to patch things up with her parents. The ball was in their court, should they decide to change their ways. Alice had assured him she'd forgiven her mum and dad, and that was progress enough. Thank heavens they hadn't spotted either him or Alice in Butleigh, though. Rio and Justin had most definitely earned their place on the VW tour in that respect, guiding the singing hopefuls to the stage and back off it again. Thankfully, the public vote hadn't declared Mr and Mrs Goldsmith victorious that evening. The grinning pottery lady with the lion's mane of hair had swooped that accolade instead.

"Is everything in place for tomorrow?" River grilled Rio and Justin once they'd pulled together the sliding doors.

His friends side-eyed one another. Justin began to twist and pull at his thumb. Rio chewed a fingernail.

"But we thought you only wanted to discuss our potential list of new acts. We didn't realise we needed to have singled one out yet." That was Justin, who had now moved on to splaying his fingers and stretching each one individually with his opposite hand.

"Not for the Twinkle, Twinkle show! I'm talking about the other show; the rather significant other show!"

"Oh, that." Rio nudged Justin.

"Yes *that*."

"Everything is one hundred percent sorted," Justin announced.

"Two hundred percent sorted, in fact." Rio interjected. "Now come back outside, lie in the sweet December sun and imagine you're revving up to watch Stormzy on the pyramid stage."

"Great. So what do I have to do when we arrive?" River ignored Rio's grime adoration, although he was secretly a fan of the rapper and his music genre himself.

Bruno bristled past the camper van's window then, so Rio whispered the answer to River.

Well, phew. Thank the universe for that.

It truly did all sound as sorted as could be. Which meant River could finally relax and try to enjoy today. He embraced his friends and even succumbed to half a smile. There might not be a proper stage performance of his own, here in these green fields that had been trodden by so many of the world's largest stars, but he'd give the villagers of Pilton a festive fun fair to remember... and a hot cocoa and gingerbread experience a gazillion times better than anything the traders could rustle up at the famous music festival. You wouldn't find one of Zara's lip-smacking cinnamon and nutmeg-infused hot chocolates there. And you wouldn't be able to track down a crumb of a turtle dove-iced gingerbread biscuit.

And then he let his grin take over his face in the realisation that the festival and its organisers owed him nothing. In fact, it was quite the opposite! For this was the very place where Avalonia began, wasn't it? Perhaps River had even pitched his tent on the exact spot where he was now standing, all those years ago? Which meant he'd actually come full circle. If it hadn't been for the chance encounter with Bear and Alex that hot and sticky June – the other band members who'd made up the rock group, along with himself and Alice – then life wouldn't have led River to this point in time. And he wouldn't be about to offer any yuletide yumminess to anyone...

CHAPTER TWENTY-FIVE
Alice

WHAT WAS THE matter with River? Was there a full moon? It was like he had ants in his pants or something. He'd half-achieved the thing he had always secretly wanted, the chance to perform at one of the biggest music festivals in the world. Okay, so he was serving up mugs of fancy cocoa and animal-shaped gingerbread biscuits, as opposed to clutching a mic and roaring his heart out to a crowd of one hundred thousand party-goers. But still. Kylie Minogue, Janet Jackson and Kanye West – three of the festival's past headline acts – certainly couldn't lay claim to the excitement and applause surrounding his current venture. And none of those megastars gave Joe Public the opportunity to put their own raw talents to the test on a stage like River did – albeit it a rickety one.

Alice was beyond proud of him. Everything he did was infused with gusto, determination, vision, and commitment. Everything he did was extraordinarily, memorably outside the box.

Files of the locals finally started to arrive in the late afternoon. A wonderful sight to behold until Alice realised, with sheer horror, that they were carrying tents! Somewhere along the lines of communication, something had gone decidedly wrong.

"Bruno!" she yelled, gesturing at the crowd on the horizon. "What the heck is this?"

"Search me?" he replied, looking genuinely petrified. "They look like they're here for *the festival* as opposed to a food and drink camper van with a stage attached to it like a piece of Lego."

"Y… yes. That's the realisation I'm swiftly coming to myself."

Oh, bleep. This did not bode well at all.

"Excellent!" River's eyebrows sailed heavenward and refused to budge, as if his moment in the spotlight had truly manifested itself after all this time, the best things coming to those who waited.

"Not really." Alice set him straight. "Not unless you want us chucked out of the place before we've even got started."

"River, mate. I have to agree with your good lady. I really think there's been a huge misunderstanding here and I fully intend to shoulder the blame for it," said Bruno, clasping River's own shoulders, trying desperately to make River look him in the eye to get a grip on reality. "You are not about to have the mini festival of your dreams. Much as I'd love you to. Much as you deserve it. We'll have to send this lot packing, and pronto. There's no way Michael would have agreed to this. Emily neither."

Emily was Michael's daughter, and nowadays very much integral to the running of the festival. River might well have attended primary school with her but that wouldn't give him any sway. There really was no way she would have agreed to this level of intrusion at such short notice, Alice acknowledged. They were blessed enough that Bruno had secured them a license to serve a few nibbles and display a little low-key local entertainment. But laying on an overnight campsite for the entire village? No, that was ridiculous.

Bruno marched forward to the approaching throng, Rio and Justin either side of him, ready to do battle. Alice couldn't bear to watch from the sidelines and left River to his delusions. She rolled her sweater sleeves up, ready to put her negotiating skills to the test.

"*Avalonia! Avalonia!*" the crowd chanted the closer they got, interspersed with squeals of "Oh my God, it *is* Alice Goldsmith!" and "Don't be uncouth, put your phone away… we'll ask if we can get a selfie with her later."

Alice felt like she was stranded in a nightmare with no escape. She'd completely forgotten how diehard indie fans could be in these parts. The constant recognition of her face may have rapidly diminished elsewhere in the world, but Pilton village was the beating heart of the independent music scene. Most of the villagers embraced every aspect of their home's heritage. In other words, they were fans who didn't forget those who had walked the alternative arts path. Even if you had only made a modest name for yourself, and mainly in America, you were still hailed here as heroic.

Alice pinched herself as she ran to catch up with the boys, but it was no use. This was no nightmare, much less a dream that she could wake up from. The field still rolled on, putting the distance between them, the revellers marching ever deeper into it with their colourful paraphernalia stubbornly strapped to their backs and gripped in their hands. Eyes wild with expectation at the private party they were privy to.

Alice stumbled on an earthy mound. Now her trainer lace needed re-tying, granting the guys even more of a head start. She decided she could do no more than freeze on the spot instead. At which point the speck of a vehicle appeared on the horizon. She knew it was curtains for their plans, the Land Rover quickly covering the distance to stop the crowd. Her heart sagged. Though quite how the permanent festival crew who looked after the enormous site could break up this group of fifty or so people, she had no idea.

That was when the strangest thing happened.

Bruno, Rio, and Justin, upon confronting the first of the campers, jumped up and down in unison with cheers of 'no way', 'oh, my God, that's amazing' and 'fuck, YES!'

They turned to somehow transmit the revelation to River, but spotted Alice was closer and sprinted to her instead, barely able to catch their breath, stumbling across the clumpy patches in the grass as Alice had done.

"Michael d... didn't... he didn't grant us permission for a c... camper van and a little talent trailer!" shouted Bruno.

See. Alice knew it was too good to be true. Like the Butleigh stop last night, they should have erased Pilton from their map. There were plenty of other villages to choose from instead. This journey was supposed to be about bringing the community together in remote places where the pubs had been closed. Well, they were alive and kicking in Butleigh *and* Pilton. So much so, these pubs had skittle and darts teams. All of which meant they were going off at tangents with this madcap venture, and enough was enough. She turned to break the news to River. It had been nice to catch a few rays and appreciate the even greater view here of Glastonbury Tor in the distance, but the true meaning of the mission was ebbing away. If they packed up now, hopefully they could avoid the embarrassment of the fast-approaching Land Rover and its crew, who undoubtedly had their loudspeakers at the ready to evict them from this sacred land.

"He granted us permission for an overnight hot chocolate, gingerbread and music partaaaaayyyyyyy!" screamed Rio.

Alice swivelled, heart beating ten to the dozen, unable to process her friend's words and the encroaching scene. The Land Rover had overtaken the villagers by now, and in it, right at the very front and behind the steering wheel, was none other than the great festival organiser himself!

Sir Michael waved excitedly at Alice and kept driving pointedly towards River and Twinkle, Twinkle. Of all the pictures that had been taken of her boyfriend over the years; the black and white snapshots of him belting out impassioned lyrics; toplessly dousing his beard and his tresses with bottles of iced water to keep cool in between numbers on stage in the South American sun; strumming his guitar with his eyes closed deep in the flow of the music; congratulating the White Stripes in the middle of a group hug at an award ceremony, and reacting to a rapturous Avalonia crowd, she didn't think she'd ever seen him as euphoric as this. Where was a zoom lens when you needed one? She guessed some of the motley crew behind her would have captured a whisper of the essence on their mobile phones.

THE AFTERNOON AND evening flashed by in a blur. A bit like

a wedding, for the bridal couple. *Well, Alice could always imagine.* No time to greet all the friendly faces or adequately savour every magical moment. Once tents had been pitched – neatly, with the greatest respect for the landscape – and once River had given in to public demand for an impromptu medley of Avalonia's hits (a public which included an eager and beaming-eyed Sir Michael), everyone had needed feeding. The orderly queues belied anything that might have been found at the real festival, and it was then that Alice had truly been able to relax, watching the villagers swoon over their gingerbread creations and Christmassy drinks. Fuelled with rich food and drink, the people of Pilton formed another orderly queue for the stage, ready to showcase their unique talents. Rio and Justin had been a little put out that they weren't getting the opportunity to perform their break dance finale until midnight, but it had been its own kind of special beneath the gaze of the moon and stars. Talking of the latter, Alice thanked *her* lucky stars that the next time her friends took to the stage there would be no more five-octave range warbles and cookie cutter clanging, the Mariah Carey break dance routine having finally reached its conclusion.

They'd pulled off this iconic stop, and they'd pulled it off in a way they could never have imagined in their wildest dreams. River had finally let musical grudge bygones be bygones, too. The cherry on the cake. And then came the sweet chocolate ganache: everyone had tidied up as quickly and efficiently as the birds in Disney's *Cinderella*, leaving the place spotless!

But now it was time to come back down to earth with a thud. And first things first: Hayley was unwittingly well overdue for a phone call from Alice, who was in dire need of the woman's matchmaking advice. Zara and Bruno had appeared to get on like a house, or VW camper van, on fire in Butleigh. Alice had cupped her ear to the camper's door, listening in on their harmonious way of working together outside, jumping back onto the seat to hide behind her book the moment she sensed one or the other of them would need to slip through the slimmest gap in the sliding doors (mindful of her ever present parents) for supply reinforcements. There was no doubt about their sizzling chemistry, whether they were aware of it or not. Unfortunately, time was ticking on, especially now that Zara had confirmed she'd managed to book her blimming flights after all, the price having dropped again. Alice's tongue had been loaded with expletives and she could have cried when she'd heard the tragic news. Bruno hadn't an inkling. Now she was really up against it to work some yuletide magic of her own.

Yes, Zara may well have huffed and puffed as she'd succumbed to the unexpected demand of yet another sell out roadshow, re-stocking the VW with yet more goodies, but ever since Butleigh, she'd dodged the man in question as if he were Jack Frost.

Alice tried not to sigh in despair as the camper threaded through the glorious Somerset countryside, the late morning sunshine beaming down in celestial pillars of light once again and creating something truly biblical. In contrast, she couldn't help but acknowledge how tense River was. She reached across to squeeze his thigh, quite unprepared for his snap.

"Not now, Al. I'm trying to concentrate."

Oh, this must have something to do with the up-coming

reading of his aunt Sheba's will. Alice had best not press him any further. She lost herself in the potpourri of cows and sheep in the fields instead.

"So," said River, at last.

"So?" Alice replied, wondering if she'd now be treated to an explanation for his narkiness.

"I thought it would be fun to do a couple of laps up and down Glastonbury high street before we head south east to Bishops Lydeard."

"Right, yes. I suppose."

"We can call in on Zara and relieve her of anything fresh she's prepared, maybe pop into the cocktail bar for a brief catch up with Lee and Jonie too…"

"But they won't be open. It's eleven o'clock."

"Oh, did I say that?" River laughed nervously. "I meant we could walk past the window, you know, and wave."

"Wave at *nobody*? Okaaaay. Anything goes in Glastonbury, I guess."

No, this definitely wasn't just Sheba-related. Something was off. Alice couldn't put her finger on it but her boyfriend was acting super-strange this morning, on a day when he should have been riding the wave of elation after the alchemy of all that had happened yesterday afternoon and last night. The national media had sent out its West Country journalists to capture the moment and everything, yet River had seemingly forgotten the lot, not even wanting to chew the cud over it.

Following the curve of the main road that skimmed the base of the Tor, Twinkle, Twinkle began to receive admiring glances from pedestrians and fellow motorists driving the opposite way as they entered Glastonbury. And before long, River had pulled up on the high street.

"You can't stop here! What are you like, Riv? We'll get a parking ticket... or worse still, get clamped and be unable to get to Bishops Lydeard at all!" cried Alice.

"I'm willing to wager a bet that we'll get away with it. The magic of the past twenty-four hours still feels like it's in the air."

River ignored her worries and turned off the ignition. He jumped from the camper, walked around the front of the vehicle, lips pursed as if about to whistle, opened Alice's door and came over all gentleman chauffeur, arm extended to not only kiss her hand but help her hop out, too.

She stood on the pavement in a daze. Was it just her imagination, or had time stood still? Alice could feel dozens of pairs of eyes on them, and not just because they'd parked on double yellows. Heck, so many of the locals tore up the rule book here that people wouldn't bat an eyelid because of that. But when she looked around, paranoia getting the better of her, everyone was simply going about their business: walking, shopping, juggling on the benches outside the church, cloak swirling, fairy wing wearing and wand waving. All was perfectly Glastonbury.

"Why don't I escort you over to Zara's so you can ask her if she's got any new goodies for us to take off her hands? I promised to meet Rio and Justin in one of the candle shops." *Hang on a minute. That's not what her boyfriend had said earlier when he'd waffled on about waving at the empty cocktail bar.* "They wanted to wander around the touristy shops here *en route* to our next stop. Rio... erm, he said he could use some advice on the best incense blends... and Justin has begged me to talk him out of buying a didgeridoo. I... I'm going to have my work cut out with that request. I think he's got designs on learning how to play it for a certain performance tonight."

Please, God, no.

And was it just Alice's imagination, or was River's voice seriously warbling through that strange spiel? Rio and Justin had said nothing of the sort about stopping here to shop. Last Alice heard, they were planning to go bowling in Taunton, the county town, which was a stone's throw from Bishops Lydeard village, where they were headed next, followed by an all you can eat Chinese buffet. Evidently the gingerbread and hot chocolate weren't quite hitting the spot.

River spun Alice around on the pavement, making her more confused by the second. The next thing she knew, he'd put his hand up to stop the traffic (which mysteriously didn't honk its horns) and started to foxtrot the pair of them down the centre of the street; destination – seemingly – Zara's former chocolate shop.

"What are you doing?" she shrieked, half in shock, half in jubilation, for it wasn't every day she saw such a playful side to her beau.

"Just dropping you off for a moment." He opened the door to Zara's place. Which was odd, because Zara was no longer serving the general public from her shop, so why were her premises unlocked? Before she could question River, he'd pushed Alice gently inside and vanished into thin air.

Zara had the largest smile on her face. Alice began to wonder if this version of the woman was an imposter, because she certainly hadn't looked so ecstatic to see any of their tribe last night at Worthy Farm when she'd grumpily rushed in and out, ducking and diving to get away from Bruno.

"Hi, I, erm," Alice started. "Well, I didn't realise we were coming into town today, and I'm a little puzzled at River's behaviour… wondering if he might have ingested some magic mushrooms last night, in fact."

Zara shrugged, her curious smile fixed to her face.

"I can't say I noticed any. Then again, I was in and out. Pilates to get to. Luckily I was only ten minutes late."

"Funny that… Bruno said you did yoga," said Alice absent-mindedly, turning to look out the window.

She had so desperately wanted to witness Zara's face fall then, for her to know that Alice knew she was telling complete and utter porkies about her leisurely pursuits. But a sixth sense called her. Or rather a collective energy did. She gasped. The high street was *full* of people. What was this, the Apocalypse or something? They weren't on the pavements either, but clogging up the whole road. She panicked that something had gone wrong. An accident perhaps? Maybe these were rubberneckers? What if River was stuck in the middle of this chaos? She had to get out of the shop, yet the scene before her was too strange to walk into. For the second time in as many days, her feet refused to budge from the spot.

Zara cleared her throat belatedly but Alice barely registered her saying, "people can do both forms of exercise, you know."

Slowly but surely, every one of the people blocking the road turned to face Alice in the shop window, as if she were a mannequin modelling the latest Glastonbury fashion. Then they began to motion to her with their hands, willing her to join them outside. Was this some kind of practical joke? She was too mesmerised to check with Zara and, as if they were luring her into a trance, she followed those hand gestures instead out onto the pavement. Regardless of the fact they had come from a bunch of complete strangers. The door remained wide open behind her.

Now Alice could fully appreciate the festive attire of the people in front of her. They were dressed in flowing cloaks and gowns in every shade of winter from gleaming cranberry red to eggnog gold, and holly leaf green to titanium silver. Their costumes shimmered as they twisted and turned, mixing and matching, swapping positions in precise dervish-like moves as they rotated in and out, around and around one another. They reminded her of the cogs in a well-oiled machine.

Then they were dancing.

This was like something out of a Broadway show, or the West End. Everyone was inexplicably in sync with each other. But how? How did random human beings pull this off? Sure, that could happen on the stage and with incessant rehearsals. But in real life? Could anything be so polished?

That was when Alice realised she'd stumbled across one of those flash mob performances. How cool! As if reading her mind, one of the dancers reached for Alice's hand and soon she was lost in the organised chaos. As she spun around, she gawked at Zara's open door, berating herself with every rotation for being so absorbed in these theatrics. Poor Zara didn't need all of her precious heat to leave the building when she was struggling to pay the bills.

Hold on though... Why was she struggling exactly? It was a curious time for such a thought but something about being made into a spinning top made Alice wonder how Zara could have travelled to Barbados, Dubai and Provence, and now be living on a shoestring? Well, she had said she didn't get on with her family. Gosh. Maybe she was another who'd been cut off from her trust fund?

The music changed tempo now, everything slowing down to a more gentle spin. Alice could make out the faces of Rio and Justin standing next to Zara on the pavement, all of them sporting massive grins. Lee and Jonie had joined her friends, the next time she was whirled around. If Alice wasn't mistaken, Lee had his hand outstretched offering her a cocktail. The contents of the glass resembled a Coco Loco. If only the Sugar Plum Fairy she was now partnered with would let her stop for a moment, perhaps she could go over and try it.

The music stopped, as if Alice's thoughts had commanded it. One by one, the dancers peeled away to reveal River on what looked suspiciously like... No. It couldn't be! *Yes. It was!* He was on bended knee.

A wedding proposal. All thoughts of the cocktail flew out of her head and her feet fairy-stepped their way across to him in what felt like the slowest of motion. Every bit of this strange morning was akin to an out of body experience, but Alice refused to let the wobbly sensation engulf her. If this was simply a dream, then it was the dream of a lifetime and she intended to savour every second of it.

River's eyes never left Alice as he stayed still and poised, awaiting her arrival. All around them, hundreds of breaths must have been held, the dancers and shoppers and her friends all on tenterhooks. Let them be. Alice needed to push them all to the edges of her consciousness. This moment was about her and River.

Finally, she stood before him, her nerves coiling in her stomach and limbs until excitement took over and adrenaline kicked in. In a quite enviable measure of calm, River slowly opened a little red satin box to reveal the most beautiful gem Alice had ever seen. A huge square-cut emerald engagement ring twinkled back at her.

Kate Middleton, eat your heart out.

Oh, River! It must have cost a fortune – and it would complement Twinkle, Twinkle perfectly!

"Yes, yes and YES!" Alice screamed before the proposal and the words leading to it had as much as left River's mouth, eliciting a huge roar of laughter and cheers from the many people surrounding them.

"She said YES!" a random Glastonian cried, setting everyone off again. In his red and gold circus ringmaster jacket, blue and green Scottish kilt and clogs, he could have been the mismatched emblem for all Alice and River's hometown represented. He threw down the crate he'd been carrying and thus began a 'tap dance' on, off, and around it that certainly wouldn't have made it into any Broadway shows, but was wonderfully in keeping with the town. The happy-go-lucky fellow pulled a silk rose out of his top pocket and threw it at the couple.

"Nice touch, mate," River acknowledged, turning to Alice. "Erm... he wasn't part of the show, I swear." He slipped the rock onto her finger and both of them remained speechless. It was a dazzler. A dazzler that had been well worth waiting for.

"It's okay, Riv. It's more than okay. It's brilliant! I thought you'd never flipping ask, though," she gushed. "I should have known you'd do it in inimitable style."

"Well, I did have one epic speech prepared, but you kind of made that null and void." River laughed.

"Oh no! I'm so sorry." Alice cupped his face in her hands and looked deep into his eyes. "You can tell me it tonight in bed," she whispered tenderly, and more than a little seductively in his ear.

River gulped.

"I... I was petrified I'd – or they'd," River waved a hand toward the approaching Rio, Justin, Zara, Lee and Jonie, "End up letting the cat out the bag, or not be able to get all the dancers organised in time. Never mind our little jaunt around the villages dishing out goodies, this was one of the trickiest things I've ever attempted to pull off in my life."

Heather and Terry appeared then, alongside their friends and the small group of Alice and River's nearest and dearest huddled together to raise a glass. Lee had thoughtfully provided not only Alice's Coco Loco, but River's Frisky Bison, Zara's B52, Heather's Ginger Rabbit, Terry's pint of cider (much to River's dismay, Lee had acquiesced to Terry's constant request for the 'Somerset fizz' and had a tap fitted at the end of the bar). Meanwhile, Rio and Justin were presented with a pair of Key West Coolers and looked mighty satisfied at Lee's guess at their cocktail style.

"Thanks ladies and gents!" River shouted to the vast sea of performers. "The tipples at Lee and Jonie's bar are on me, as soon as it's opening time. No more than two each, remember."

River and his cocktail connoisseur rules! The dancers roared their approval at his benevolence nonetheless.

"You will be there tomorrow, won't you, son?" Heather inquired after copious sips of her drink.

"For the reading of the will?" asked River.

Talk about turning elation on its head, but Alice supposed that Heather had to grab her moments with her boy when she could. He did have a busy schedule.

"Yes. It's best we get it out the way before Saturnalia." Heather was Pagan and didn't celebrate Christmas in the 'traditional' mainstream sense.

"I'll be there." River grasped Alice's jewelled hand. "We both will. We'll have to delay things at our next stop by a day, but that's okay. Not that I'm expecting, or entitled, to anything more than a mention of the camper van."

"It might be sensible to brace yourself." Heather fussed about with the invisible lint on River's jumper. "Like I'm pretty certain Sheba hinted in her letter."

CHAPTER TWENTY-SIX
Zara

ZARA WAS MADE up for the happy couple, of course. And thankfully Bruno hadn't been there to witness River's grand gesture of love. The flash mob had been the height of romance, performing with the sort of military precision that was up there with the changing of the guard, and all of the royal pomp and ceremony she'd watched in the flesh during her London years. Well, with the exception of the kilted and clogged tap dancer, who with his incongruous circus jacket reminded her of those dress-up paper dolls she used to play with as a kid. Still, she couldn't imagine anyone going to such lengths to declare their love for her, and she sighed in resignation.

Okay, Zara was lying. A small part of her had wanted Bruno to be there. It was the same small – and irritatingly undeniable – part of her that had begged the other bits of her to stay for longer than ten minutes at the festival site when she'd dispatched her supplies. It was the same small part of her that had enjoyed that thoroughly saucy and wicked dream about undressing Bruno.

And it could get lost. Like, totally.

Zara was not entertaining those ideas, even if this rebellious streak in her was growing bigger by the day, tempting her with longer glances at the Adonis and his unflappable, sexy quiff. How that part of her longed to run her hands through his hair to see if she could get it to move... and that was just for starters. The temptation to inch her way to other areas of his anatomy seemed to be upping its tempo by the minute.

But it was no use. Zara snapped herself out of the silly daydream. Destiny was calling and hers was in the annexe of a tumbledown villa in Tuscany, where she'd soon be shacked up with Lucy and whipping up Anglo-Italian gourmet treats... increasingly overlooking the fact that messing with the perfection of Tuscan bread, cakes, biscuits and puddings felt like high treason. First, though, she had a ridiculously long drive to Bishops Lydeard to catch up with the camper van and meet the customers' demands.

Bruno had shouted at Zara's retreating back as she'd fled from the festival site. "Let's share the drive to the next stop! You know it makes sense. Your car or mine. There's no point in us both clogging up the roads. If you don't want to talk to me on the journey, just bring a CD of your choice. I'll happily listen to the whole thing."

"No, you're all right," she'd replied. "I can smell another how-to-run-my-chocolate-business lecture from a mile away. I don't need your unsolicited advice, thanks all the same."

Zara hadn't wanted to see the expression on his face, but it had been inevitable. That devil of a smaller part of herself who was infatuated with Bruno, well, it hadn't allowed Zara to turn her cheek fast enough. The man had looked hurt and humiliated. Nevertheless, she'd stuck to her guns and driven away before she could change her mind. She simply had to get to Italy before this smaller part of herself became a third of her… then a half… then a whole, gobbling her sense up like a venus flytrap. It was not happening!

What *was* happening was this: she was going to drive all of twenty-six miles to Bishops Lydeard, on the outskirts of Taunton, (claiming for said mileage) and she was going to carefully drop off her goodies to help spread some festive cheer, then get out of there faster than Santa's reindeer.

BUT THAT WASN'T what happened, was it? Best laid bloody plans and all that. Whilst Zara had successfully carried out the drive and the drop (regardless of the fact Bruno ended up trailing her all the way along the A39, meaning they must have synced their departures), just as she was about to leave the children's park where the VW was to be stationed for the afternoon and evening, a small blonde girl with scruffy pigtails had grabbed her hand. In the other, the girl held a half-eaten gingerbread Christmas tree. A pistachio, rose and white chocolate adorned gingerbread Christmas tree. What a waste of premium ingredients. What a pushover Bruno was. Zara hoped none of her expertly-piped Cointreau and orange zest Nutcracker chocolates would meet with the same fate.

"Please will you help me? My sister is stuck in the air on the seesaw and I'm not strong enough to get her down."

"Er, where are your parents?" Zara frowned. She was ever mindful of the dangers of getting involved with children that she didn't know. One had to be so careful nowadays.

"A… at the pub."

The girl shrugged and gnawed ungratefully on the biscuit's branch. Zara realised she couldn't have been older than five or six. Poor thing.

Zara looked all around her but there was definitely nobody passing for a parent in sight. In fact the park was currently empty save for River, Alice, Bruno – and, for some reason, Hayley – who were as good as miles away over the other side of the playground, helping set up for the fast-approaching village throngs. A kiddie park was the quirkiest of places for their foodie van stop and Zara was stunned the council had allowed it. Then again, with no alcohol in the mix, and cosy hot chocs being sipped, she guessed nobody could do too much damage to themselves or the swings and slides. Not that this had stopped these children. The girl's sister looked a little older, even from afar and stuck in mid-air, and she wasn't particularly panicking, which was strange.

"Okay then." Zara relented. "Let's see what I can do."

She approached the seesaw, only to find that the right-hand seat had mysteriously been covered in clods of earth and rocks so that it was rooted to the ground. No wonder the poor mite was still airborne.

"Did you do this to your sister, sweetheart?" Zara crouched down face level with the youngster who still had a grip on her hand.

The little girl giggled. This was really weird. And why wasn't her sibling screaming or cursing, even? If Zara had pulled this stunt on either of her sisters, World War Three would have erupted.

"Okay. Yes, it was me… Auntie Hay." The child covered her mouth, eyes wide with disbelief that she'd said that bit. "I mean erm... *what do I mean again?*" She screwed up her features and looked up to her older strawberry-blonde sister for guidance.

"Tsk!" The bigger and freckled girl adopted a cross-legged pose now on the airborne seesaw seat and Zara's heart was in her mouth that she'd topple off and break a leg. "You mean you have been *really naughty* and caused the kind of chaos that will need *one or more people* to rescue me. Quick, Zara: you'd better go and get help! Oh, look, that man over there with the sticking-up hair looks like he might be able to save me."

Zara was about to storm off. Someone was definitely having a laugh at her expense. These kids knew her name. And 'Auntie Hay' sounded suspiciously like a certain Hayley. She didn't see any other contenders for that role in this park, besides that biscuit-loving taxi driver friend of River and Alice's. But why on earth would Hayley encourage them to muck about like this? It was dangerous.

The older girl indulged in some acrobatics now and Zara began to panic.

"Sit properly and hold tight. I'll have you down in a second."

Zara took off her gloves and stuffed them in her coat pocket, preferring to get her hands dirty instead as she gradually removed the various mounds to restore the seesaw's balance and gently bring the rebellious kid back down to earth. Huffing and puffing, Zara had to hand it to the little sister, she'd done her groundwork, so to speak. Zara flung a huge rock to the right of her, only to be greeted by a searing yelp.

"And she strikes a-bleeping-gain!" said a male voice that

appeared to be in agony.

Zara shrieked. She hadn't heard anybody approaching her. The girls snorted with laughter and the eldest dismounted the seesaw with the grace of a gymnast. Zara tried to suppress the anger that threatened to expel from her nose like a dragon. How dare the little brats! The girls scarpered intuitively, leaving her to deal with a pain-stricken Bruno, who was hopping about on one foot.

"What the hell is going on? I have better things to do with my time than deal with this nonsense," Zara screamed, hands flapping about.

"Ha, I might well ask you the blood… I mean the… the same. Ow! Goddammit, you'd be a demon with a shot put in the Olympics, Zara."

Zara wanted to eyeroll Bruno's theatrics, except it was a whopping great rock she'd unwittingly flung at his foot and the small part of her that yearned for Bruno was delighted to witness the bloom in her heart. The other parts of Zara mentally kicked her emotions into touch. Never mind romance. Where had the small girl found that large rock? And how the frick had she carried it? Never mind the mystery of Stonehenge's formation. This was truly inexplicable.

Bruno hopped backwards to the nearest bench, Zara following him. He removed his trainer and rubbed his socked foot.

"Are you sure you don't have a secret foot fetish? It's just you can't seem to stop injuring mine. First backing into the VW in those clodhopper Wellington boots, and now this. I can show you in the flesh if you like. I promise I've cut my nails."

"Please don't."

Zara tried to keep at bay images of other parts of his body she really wouldn't mind casting her gaze over. She could feel her cheeks burning up without confirmation from a mirror. Thank God she could blame the cold weather, which always did that to her anyway.

"They're Hayley's nieces," Bruno explained. "They live nearby and are home-schooled by their mum, hence being here for playtime. Hayley hadn't seen them in ages so decided to pop down and kill two birds… gingerbread and a girlie get-together."

"Yes, I see they've got their paws on your biscuits already."

"They're quirky little characters." Bruno laughed. "A right pair of scallywags."

"I can think of stronger words, for stressing me out like that."

Zara put her gloves back on and began to march off.

"Wait, Zara. I… erm… I'm not actually planning on staying myself." She stopped in her tracks and slowly turned to take in his devilish good looks again. "I really need to get back home. I'm not sure how badly you've damaged my toe, so, well… I hate to burden you but might I ask for a lift? I can leave my car here and make my way back tomorrow."

"Seriously? It's hardly broken!"

"Oh, you'd be surprised. I mean, you hear of people breaking their toes all the time without realising it. It's certainly sprained. I'll just need to rest it for twenty-four hours. That's all. You wouldn't want me to have a traffic accident, would you?"

And there Zara found herself at another crossroads. To be the ice maiden, or not to be?

At the exact same moment, a very smug-looking, incorrigible Hayley and her meddlesome nieces waltzed by. Scratch giving the woman the satisfaction – since when had Zara's love life been any of her business anyway? – and scratch the Shakespearean pondering. Zara would save that up for a romantic trip to Verona when she was living in Italy. On that note, it was time for Bruno to know the score. She waited for Hayley and co to clear off and took a deep breath.

"I'm sorry, Bruno but the answer's no. I'm sure Hayley's going back that way later. Look, I have things to do. Important things. I'm off to Taunton to pick up my Euros and stock up on a few quintessentially British bits and pieces."

"You're going on holiday? Ooh, save room in your suitcase for me."

Bruno's face lit up.

"I'm going on a very long holiday. Alone. And I don't intend to come back. I'm moving to Italy."

Bruno's jaw dropped and the light left his eyes. His face turned white as the buffalo mozzarella Zara would soon begrudgingly be swapping for Cheddar cheese in her new culinary venture at Lucy's. A pitifully terrible analogy, but an accurate one.

"Oh, I see. Does Alice know? River? Hayley?"

"Alice knows, yes. Not that it's really anybody's concern. I fly to Pisa on January the fifth. It's a good opportunity."

"You don't sound convinced."

Zara laughed.

"For some warped reason, *you* seem convinced you can

read me like a book – quite aside from lecturing me about my career path. I think I know what's right for me and what's not, *grazie mille*."

"I think we could be *anime gemelle*."

"You what?"

It sounded like a culinary term he was trying to show off with.

"We have a connection. One hell of a spark. Whilst I think that would burn just as brightly between us across the miles; whilst I know that absence makes the heart grow stronger, I really can't see the point in either of us denying it or prolonging the pretence."

"I think you're…" *right, she had wanted to say.* "M…mistaken. Like massively." She laughed again, because it was that or she'd cry at his accuracy and intuition. "We're work colleagues. Temporary ones at that. Look, I wouldn't get carried away with the romance of River's proposal to Alice." Zara shrugged.

"How can I? I didn't see it." Bruno looked at her earnestly. Foot back in its trainer now, and remarkably recovered. He steepled his fingers and lifted up his chin as if he could read her innermost thoughts. Athena would have captured this moment in A3, if they were still in business, giving their iconic 'Man and Baby' poster some serious competition, making themselves millions. Zara could have relented and plastered her bedroom walls and ceiling with it, undressing in front of Bruno's sexy, dark eyes, before splaying herself on her bed and…

She felt her cheeks burning hotter. This conversation was done. Her flight was booked. There was no going back. She proffered a sympathetic smile and marched to her car.

CHAPTER TWENTY-SEVEN
River

RIVER TURNED THE steering wheel to round another bend, wondering if Alice and Bruno had looked at the map upside down. Meare and Wedmore, their next two stops, might be close to one another, but they were virtually the other side of Somerset from Bishops Lydeard, Beer Hackett, and The Caundles, where the camper had laid out its wintery wares to the delight of the villagers.

Oh, well. They were certainly seeing a lot of the countryside in between, and this trip had been as much about that as anything else. It was also giving River time to process the rollercoaster of emotions of the past few days. *Alice had said yes*. River smiled as he re-played the magic of the flash mob proposal. Aside from the random dude who just couldn't help but join in with his crazy clog dance, everything had run like clockwork. And now they had a wedding to plan. Soon after that he could think of nothing in this life he'd love more than to make babies, and there was nobody he'd rather do that with than his beautiful Alice. He'd grown up at last. That ring had eaten into his savings, admittedly, but it had been worth it to see the look on her face.

Then had come the revelation of the will. River was still

struggling to process his fate. Not only was he the owner of a VW camper van, but now he'd inherited a cat... with the exact same name as one of Alice's horses. Quite where they were supposed to keep Blossom, he had no idea, although Alice had been delighted. She adored that feline. Oh, and then there had been an *entire* campsite bequeathed to him, with express permission to turn it into a home with stables should he and Alice so wish... on the proviso that the scant few part-time staff members were paid off fairly or hired for the new venture.

It was a lot to take on board. It would certainly settle their hunt for a long-term home with enough acreage for some stables. Blossom would be in her element, following horses around as opposed to holidaymakers. River felt a stab of guilt at the idea of ripping the static caravans out and starting all over again on the land where his aunt had shed so much blood, sweat and tears, but then again, tourist numbers had been down for a while, since Glastonbury now offered so many alternative kinds of accommodation. The advent of Airbnb was a wonderful thing, but not when you were the owner of a caravan park. They could sell off the caravans, keeping them intact, using the money to fund perhaps a renovation of his aunt's existing bungalow, plus of course the construction of the stables. Alice had hinted at the possibility of running a proper riding school there, since Glastonbury had nothing along those lines to date. And River was already starting to dream about some kind of companion eatery attached to its side. Maybe somewhere with a view of the paddocks?

He looked at his dozing wife-to-be, in the passenger seat.

She really was the epitome of a sleeping beauty and River was glad she was taking this opportunity for a catnap. They were now a fortnight into their adventure and the itinerary was starting to take its toll, as much as it was exciting.

Eventually they passed the sign for Meare. River was proud of himself for single-handedly sorting out the logistics for this stop. Harry, a musician friend, owned a stunner of a house here, complete with an orchard that went on forever and backed onto the river. It was a glorious spot, although it didn't quite sit with the ethics of the tour because Harry insisted on cherry-picking the villagers invited onto his property. River would just have to trust that he had selected a good mix of people in need of community spirit and deserving of a lift. Preferably people who had a sideline in entertaining too. As quaint as those last stops had been, the talent was somewhat lacking, making Rio and Justin's brand new drag act an Oscar-worthy performance.

Alice stirred at River's side as Harry came out of his property to greet them, opening up swinging blue gates to reveal a driveway encrusted in moss which led to the orchard's entrance. Not long after they'd parked up beneath the boughs of the apple trees, Harry wined and dined them in his grand house and, in a break with tradition, River and Alice made the most of having the rest of the evening to themselves in the camper. After an epic sex marathon (River would propose to Alice more often if it gave her that much energy and instigated that many positions!), and a couple of Bailey's hot chocolates (he'd never have served anything so mainstream in his cocktail bar but heck, it was Christmas, and in a cocoa it was rather sublime) he couldn't help but notice his fiancée's glum expression.

"Oh. Wasn't it good for you then?" He frowned.

"Are you kidding?" Alice proffered a shy smile. "That was incredible. I'm going to ache tomorrow but it was worth it." She bit her lip, and frankly River could have whipped off her clothes all over again.

"What's up then, honey?" He kissed her on the forehead instead, trying to will away his wicked thoughts of seduction.

"It's Bruno."

River's heart thudded. Damn. He knew the way his life was currently panning out was too good to be true. Alice was having an affair.

"Noooo!" Alice covered her hand with her mouth as if she'd seen him mentally join up the dots. "It's Bruno and it's Zara!"

"They've finally got it on?" River sighed in relief.

"I wish. Far from it, in fact. She only went and told him about Italy."

"Ah, right. That. Well, I guess it makes sense. I mean, you did tell me Zara had accepted her friend's offer and booked the flight."

"I thought they'd be great together. And I thought she'd change her mind, give him half a chance. It's only a flight. It's hardly setting the course of her life in stone. Oh, why is she so damned stubborn, Riv? I can't bear to play witness to his heartbreak and her petulant denial."

"Look, Al, it's not your job to change the world. You have to focus on you. On us. You've tried... I mean I'm guessing that freak seesaw fiasco was something cooked up between you and Hayley?"

"Absolutely not." Alice grimaced. "I might have had a little word with her, but I thought Hayley operated more smoothly than that."

"This is Hayley we're talking about." River laughed. "She has her own very distinct way of doing things. That said, ninety-nine percent of the time, somehow it works. Maybe we just need her to come up with something else?"

"After the way she got the customers in on the act at Beer Hackett? No way. What a disaster." Alice looked startled, and rightly so. River hadn't initially realised it was Hayley who had bribed a number of customers to find continuous problems with their orders, the minute he and Alice were doing their utmost to lure would-be performers to the stage area. Normally that would be Rio and Justin's task, but the amount of makeup they were caking on themselves back at their lodgings in readiness for their act was seriously time-consuming. And so Bruno and Zara, who had arrived separately, as usual – not for want of Bruno trying to carpool – found themselves lumbered with serving the customers. Something Zara had made very clear to River and to Alice that she wasn't prepared to do again. This had led to some frantic scurrying in and out of the camper van to sort out the demanding queue of villagers' requirements… and an inevitable 'accident'.

Hayley's recruits had apparently interpreted it as a bodily collision between Bruno and Zara, followed by a brief but very passionate kiss that Zara had been the first to pull away from. At least that's the version of events that had made its way through the grapevine and back to River and Alice. River could see where Alice was coming from. A little more subtlety wouldn't have gone amiss, but since time was of the essence, Hayley had evidently ramped her brainwaves into top gear, with half a result.

Or perhaps it was just that his friend had never encountered anyone as obstinate as Zara? River was no dating guru but it was plain to see the attraction between Zara and Bruno. The pair of them had looked utterly miserable the past couple of days and they'd have to jolly well sort that before they scared the customers off. Not that Zara ever hung around for long if she could help it.

"I'll ask Hayley to calm things down tonight," said River. "It's not just Rio and Justin who are bees around a honeypot when it comes to this old camper van." He patted Twinkle, Twinkle's roof affectionately. "Hayley's obsessed. The lengths that lady will go to for her cocoa and gingerbread fix. No matter where we've been set up in Somerset, I don't think she's missed an afternoon or evening with us since she drove Mum and Terry over to Bruno's folks' farm that day. If she wants her Tuesday sugar rush, she'll have to promise to stop trying with Bruno and Zara."

Alice broke into fits of giggles. "Well, you did say you wanted to create some community spirit. And we've definitely got some fans."

"Local community spirit. Very local. Christ, imagine if everyone else in Somerset and Cornwall had the same idea and trailed us around like foodie groupies!"

THE NEXT MORNING got off to a drizzly start, but fortunately things quickly cleared up, and the shelter of the apple trees helped stave off the pitter-patter.

"Promise me you'll have that chat with Hayley," said Alice. "I've given up all hope of Zara and Bruno getting together now so it's best to nip any more wacky ideas in the bud before things get out of hand and Zara wants to kill him."

"Will do." River saluted her, and set to unfolding and setting up the stage for what felt like the millionth time.

Harry arrived to inspect the finishing touches and, once satisfied, he opened his gates to let the select revellers in. They were the perfect assortment of people, to be fair. And, whilst none of them were dressed in Victorian couture, something about their demeanour, spirit, and the rainbow colours of their hats, scarves, mittens, and coats put River in mind of the characters and shiny foil wrappers of a vintage Christmas Quality Streets tin. Everybody mingled jovially, the iced polar bear biscuits and praline hot chocolate stirrers were a definite afternoon hit, and even the entertainment got off to a cracking start. The all-you-can-eat ghost chili pepper and ice cream buffet performance was a new one on River! He could only admire the tenacity of the three local brothers who'd showcased it on his rustic stage.

"I've got the most awesome surprise for you guys," said Hayley on arrival, pushing past the queuing customers to River and Alice. They were serving together in a break with tradition, since Rio and Justin had finally nailed their makeup routine, giving River some respite from stage management. "Just call me a genius!" She held her hands up in surrender.

River gulped. Alice's eyes took on a startled expression that made her look as fragile as a china doll. She snapped herself back to dealing with the customers, and River took the giant hint that he needed to do some dealing of his own: a blow to Hayley's plans. He led his friend aside.

"Hayley, I know Alice enlisted your help... but it's time to give up. It's never going to happen. Zara and Bruno are adults and if they'd wanted to get together, they would have found a way by now. They've certainly had enough chances."

There. Not even Hayley could argue with that. But in fact she batted his words away as if she had a completely different matter on her mind altogether.

"Yeah, yeah. Whatever. This is much more exciting." She stopped to take a breath, eyes brimming with glee. "What it is... ooh, I can't wait to tell you."

"I'm listening."

"Eek! My uncle used to play Santa for the kids at some of the local primary schools."

"And?"

"And... I got chatting to him last night on the phone."

Hayley rolled her hands dramatically as if that should make everything clear.

"Okay."

"River, he's only agreed to dust down his outfit and grotto to loan them to us for the afternoon and evening! He'll sort all the gifts too, don't worry. He's got some left over from the late eighties, all still in their original wrapping paper."

"I'm not sure they'll still be in fash..."

"Honestly, River," Hayley tutted. "Every child knows it's not the real Father Christmas, this many days before the twenty-fifth. They also know to be grateful for the token. It's the novelty effect, that's all. Who doesn't love finding out if they've made the naughty or nice list, and telling Santa what they want for Christmas in his grotto?"

"Go on."

River braced himself for the sudden catch. But miraculously there didn't seem to be one. In fact, it was a marvellous idea and Hayley had completely redeemed herself. They might have got lucky with a couple of inventive talent show performances this afternoon, but he couldn't rest on his laurels. If Meare's evening acts were as dismal as the last stops, Santa and his grotto would neatly take the attention away from the naff performances. Hayley's dad was even bringing his new – and decidedly younger – wife with him to be the elf. What could possibly go wrong?

CHAPTER TWENTY-EIGHT
Alice

ALICE IMMERSED HERSELF in the orders as best she could but her mind was consumed, wedding ideas tumbling like confetti, not to mention the excitement over the land River had inherited. And little Blossom. And now her not-so-little herd of horses really would have a forever home, if they could renovate the caravan park and turn it into stables. Her good fortune was dappled with guilt, though. Until Alice pictured Sheba giving her a stern telling off. She was right, feeling unworthy didn't suit her, neither had it ever benefitted a soul. She'd gratefully receive these gifts and give back what she could to the community. Fairly-priced riding lessons available to underprivileged kids would be an excellent start.

Back to the wedding, though, and there was so much to think about. Should they go with the romance of a hay barn and opt for something boho rustic, draped with bunting and festooned with tea lights in jars? Alice could just imagine herself in a simple white dress with a flowery halo, cute and mischievous bridesmaids trailing at her feet. There were certainly plenty of picture perfect locations. They'd pitched themselves up in any number of them on this trip alone.

Or perhaps they should move a little more upmarket?

She'd heard boho luxe was the latest trend, with wedding tableaus bedecked with giant peach, pink, and cream peony-studded arches, overflowing table runners, and mini-Cath Kidston tepees for children. Oh, but what about the romance of a castle? The guests could wear medieval outfits and the feast would be fit for a king. Actually, they could theme it around the legend of King Arthur who was said to be buried in Glastonbury's Abbey (as well as Mount Etna, Richmond Castle et al).

Mercifully, Bruno arrived then, restoring Alice's sanity with his additional gingerbread supplies just as she was feeling the pressure of the ever-growing queue. How many 'select' villagers had Harry invited? It seemed like everybody and their pooches were here this afternoon.

"Hey," Bruno high-fived her on his way into the camper van. "Looks like you need some help. Let me drop these off and I'll be right with you."

Why couldn't Zara see what a catch he was? It bugged Alice and seemed so unfair to Bruno, when here she was getting giddily carried away with planning her nuptials. Although Bruno had, of course, been married before.

Alice diligently added whipped cream and salted caramel sauce to the order of the elderly lady standing before her, lifting the cute pine-green mug with its red ribbon adornment to pass to her – then she almost tipped the lot over the serving table and the woman's duffle coat. Just over the old lady's shoulder, she could see Hayley pressing her foot on a pump; a pump which was inflating a quite hideous-looking plastic Santa Claus. Alice watched in horror. That was bad enough, and a total clash with the vintage decor of the VW. But to

Santa's side sat a pile of other decidedly deflated objects, waiting to become just as plump.

"Bruno!" she hissed. "Get here now!"

"All right, coming." He jumped out of the camper as instructed, his gaze immediately following Alice's to take in the bouncy snowglobe that'd now randomly appeared next to the jolly awful, jolly wobbly Father Christmas.

"Would you try and get to the bottom of this? If I go over to see what the heck is going on, I'll be taking this cake knife with me to pop those blimming things," said Alice as graciously as one could when one was furious in front of customers. "With any luck, Zara will be here any minute now and I'll ask her to help me serve if the pace continues. I know she made it clear last time was the final favour, but I've no idea what's happened to River so I can't ask him, and Rio and Justin haven't quite finished applying their warpaint."

River's chat with Hayley had evidently served to make things worse. Not that these garish inflatables had anything to do with her attempting to play Cupid. But the outdated eighties taste definitely didn't belong in this shabby chic yuletide-themed orchard, that much was clear.

"No problem. Leave it with me. Oh, and erm… I'll probably stay clear of the camper until Zara's gone, if that's okay with you. All I seem to do is annoy her lately."

Alice frowned as Bruno walked off in Hayley's direction.

"Of course," was all she could muster, for there was no point stringing him along anymore, after all. He'd best dust down the Tinder app.

"Cheer up, love, it might never happen," said a middle-aged man.

Gawd, wasn't that just the most button-pushing statement? Alice smiled serenely anyway and took his order for a bog standard hot chocolate and a bog standard gingerbread man. Boring fart. That said it all.

She continued to work her way through the queue. Bruno still hadn't managed to extricate himself from Hayley, and now an entire blasted 'grotto' had been erected. Quite the height of tacky, and a million miles from the gorgeously rustic wooden shacks that stylish Santas tended to frequent with their helpers nowadays. Alice was livid. This was a total one-off. No way was Hayley ruining the ambiance like this again.

A small ray of light appeared on the horizon, and not before time. Zara bent her head upon spotting Hayley, pushing her trolley in front of her as if she were in a chariot race in ancient Rome. Evidently the rumours about Hayley encouraging the customers to find fault with their biscuits and drinks whilst Zara and Bruno were serving, instigating their head-on collision and kiss, had made their way back to Zara.

Hayley whipped her head around, pulled a phone from her pocket, checked left and right that nobody was privy to her antics (completely missing Alice, who could detect a fake phone call a mile off), looked at the screen, slapped a hand to her forehead and made a giant (and very woodenly-acted) O with her mouth, dived into the grotto, re-emerged with a costume in each hand, flung the red and white one at Bruno who had now re-appeared from behind the grotto (Alice guessed he'd spotted Zara's approach before anybody else had), and sprinted after the oblivious Zara with the green and red number…

CHAPTER TWENTY-NINE
Zara

THE BADGER HOLES were a nightmare, especially when you had a fringe in desperate need of a chop, and there were nettles popping up everywhere under your Wellington boots. No wonder it was a private event. Zara couldn't see what she was treading on, and nor could she see how health and safety had approved any of this set-up. Upon spying Hayley and a questionable range of festive inflatables to her left, she ramped things up a notch, cowering so as not to be spotted as she trotted to the VW to refuel it with cocoa.

Something strange happened as she got closer to Alice. She couldn't help but take in her swift succession of facial expressions. Had Zara sprouted a tail since her last visit to the camper van? She turned to be sure. No, there was no physical tail. But there was definitely someone on her proverbial tail.

Hayley. Hayley and a brightly-coloured, uber-cheery felt costume. Hayley, wearing a crooked, non-negotiable smile as she extended said brightly-coloured, uber-cheery felt costume in Zara's direction. The bitch.

"Santa's helper couldn't make it. Flat tyre." Hayley arched a brow that warned Zara not to dare challenge a word. "You're the only one of Team Twinkle who can fit into this little number. Alice might have just as enviable a waistline as yourself, but sadly she's too tall."

"Oh, no, no, no." Zara laughed bitterly although she knew she'd lost already. "There's no way I'm falling for that."

"Hands up," Hayley raised hers then, waggling the garment about as if she were attempting to hypnotise Zara, "I should never have interfered in matters of the heart. I'm sorry. There. You're one of only a tiny number of people who has ever heard those words escape my lips."

"Seriously?"

"Straight up."

Somehow Zara didn't doubt it.

"But on the subject of apologies," Hayley continued, "you'll regret it for the rest of your life if you break *their* hearts." She pointed at a gathering of inquisitive faces who were eyeballing the grotto. Huh, they were probably looking for the airhole so they could deflate the eyesore.

There was no point arguing, though. Zara had quickly worked out that the savvy chose their battles carefully when it came to Hayley. That said, the woman was not getting away with this. There would be inevitable payback and Zara could think of nothing more fitting than to serve up her revenge not in a cold dish, but a fiery hot cup of cocoa. Coincidentally, Zara had bumped into a certain trio of Scoville-defying brothers at the orchard's entrance; they were still plying themselves with ice cream to cool down their tongues after their earlier, and very niche chili pepper stage performance. The brothers had got chatting with Zara and offered to supply her with extra special chili for her foodie venture, something she might be taking them up on very soon.

Actually, no. On reflection that was taking things too far. Zara shook the Grinch-like behaviour out of her fringe and her braids, resolving to get into the spirit. Hayley sounded genuine, didn't she? One had to admire the way she was lending a hand, not only by making things as magical as possible for the children, but by dragging those eighties mementoes along to today's event, pumping them up, and helping so many grown-ups relive the magic of the season. In any case, just another ten days until Christmas, and then she could be out of here. *She could do this.* She'd never have to put herself through a similar malarkey in Italy, after all. This act of benevolence would be over in the blink of an eye, and the last thing anyone would be able to call her was selfish (or indeed elfish).

Zara sighed and accepted the red and green ensemble, complete with its hat and boots. She guessed there were worse ways to spend a Tuesday afternoon and evening. Turning her back on Hayley, she continued with her customary drill, dropping off all of the supplies and milk alternatives as a puzzled Alice looked on in between serving the growing but patiently waiting crowd. They exchanged smiles and Alice went to open her mouth as if to ask something – Zara could pretty much guess it was 'can you stay here and help me…? I promise it *really* is the last time!' – but then thought better of it. Zara walked quickly to the grotto before Alice changed her mind, and before she changed *her* mind. Santa had better not be an old pervert, else she was out of there.

There was nobody inside the inflatable grotto, and thankfully no sign of Bruno, who had deposited his fresh gingerbread supplies in the camper already. Zara had set her goodies next to them. Plus his car wasn't in the yard. He was obviously long gone. Since the closed sign was up and there wasn't exactly anywhere else to transform herself from chocolatier to elf, she deftly switched from one outfit to another. What a blessing there were no mirrors, she didn't want to think about how ridiculous she looked. She patted herself down, checked her plaits felt in place, and sat quietly awaiting the big man's arrival. The anticipation almost felt like Christmas Eve. A synthetic Christmas tree twinkled with eighties floral-shaped bulbs in pinks, blues, reds, greens, and ambers. The gold latticed tinsel, that she remembered had once seemed so modern, hung overhead. Hmm... Santa's dated, orange and brown flowered deckchair was a little too reclined. Zara decided to adjust it so it resembled less bed, more chair.

She was about to rearrange the higgledy-piggledy pile of tissue-thin, retro gift-wrapped presents, which were flooding her with happier throwback family memories, when she heard something outside in the long grass. Two sets of footsteps approached the grotto, the shadow of their owners looming ever larger, until they stopped right outside. Zara felt like she was watching one of those silhouette shows you sometimes get at Glastonbury festival in the theatre and circus field. One performer was definitely Hayley. The other, standing in profile, was wearing a beard and had a distinct Santa outline, complete with a sack. Her heart thudded. So silly. It wasn't the man himself!

"Ho, ho, ho! Let's get this show-ho-ho started," he boomed in an American accent that was either a below average impersonation of Kurt Russell in *The Christmas Chronicles,* or a Santa with a blended American/Irish/Indian/Italian/Welsh lilt, who'd had one too many sherries.

Zara swallowed nervously as she readied herself for his entrance, mindful that she'd be stuck with him until the presents ran out. She hoped they'd have good chemistry. Hayley appeared first through the inflatable door, a smile tugging at her lips.

"Santa had a flat tyre too," she snort-laughed.

"He what?"

Zara knitted her brows. That was more than a coincidence, surely. *Then who was playing Santa?*

The eyes were the giveaway to that answer. Santa's were bright, expectant, twinkly, and challenging, taking in the whole grotto before edging through the door with his sack. Santa, of course, was bloody Bruno.

Honestly! How gullible could Zara get?

"B... but I didn't see your car here?" she quizzed him, mad at herself for tripping over her words.

"It's in for a service." Bruno offloaded his sack next to the garish deckchair, plonking himself in it as if he'd already visited a thousand households. Next thing he'd be demanding a mince pie and Babycham. "I decided it was no use ringing to see if you'd break your self-imposed rules and agree to ferry me here just this once... When I called Hayley instead, she turned up in one of those big MPV cabs and she had all the grotto paraphernalia in the back."

Another crossroads. Just when Zara had managed to get that searingly short but sweet kiss they'd recently – and *very accidentally* shared – out of her head... for the briefest of interludes. The same kiss that was keeping her up every night because, loath as she was to admit it, it had been the best kiss of her life; its passion, tenderness, and fire somehow all fusing together in those few seconds to drop her a very large hint as to how good this could feel on a regular basis.

Zara bent to straighten the wayward bells on her felt boots. This was her only opportunity to compose herself, now she was in the same room as Bruno. Again. Once she raised her head to look at the man who could melt her insides, that would be it. It was imperative she decided whether to turn left, right or head straight down the middle.

She stood tall, plastered on a fake smile, and dusted down the naughty elf idea of not so long ago. There was only one thing she could do. The same thing the pop culture elf on the shelf doll would do, if he found himself in her winklepickers…

"Oh what fun we're going to have!" Zara exclaimed.

She rubbed her hands in front of a pleasantly surprised Bruno, who evidently thought all his Christmases had come at once and she was hinting at the flirt marathon awaiting him. He should be so lucky.

"Really?" He winked. "You're not mad at Hayley? Not that I had anything to do with this or saw it coming but now it's blatantly obvious she's trying to set us up… yet again." He smirked, clearly delighted that the infuriating woman didn't know when to put a Christmas stocking in it.

"Absolutely, and I think we really ought to toast to that," Zara agreed. "Hold the fort, Santa Baby. I'll be back with the *hot* drinks."

Zara grabbed her purse from her bag, tucked it into her handy elf pocket, sprinted over to the chili pepper dealing brothers, secured herself some ground Carolina Reaper pepper, tucked it into her other elf pocket and headed to the VW to make Hayley a hot cocoa special.

CHAPTER THIRTY
River

WITH WEDMORE AND another couple of Somerset Levels villages under their belt, and the fire of the chili pepper surprise finally being extinguished in Meare's apple orchards (Hayley's cries could have been heard as far away as Glastonbury Tor, and had River wondering how Bruno could have the hots for someone as dangerous as Zara – a terrible quip, but it definitely fit the circumstances), it was time to head to the coast at last.

River, Alice, Twinkle, Twinkle and the ragtag gang were to spend two nights in Brean. And when he said ragtag gang, he meant ragtag gang minus Hayley. They were so close to the finishing line of this Christmas roadshow, and he preferred that they crossed it in one piece. Zara might have rubbed along with Bruno in the grotto, but Hayley's unsolicited action had sabotaged things before they had even started. Far from being the initial doormat River had thought she was, Zara was one of the most strong-willed and unpredictable people he'd ever met, totally up there with Hayley herself. His taxi driver friend had definitely met her match – never mind her attempts at matchmaking. The focus now wasn't so much on bringing Zara and Bruno together, but on keeping them apart. And the focus was also on keeping up the good quality gingerbread, chocolate, and service. Needless to say, after the orchard shenanigans, there was some way to go with the latter: an unforgivable number of children had scarpered from Harry's place without any presents; their parents joining them.

"It was obvious history was going to repeat itself, River. You're too damned malleable! I was having kittens watching that woman pump up all those tacky inflatables. It was always going to end in disaster one way or another, and here we go, she got her just desserts. In many ways, I don't actually blame Zara."

It was a bit hypocritical of Alice, seeing as she was the one who had set Hayley off in the first place, but the last thing River wanted was confrontation with his bride-to-be.

Pulling onto Brean's Lotus Biscoff-coloured beach (once again, they had magically been granted permission to park here and host the event), River let out the giant breath he didn't know he'd been holding. The salty sea air would do everyone good. Brean's sands were one of the longest stretches of beach in Europe, complete with irresistible dunes. Distant Lundy island and her puffin colonies sat out to sea, and all of it was backed up by an expanse of blinding green. He could tell the sunsets here would be amazing – on the rare days the golden ball put in an appearance, at least.

Just a trickle of people showed up on day one, helping to restore everyone's equilibrium, and meaning neither of River's foodie and drinkie suppliers needed to trouble themselves trucking supplies all this way. Well, *every cloud* after their last interactions! Although, interestingly, Zara only held a grudge against Hayley, who she'd vowed never to speak to again.

Yes, Brean's smaller crowds were just the ticket: full of *joie de vivre* and champing at the bit to embrace the fun, once they'd had their fill of gingerbread and cocoa. The stage-hosted sandcastle building competition was a blast, and the shell mandala performance calmly inspirational. They'd been unbelievably lucky in the evening, with a spectacular sundown, and River had felt the rare pull to get his guitar out to serenade the small miracle, as well as the tiny crowd. To cap it all off, Rio and Justin had moved on to a more sedate performance this week. Inspired by the sand at their feet, they'd made timers and invented a double act that saw them debate a subject of the audience's choice for a minute. Thankfully, the spectators had steered away from politics, the Royal Family, and conspiracy theories surrounding Covid-19. River hoped that's how it would stay at their next stops.

Alas, on day two River wondered if he was living in a parallel universe. Rio and Justin, who'd been staying at one of the old-fashioned beachfront hotels in the neighbouring resort, knocked on the door of the VW to present River and Alice with a letter. Brean's leisure park had cordially invited them all to spend the afternoon and evening on site.

"How did this happen?"

River was perplexed, unsure whether he wanted things to take this mainstream turn. Whilst he'd defy anyone to order burger, chips, and fizzy drinks when there was gourmet gingerbread and hot chocolate on the menu, how could his miniature stage hold its own when there were rollercoasters and dodgems to play on?

"Fiona extended her West Country stay, apparently," Justin explained. "Before she started the foodie and travel blog, she worked in the leisure industry and she happens to know one of the park's managers well. She paid a quick visit earlier in the month and told them to look out for us, as she had an inkling we'd be heading somewhere this way. And here we go."

"You'll – *we'll*," Rio hugged his partner, "have the entire place to ourselves. Villagers and the few winter holidaymakers in the resort can enter for free and earn themselves a ride for every Twinkle, Twinkle food or drink purchase and stage performance. None of the park's eateries will be open, so it's win-win. Plus it's now the official home of Sooty, Sweep and Soo!"

Rio and Justin both jumped up and down excitedly.

"Wow. That's amazing!" said River.

Even he'd had a penchant for those puppets during his childhood. Although Heather had rarely let River watch TV because of its 'mind numbing tendencies', she approved of The Sooty Show so it had been one of his treats. It was no mean feat that Terry had managed to smuggle a large flat screen telly into the house he now shared with River's mum.

Bruno might have his contacts, but flipping heck, the ripples from Fiona's blog had really opened doors for them. And now, apparently, leisure park gates.

"Alice, does all of this sound okay to you?"

River couldn't take it for granted it would be up Alice's street, but it would certainly add some variety to the trip. No matter how much the pair of them loved nature and fields, River was feeling not so much mellowed out as meadowed out. It would actually be good to see a bit of concrete for a change.

"It sounds like a day out at Disneyland. What an honour that they'd go to these lengths for us and our little camper," Alice replied, much to his relief. "We really need to find Fiona's address and send her a massive bouquet of flowers for everything she's done for us."

River inwardly swatted away his guilty feelings toward Hayley. She'd be in her element. But it was just too dangerous. Besides, surely she had people to ferry about in Glastonbury? Better for her to stick to her day – and night – job.

Once they'd devoured their scrambled eggs and hash browns and washed them down with tea, it was time to bid farewell to the rolling waves and seagulls and make the short journey down the road to the leisure park. Rio and Justin were waiting for them at the gates, as were the local and national press. River felt like they were being granted access to Willy Wonka's factory – well, the small theme park version, anyway. He could never have envisaged these kinds of capers at the beginning of this idea.

Setting up was quick and easy, and then it was time to take advantage of the once-in-a-lifetime offer of having the rides all to themselves. Again, he felt as if he were committing a sin not inviting Hayley, but the mission was about the local people, he reminded himself. Bruno and Zara had been notified of today's change of address and both were now offloading their biscuits, cakes, cocoa mixes, stirrers and melts – not quite at the distance he'd like to keep them apart, but civilly at least. River could already tell that the villagers would clean them out as efficiently as locusts, and the pair would definitely need to revisit at tomorrow's stop.

"And that's all the more reason why you should both enjoy yourselves here today… at least for half an hour," River insisted.

"Do you have any idea how long it takes me to make these chocolates?" Zara retorted. "I love a funfair as much as the next girl but it's just not possible with all the work awaiting me. Not to mention factoring in the journey."

"Come on, Zara," Bruno added. "You know what they say about all work and no play… and you have to admit, we got on like a grotto on fire last time we had some fun."

River gritted his teeth. Why hadn't he thought through that daft suggestion? He was meant to be creating a wedge between them, not cajoling them to try the Tunnel of Love.

"Do not remind me," said Alice. River's ears throbbed with the memory of Hayley's screams. His fiancée just shuddered.

"No, I'm heading off." Zara was adamant as ever. "I've got to start boxing up my stuff for storage and packing my cases as well, while I play my Italian language CD."

"Why don't you let me teach you?"

Zara looked at Bruno blankly. She had finally opened her mouth to answer when one of the fairground ride operators sauntered up to their group and cheekily whisked Alice and Bruno away. What the heck? River hated the complex Bruno occasionally gave him by being the best-looking guy in Somerset, and now his thoughts turned on themselves. He wished that Bruno and Zara would hurry up and get it on so it'd be obvious his girl was not up for grabs.

He waved Zara off to her little red Ka anyway, noticing that her path back to the carpark had to take her past the brand new attraction of the spinning teacups, where that annoying leisure park twit had now secured a bar across Alice and Bruno's laps.

A duo of shrieks permeated the air and River looked up to spot Rio and Justin plummeting from the fear-inducing height of forty metres on the Xtreme attraction, a rotating 'booster' ride that certainly wouldn't do much to lift River's spirits. But then the teacup dude inadvertently redeemed himself, snapping River's attention back to his love. Upon clocking Zara thinking she'd got away with not joining in, the ride's operator manually halted the cup's spin, beckoned to Zara suggesting that somebody had 'dropped some money' next to the ride – it was an impressive display of hand gestures, River had to *hand* it to the guy. Alice immediately saw her chance to hop out of the cup, Bruno instinctively shuffled along the seat and patted the space next to him, the owner had somehow coaxed Zara in and sealed her fate with the safety bar, while Alice took care of the empty gingerbread trolley.

The stereo blasted out Dean Martin's *That's Amore*, which was a marked improvement on the usual thrum of a modern fairground's acoustics, and River marvelled once again at the way Zara's defiance was being quashed by so many 'coincidences'. Meanwhile, a wobbly but very happy Rio and Justin stumbled into the serving table, which thankfully wasn't yet groaning under its usual weight of saccharine goodness.

"We love you, River! Let's do this every Christmas!" Justin cried.

"Speaking of which," said Rio. "What are you doing on the big day itself? All that flying through the air has given us an idea…"

CHAPTER THIRTY-ONE
Alice

ALICE DIDN'T HAVE the fondest memories of Westonzoyland. Somehow the airfield had become an iconic Somerset space for learner drivers to finesse the art of going up the gear changes. Her sister, Tamara, had brought her here when she was learning, and banshee-screamed at her until she'd sobbed and jumped out of the driver's seat, slamming the car door behind her, convinced that she would never pass her test. Even so, the place had still retained its status as a take-off and landing strip for Civil Air Patrol activities. The mind boggled.

But the festive season had produced the goods once again and they'd been given the green light to base themselves here for the afternoon and evening. Most villagers would need to get in their own cars to reach Twinkle, Twinkle, but it was kind of refreshing to set up in yet another different landscape. The flat vastness of the Somerset levels brought with it some much-needed perspective, and suddenly all the silly drama between Zara and Bruno (much eggnogged-on by Hayley's interference) felt as small and as insignificant as a snowflake.

"Time is ticking and as a token of our appreciation, Riv and I wanted to give you these as an early Christmas present."

Alice passed Rio, Justin, Zara, and Bruno a handmade

ceramic replica of the camper van complete with all the Yuletide bells and whistles on it – as intricately designed as one of Bruno's mini gingerbread houses. She hoped they'd appreciate the thought that had gone into it, for these had been custom-made by a Somerset ceramicist and were a hundred times removed from the cheap souvenirs for sale in the seaside shops.

"We've kept one back for Jimmy... and, erm, Hayley. Well, she has been helpful sometimes."

Zara's eyes were on stalks at the Hayley comment. She stashed the gift away and, frustratingly, predictably as ever, made her excuses and left. Bruno looked forlorn. Rio and Jimmy shook their heads despondently, and River had to work extra hard then to chivvy everyone along and get the stage set up. A stream of customers was already heading their way, and they'd still not prepared the food and drink.

"Oh, and we've been thinking about your Christmas dinner idea, boys," said Alice. Rio and Jimmy turned to her so quickly and expectantly that she was relieved they'd decided to say yes, despite the arm twisting it had taken on River's part, because turning them down and witnessing their disappointment didn't bear thinking about.

"Hooray!" the happy couple high-fived each of her palms. "It'll be epic, we promise! We've got so many party games for tea-time."

Great. She'd best forewarn Heather and Terry. Christmas was likely to be at their place.

"Erm, Bruno? You're more than welcome to join us."

Bruno appeared to mull things over for a while before saying, much to Alice's surprise, "I'd like that. But if it's okay with you, I'll pop over for Christmas tea with a panettone, some torrone and a few ricotta fritters. I really ought to be with my parents and Nolan at lunchtime."

"Excellent!" Alice chirruped, the damned cogs in her head working on overdrive to find a way to bribe Zara. She knew she shouldn't, and that she was being the biggest hypocrite after all she'd said to River; after he'd supposedly parroted that same advice on to Hayley – but she couldn't help herself. Scenarios of romantic Christmas cracker-pulling, cosy *Love, Actually* viewing (whilst everybody else furtively slipped out of the room for a variety of genuine reasons), and both the lovebirds-to-be getting nominated for non-negotiable washing-up chores flooded her mind.

How fitting that the theme of the Wright Brothers inspired most of Westonzoyland's acts that evening. The local people who arrived in feathered outfits and questionable-looking cardboard box 'flying machines', face planting the tarmac spectacularly in their attempts to get airborne, were like an illustration of the gang's Cupid attempts… so far. Alas, their messages of never giving up, no matter how insurmountable the challenge first appeared, could only spur Alice on until this relationship was in the bag.

ADMITTEDLY, THEY WERE cheating just a little bit when it came to Watchet. The tiny town might have a village feel to it, but it wasn't one. River desperately wanted to deliver his vision to a harbour, though. Brean and her wide sands had been the perfect contrast to the landlocked Somerset villages thus far but as travelling foodies, both River and Alice were keen to break their self-imposed rules. They'd even been granted special harbourside access so they could camp by the boats for the night; every destination on their wish list doing all that it could to accommodate them. And Jimmy had made the trek once again from Cornwall, unable to resist the chance to perform a brand new sea shanty amidst the backdrop of bobbing, tinsel-draped boats.

The West Somerset Railway had also set up a special service for villagers to hop onto the various stops on its line, which called into Watchet. Actually, it was food and travel expert Fiona who'd organised and co-ordinated this with the volunteers who ran the railway as a surprise – Bruno having fessed up to being the one who'd filled her in on Twinkle, Twinkle's planned itinerary. Which was great, amazing, fabulous and all the superlatives... except the expectation this had understandably generated was leaving River quite tetchy. How would they ever fulfil it? Some of their esteemed clientele were used to seamless service on the vintage train – Murder Mystery and a three course meal, or fish and chip suppers, or Santa specials with a Christmas dinner and all the trimmings. What would happen when they alighted at Watchet and discovered that River was clean out of cocoa, and the gingerbread had all been guzzled?

"You're panicking over nothing, Riv. You've got to remember, the talent contest and the festive camaraderie are what people are really coming for, from all the little pockets of Somerset. Besides, there are newsagents and eateries open in the evening, too, so nobody's going to starve. We'll bring supplies in by speedboat from nearby Minehead if the train tracks and roads get clogged up with hot chocolate and gingerbread fiends." Alice had laughed but River couldn't understand why that terrifying image was so funny.

It all came back to perspective.

The only thing Alice found scary was trying to pin Zara down about Christmas dinner. Forget River's visions for his travelling food and drink van, this was going to be a mission unlike any other…

CHAPTER THIRTY-TWO
Zara

NOTHING SURPRISED ZARA anymore when it came to the infinite variety of ways people could find to try and get her and Bruno together. Nevertheless, she had prided herself on getting away without bumping into the guy for the past couple of drop-offs. Okay, she'd had to go through the motions of hanging around with the others to show gratitude for the gift at the airfield, but other than that, she'd excelled herself. Which made her fast-approaching clean break to Italy all the easier. She might be thinking about Bruno twenty-four-seven (she'd even piped quiffs on a number of her Nutcracker soldiers, instead of adding details to their hats!) but she had managed to outsmart these silly will-they-won't-they situations that those around them felt obliged to continuously make manifest.

But then Zara's car wouldn't start. Perhaps it wasn't surprising, with all the scurrying backwards and forwards across the county. She'd put more miles on it in a month than in the past year.

Determined to avoid Glastonbury and its 'solutions' at all costs, she called both the neighbouring Street and Wells' handful of taxi companies. Nothing. All lines engaged, or all drivers out/unprepared to drive so far out of the area. Reluctantly, Zara called Glastonbury's one and only taxi company and prayed she would get a male.

The receptionist sounded confused: "What an unusual request, to ask for a bloke. Normally it's the other way around, certain clients feel more at ease with a lady driver… not that we employ anybody dodgy, be they male, female, transgender, gender neutral, non-binary, two-spirit, or gender fluid. Forgive me for not mentioning all fifty-eight genders, but I think you get my gist… we're a taxi company that prides itself on safety *and* equality. Just as long as you promise not to hit on my colleagues, and that's not the reason you're asking for a man, I'll see what I can do."

Surprise, surprise, it was Hayley who honked her horn outside Zara's apartment and empty chocolate premises fifteen minutes later, and Zara cursed herself for her bizarre request, which had clearly sounded suspicious. No matter, she wouldn't be hopping in the cab herself.

"Best jump in then," Hayley instructed her without making eye contact. Zara guessed she was still reeling from the chili saga, not to mention being cut out of the leisure park fun. "It was me who volunteered my services by the way." Zara sighed audibly at that. "Your call came in on loudspeaker when I was making Kath, our receptionist, a cuppa. It feels like ages since I caught up with River, Alice, and the lads. And I've got a soft spot for Watchet and its little harbourside ice cream huts… even more so after *somebody* burnt my tongue and made me yearn for cool desserts in the depths of winter. Yes, this afternoon was obviously meant to be."

"Capsaicin's effects don't last for longer than twenty-four

hours," Zara said firmly. "Oh, and there's really no need for me to accompany you, then. You can just take the goodies off my hands and pack them into the boot, since you're going that way yourself."

"Do I look like the sort of woman who can be trusted with a boot full of sexy chocolate Nutcracker soldiers? I love a man in uniform a bit too much. Give me a cocoa version and I'll rip his head off and make short work of him for breakfast. No. You're coming with me, missy."

Sulking was futile. Zara got into the back of the taxi as Hayley packed her boxes into the boot. She feigned sleep for the duration of the journey. Well, that's how it had started, but before long, Hayley was prodding her disoriented client in the ribs, and Zara woke, mortified to realise she'd really been out for the count and that they'd pulled up at the closest car park to the harbour already. Furtively, she checked her face for dribble. Phew. All good. Zara blinked the remnants of sleep away, marvelling at the fact she hadn't taken more catnaps over this labour-intensive month, and went to the boot to load up her trolley, following Hayley to the harbour silently, thankful at least that the woman had finally got the message and appeared to have put down her metaphorical Cupid's bow and arrow.

Bruno would inevitably turn up at some point, though. And now she was refreshed from her slumber Zara realised, to her horror, that with no wheels of her own other than those attached to her trolley, she was stuck here for the duration.

River and Alice spotted the pair of them approaching and scurried to their aid, eyes wide with trepidation, presumably because the last thing they'd expected was to see Hayley and

Zara arrive together.

"That's great. Thanks, both," said Alice. "Unexpected to er... to see you in such close proximity... and unexpected to see you at all, Hayley."

"Yeah, well, madam's car wouldn't start and I fancied a trip this way. No laws against that, are there? Anyway, what's cooking? You owe me a few treats on the house, methinks." Hayley cupped her hand to her chin and began to peruse the menu. "Rumour has it I missed out on a *rollercoaster* of a week."

River's Adam's apple did its bouncing thing. "Sure, Hayley. The goodies are on me," he squeaked. "Take your pick now before the steam train arrives."

"Say what?" Hayley looked confused.

"Not only do we have the usual local crowd arriving this afternoon and tonight," Alice explained. "But the steam train has put on a foodie and drinkie special, dropping railway enthusiasts off here for a quick stroll to the harbour where they can get a hot cocoa and gingerbread biscuit of their choice before jumping back on board."

"Blimey. I'd better have first dibs. It sounds like you're going to be swamped."

"Yeah, that's what I'm worried about, too," said River, his forehead creasing.

Zara set to it, offloading her supplies in the VW, which would hopefully help to reassure him.

"Where's Bruno?" she could hear Hayley mumbling between mouthfuls outside. Jeez, that woman wasted no time in honing in on a feast or the opportunity to gossip.

Curiosity got the better of Zara and she crouched down

by the side of the door to listen in on the conversation.

"Shhh," River answered. "I tried to tell you back at the orchard before you got carried away with that freaking grotto idea," he continued in a whisper. "We've given up on the matchmaking, not that any of this had anything to do with me in the first place. Between you and me, Alice has made a right mess of things, although to give her her due, Bruno did hint he was looking for love when we bumped into him at the start of all of this. Yes, it's blatantly obvious he and Zara both fancy each other." *Shit, was it really?* "But it's not our place to keep forcing it. Now please, let's forget all about happily-ever-afters or setting up epic meet-cutes." Zara was impressed that River knew of the latter term, but not so thrilled he'd voiced the idea, which was certain to plant a fresh seed. "And focus on community magic-making instead. That's what all of this is about and to be honest I'm getting quite pissed off with the hidden lurve agenda hijacking everything."

"You and me both," Zara whispered to herself inside the van.

"Whatever," Hayley replied, and Zara could well imagine the shrug that accompanied it.

She could have jumped out and hugged River, then. Now she could finally relax, and just as well, seeing as she was here for the evening. Yes, Bruno would turn up at some point with his gingerbread, but at least now she didn't have to look over her shoulder perpetually for fear of a wannabe Paddy McGuinness trying to pair them up on a date and send them off to the fictional 'Isle of Fernando's'.

"What can I do to help out?" Zara asked River, once the coast was clear and Hayley was dangling her legs over the harbour wall with her row of foodie treasures to the left and a mammoth hot cocoa to the right of her.

"I know you said it was the last time you'd step in," said River tentatively, "but if you are here for the evening – I mean, I'm assuming you're getting a lift back with Hayley – then Alice would love you forever if you wouldn't mind giving her some respite and serving the customers for an hour or so."

"No problem, I can do that," Christmas Cheer Zara replied, much to River's amazement, and much to Zara's own.

With the day trippers taking it in turns to wander around the quaint harbour, visit the cute shops, and queue for their camper van food and drink purchases, Zara had to admit it was all rather satisfying. The smiles that lit up the customers' faces as they watched their chocolate stirrers dissolve into their drinks… and then tasted the decadent and heavenly result, was extremely rewarding. Zara had never given any of this five minutes consideration before, mainly because she'd been lumbered with Bruno, more concerned about her body language, or rushing around like a headless chicken correcting orders that were never faulty in the first place, courtesy of Hayley and her mischief.

"What you're doing here is wonderful," said a woman more or less Zara's age, snapping her from her daydream. "Are these local ingredients?"

"Ninety-five percent of what I use is from the area, yes," said Zara proudly.

"The same goes for my gingerbread," Bruno added, making Zara's heart jump and her face flush.

"Well, keep doing what you're doing. It's awesome. Nothing beats it. So many small businesses benefit that way, too."

"She's right," Bruno acknowledged once the happy customer had departed with her bag of chocolate tree decorations, a trio of gingerbread cupcakes, and one of Zara's decadent Bailey's hot chocolates.

"I know she is."

And Zara found she could even look Bruno in the eye with a smile to show she meant it. She'd done nothing but churn his brainwave of a week ago over and over in her mind. Had she not signed herself up for Italy, she might well have been persuaded to rebel against her own rules, tapping into her trust fund to set up a business like no other; a business selling locally sourced Glastonbury cocoa mixes, chocolate, cakes and biscuits all over the world.

She had more than enough money at her disposal to hire a team – all right, just as Blake had rightly suggested a couple of years ago. She could start off nationally, and then she could imagine things taking off exponentially, to become globally successful. Just because the initial idea had been given to her, it didn't mean it wasn't hers for the taking and the evolving.

In only a week, Zara had subconsciously let the seed of that idea propel her forward, and she'd found herself doodling her way through an entire notebook, with themed sketches of welly boot hot chocolate stirrers, chocolate rock and pop icons who'd appeared at Glastonbury festival over the years (she'd been particularly excited about the David Bowie one), cow-shaped biscuits, rainbow cupcakes, and 'mud' puddings. Then there were the notes she'd scribbled, about potential Bundt cake tin makers who might be able to custom-design a mould for a Glastonbury festival pyramid stage and yes, absolutely, a giant and very moreish Glastonbury Tor.

So it was okay to catch hold of an idea as if it was a baton in a relay race, speeding ahead with it at your own tempo. Except Zara didn't want to pass this one on to anybody else.

Yes, it was perfectly okay to accept another person's idea. After all, it was hardly Zara who'd approached Lucy with the suggestion to join forces and concoct Anglo-Italian pastries in Tuscany, was it?

Watching the gulls dive and soar above Hayley, who was having to work fast to dispose of her treats, Zara quietly admitted to herself that she really would turn back the clock if she could. She'd follow her heart. Not her romantic one, but her creative one.

It was too late now, though. Not only had the flight been booked, and many of her worldly possessions put into storage, but she'd be letting Lucy down big-time. Her friend had impressive plans and Zara was a key part of them – not that Lucy was particularly giving her any input, but still. It was Italy, for goodness sake. One could make so many allowances for a life in Italy, couldn't one?

Amazingly, Bruno didn't push the business talk any further. He continued to chat amicably instead and, as if someone had waved a wand over them, Zara felt the pressure of the last few weeks ease. Hayley still had her back to them. Alice had apparently given up on them too. And River was River, as chilled as could be and reluctant to meddle in their affairs in the first place. There was nobody to bother them and nobody to spy on them. So why was Zara putting so much emphasis on *them*? It was like she was intent on making herself and Bruno a couple after all.

She clenched her fists as if the action might drum some

sense into her body. No, they were not a couple. Not in the slightest. They were simply getting on with things; two colleagues hired to do what they did best: catering... for a Christmas camper van. At least that's how the afternoon continued to pan out, anyway.

But once River was properly away from the serving area and taking care of the acts, welcoming Jimmy back into the fold, and briefing Rio and Justin as to how they should handle any strange debating topics for their performance, Zara quickly realised it was all too good to be true; the marathon sugar hit of the afternoon had kicked in and Hayley had her beady eye on Zara and Bruno's every movement all over again.

That was one thing. But soon, between boiling milk and pouring it for orders, Zara noticed Alice and Hayley in some strange kind of whispering cahoots.

"Something's come up," she told Bruno. "I'll be two minutes."

She hung up her apron on the camper van door to show she meant business to the busybodies, and marched across to Alice and Hayley.

"I think it's time we spoke of the elephant in the harbour," Zara boldly announced.

Alice blanched. Hayley sucked in her cheeks as if she'd been scoffing not gingerbread but lemons.

"Let's just get one thing straight, shall we?" Zara stopped to look both women up and down. She couldn't give a monkey's that Alice was a former rock star and Hayley the UK's toughest taxi driver (the latter according to River, anyhow). "I am providing a catering service for you, Alice. I did not sign myself up for this! I'm a grown woman who is quite capable of choosing her own potential boyfriend material. This constant interference from everybody – no matter how pure their intentions – has got to stop."

Alice slowly nodded her head. Hayley looked left to right as if seeking fresh comebacks.

"Great. I'm glad we got that little matter cleared up. I'll go back to the customers now and carry on with my job."

Zara felt elated, chuffed to bits with herself. Why hadn't she said all of that sooner? It couldn't have been easier to spell things out. She turned on her heel and was just about to make for the camper van.

"Erherm. Capable, with the exception of Blake," Hayley muttered, blatantly referring to Zara's poor choice of past partner.

"What was that?" Zara pivoted to eyeball her.

"I was just saying to Alice that I'm more than capable of slicing my cake… and erm, I'm coming over to do that right now."

My backside you did, thought Zara.

Alice's expression begged to differ too, and Zara had to hand it to Hayley, she was quicker with the quips than that wild-haired, loud-shirted comedian, Milton Jones.

Hayley sped off in front of Zara anyway and made a grab for a knife, hacking away at Bruno's infamous gingerbread and mascarpone layer cake, much to his annoyance and the raised eyebrows of the patiently queuing customers.

Zara had only just calmed down by the time River and Alice returned to the camper to check how things were going.

"Two's company, three's a crowd," said Bruno.

A group of local teens briskly snapped everyone out of

their complaints; their swagger proprietary as they approached the camper and its menu board.

"Well, this is a load of poxy old shit, if ever I saw it." The spotty, slick-haired 'leader' kicked some loose stones at the base of the serving table, and the queue of foodies waiting to be served lurched intuitively to the left.

"Yer, we don't need outsiders coming here and telling us how to celebrate Crimbo," piped up one of his sidekicks.

"Jackson's a sad and desperate joke of an old-timer with his piss-poor music," said another.

"I'd give that Alice a good seeing-to, though," the oily teen snickered, looking River right in the eye.

"You and me both, mate. Phwoar!" came a voice from the back of the gang.

"Hands off. She's mine. I don't do threesomes," lead teen commanded, amidst a boom of belly laughs.

River was about to explode. Zara, Alice, and Bruno were speechless.

Hayley, not quite so much. "Wash your mouths out this instant before I get a bar of soap and do it myself, you bunch of tosspots."

"Is that a threat, fatty?"

"It's a promise." Hayley's face and neck turned dart frog red, warning of poison and paralysis as she inched closer to the gang, who let out a collective "ooooh!"

"That's the best piece of talent I've seen here all night," cheeked the ringleader.

"Oh, you ain't seen nothing yet, sweetheart." Hayley cracked her knuckles.

Zara's heart began to race. Shit, this was not looking

good. Surely there were some local police they could call to break things up before they got started? And surely River and Alice had dealt with a few things like this in their time on the road? Didn't anyone have any better ideas? Hayley would get herself beaten to a pulp by those kids. One on one, maybe not, but here, she was outnumbered. Zara wished she had learnt some self-defence moves. Alas when it came to physical confrontation, she preferred to retreat. Bruno was clearly of the same ilk and something about that reassured her, even if it did make him look a tad lame. Whilst Blake and her other past boyfriends had certainly never laid a finger on her, they had all been involved in skirmishes in the town's pubs from time to time.

"Pfft. I bet none of you can parkour over boats with a firework in one hand and a cider in the other," the leader challenged, "that's real talent!" He pulled a can out of his pocket and tugged the ring pull off.

"Dear God, tell me he's joking." Zara gasped, eyes glued to his other pocket, lest it go up in flames as she allowed Bruno to steer her to safety behind the camper van.

On cue, tyres screeched and an electric blue Nissan Skyline began zooming around the bins. How it had gained access to the harbour was a mystery but it provided the ultimate backdrop of excitement to the teens' rebellion, and evidently contained even more friends. Lead teen approached it with his sheep trailing behind him, and something looking decidedly powerful was passed to him through the window.

"There's always one who's gotta push it too far," stated Hayley calmly.

She removed her gloves and pressed her palms together as

if to prepare herself for battle. This was insane. Yes, she was a sturdy woman and Zara didn't doubt she could pack a punch, but the idiotic lad was threatening to light a firework, for goodness sake. This was no time for second guessing. Zara had been haunted by those scary fireworks adverts of the past.

"Ladies and gents," Hayley began, taking in the startled expressions of the audience surrounding her. "If you'll kindly bear with me for a moment, I'm just off to fish for the catch of the day, and we'll be on stage for you in moments."

"She said what?"

Zara lunged forward to save Hayley from the fate that surely awaited her.

Bruno sprinted after her. "Zara, no!"

The young lad, true to his word, had already started to follow through on his delusional plan. Having snatched the gift from the Nissan's driver, he ran down the steep ramp to the marina, lit the firework and jumped into a boat, his can of fizz held high in the air like a trophy. He swirled it and grinned, teetering, toppling.

"He's plastered already. He won't last long and hopefully he'll drop the rocket in the sea." At least it looked to be one of those unassuming rockets, which, before it was lit, resembled a cute colouring pencil. "Now stand back, Hayley, don't be stupid," Zara pleaded as she followed Hayley down the same ramp after him. Despite the woman's annoying and unsolicited matchmaking skills, she couldn't let her endanger herself like this.

"Bruno, keep her away," Hayley yelled back over her shoulder. "This zone is for experts only."

But it was too late, the teen had already fallen into the

water, thankfully taking his planned pyrotechnics with him. Zara could hear the scream of the crowd and the deep laughter and whoops of his friends, who were in their element watching over the railings above them.

Before Zara could shrug Bruno's hold away, Hayley had leapt onto the same boat, as if she were a polished body double in the movies, and heaved the lad out before his face had gone under the water's surface. Scooping him up and into the small vessel as if he weighed nothing more than a puppy, his weedy body protesting, limbs flailing, she removed her jacket to dry him off, and then proceeded to transport him past a stunned Zara and Bruno and up to the stage, where she stood him upright and said, "Now repeat those words again loud and clear in front of the good people of Watchet."

The fool attempted to mouth off again, adding a number of pathetic kicks to Hayley's legs, only to be countered by some unidentifiable and seriously impressive self-defence moves, finally surrendering and falling into a heap on the floor.

"Krav maga," River enlightened Zara and Bruno – whose protective arm was still wrapped around Zara, and felt so very right. "Hayley's an expert in all sorts of these things. She trained to be a bodyguard before her career changed to cabs." Woah, seems Zara had totally underestimated Hayley. "You probably want to cover your ears for this bit, Zara, but that hook punch move you've just witnessed is exactly how she turfed Blake out of the church when he and Georgina barged in on Lee and Jonie's wedding ceremony, just as the vicar asked if anyone knew of any reason for the marriage not to go ahead."

"Ah, right."

How embarrassing. Bruno must think Zara was such a fool herself falling for someone as klutzy as the character everyone was booing on the stage (Blake's TV show resurrection and £100k win notwithstanding). She shrugged Bruno's arm away. Whilst she was on the fool subject, there was no point in fooling herself. She was off to Italy. Within days now, not weeks.

Cheers burst out all around them and the locals and day trippers got back to the business of enjoying the festivities.

"Not only is Krav maga an excellent form of self-defence," Hayley continued to prattle on regardless, now with the aid of a mic, "but in situations like this one, it can soon bring a drunk and disorderly plonker to his senses."

The teen sat up now, nodding his head in agreement of her assessment. There was no doubt about it, Hayley had won the talent contest this day, week, and month.

"Just one last thing before I retire to the VW for a well-deserved gingerbread man and a deluxe hot cocoa decorated with a village of mini 3D gingerbread houses… nudge, nudge River and Alice… get them lined up for me now."

"Right you are, Hayley. Your wish is my command," said River.

The Christmas crowds halted their conversations as Hayley charged over to the Nissan and turned off the irritating rave music.

She returned to the stage to pick up the mic one last time:

"Polite PS: Nobody disses my mate River Jackson's music."

Another hearty cheer ricocheted along the harbour and

Jimmy took to the stage to get the locals revved up for their own performances, his brand new sea shanty and spoon medley going down a treat.

ZARA RESUMED HER place in the back of the taxi on the way home, while the teen, after semi-righting his wrongs by gifting gingerbread and cocoa to the revellers, sat in the front alongside Hayley, who issued him an ultimatum. "Parents' house or police station."

"Oh, man! I mean l... lady. Please just drop me off at my folks' place and I promise never to get into trouble again."

"What do you think, Zara?"

Zara thought she'd ended up in the kind of warped dream that could rival a scene on the croquet lawn of the Queen of Hearts' palace in *Alice in Wonderland*. Admittedly, Hayley was amazeballs but Zara had no illusions about her: if the woman wasn't amused by somebody's antics, she was apt to decide it was 'off with their heads.'

"Me?" Zara stifled a yawn, which she hoped would indicate her intention to sleep all the way back to Glastonbury once they'd deposited the teen wherever Hayley saw fit. "Well, erm, I reckon he's seen the error of his ways... like he said. I'm sure the CCTV in town can be the judge of the way forward from here. Maybe just drop him at home?"

"Great minds," Hayley agreed, much to Zara and the teen's surprise.

The taxi pulled up at the address the reformed character had given them, and the boy high-fived Hayley, not before diving back into the car and engulfing her in a massive hug.

"Thanks," he spluttered, tears in his eyes. "I'm sorry for behaving like a total dick. My parents are on the verge of splitting up and I couldn't face being at home to watch another domestic. My girlfriend dumped me last week, and I'm still on the dole with no prospect of getting a place of my own... not until I turn eighteen."

Zara swallowed down the lump in her throat. If only she carried her trust fund around in a purse, she'd shower this youngster with the money he needed to get himself some qualifications and set up on his own as soon as possible. It broke her heart. Only those who were damaged themselves continued to inflict pain.

"There, there: things will look up now." Hayley patted him and gently shoved him off her heaving chest. "Let tonight be a warning that there is a better way... and behaving like a twit in public isn't the answer."

He waved them off and Zara's heart shattered all over again, wondering what would be waiting for the kid on the other side of the front door. It was a wake-up call and a half. At least leaving her family home had been a real choice and something she'd waited until her early twenties to do. Things had never been so bad that she couldn't have tucked herself away from her family in her sprawling quarters. She simply wasn't cut from the same toffee-nosed cloth, that was all.

"Wow," was all she could say, as they hit the road to return to Glastonbury.

"Indeed," said Hayley. "Who needs Netflix for entertainment."

✧ ✧ ✧

"Picking up from where we left off on the entertainment subject…"

Hayley's voice didn't so much rouse Zara from her Bruno-filled slumbers, as make her jump out of her skin.

Where in the hell was she? Dazed, Zara adjusted her eyes to the darkness and realised Hayley had pulled up in the carpark at the rear of her flat.

"Thanks, right. I believe River and Alice have offered to pay for my fare so I'll see you at one of the next Twinkle, Twinkle stops no doubt." Zara went to open the door but Hayley pressed a finger on the child lock button and kept it there.

"What the actual fu—?"

Why did Zara feel like a fly trapped in a spider's web of interrogation already? Bloody great.

"Why?" Hayley demanded, eyes boring into her very soul through the driver's mirror as if searching for lost treasure.

Yes, 'why' pretty much summed this freakish situation up.

"I beg your pardon?"

"You heard me the first time, Zara."

"I did?"

"Oh, yes."

"Erm." Zara shrugged. "Why do teenage boys act like such fools?" She giggled nervously. "Look, you're more than welcome to come in for a coffee so we can debate it, but please let me out of the taxi."

"Not teenage boys," Hayley ignored her request. "I expect that sort of shoddy behaviour from teenage boys. I'm talking about grown women who are old enough to know better. I'm talking about *you*."

"Well, I'm sorry, Hayley. But I'm at a loss. I have no idea what you're blathering on about."

She really did.

Hayley tutted. "Do we have to drag this out?"

"Okay, then. Here's why." Zara suddenly felt she might spontaneously combust with anger. *Who was this woman and what right did she have to hold her hostage?* Especially after her holier-than-thou lecture to that poor kid. She was meant to drive cabs, for goodness sake, not flit between thinking she was starring in a Bond movie, or some kind of agony aunt for a newspaper column... although Zara had to admit it: her fighting skills were badass.

"I'm moving to Italy, that's why." Zara threw her hands up in the air with an Italian-infused gesticulation. Hayley's eyes narrowed, unable to process this sudden turn of events which it appeared nobody else had told her about. "I leave on January the fifth and I'm flying miles away to a place that couldn't be more quintessentially Tuscany if it tried. I've been invited by a friend – a female one, in case you wanted to make yet more enquiries into my love life... not that my sexual orientation is any of your business – to help her run her bakery empire. There. Conversation over. Now please let me out."

"'Tis the people that make a place."

"That's, erm, poetic." Zara thought London cabbies were bad enough at jabbering on. Did Hayley do this to all her clients? "And you're right. Tuscany will be full of lovely people."

"People go to the Maldives on holiday, it doesn't mean they could live there."

"I've been to Tuscany many times when I was younger, Hayley. I know what I'm getting myself into. Peace and quiet. Utter bliss."

"Solitude? Hayley laughed. "Throwing away the chance of a good relationship sounds more accurate to me."

But Hayley released the child lock, shook her head in defeat, and finally let Zara step out.

CHAPTER THIRTY-THREE
River

RIVER STILL WASN'T best pleased about the way they'd agreed to spend Christmas day. Yes, it was for families – blood and extended – but truth be told, he'd wanted Alice all to himself. In a proper bed. In a hotel bed. Over and over. And over.

Rio and Justin, Jimmy, his mum, and Terry, well, they'd all had other ideas. Heather and Terry had won on that front in the end, insisting upon a traditional Christmas lunch for everybody at their place, complete with board games, trifle, and drinks in the evening. Mercifully, River and Alice managed to escape their first truce of a Christmas with Blake – and his Kiwi/Brit girlfriend, Ali. The happy couple had decided to spend the holidays in Auckland, packing up Ali's flat ready for her relocation to the UK. Mercifully, Jimmy didn't sing a single note of a sea shanty when Heather presented him with a beautifully wrapped gift of new spoons… instead he tapped them to Cliff Richard's *Mistletoe and Wine* whilst everybody pretended to smile in appreciation, closed-mouthed to cover their gritted teeth. And Rio and Justin didn't insist upon putting everyone through renditions of their new Boxing Day party piece, which would be performed the following evening at their family's house.

"There's really no need to showcase it for you," said Rio, as if trying to convince River that it was for the best. River chewed hard on his fit of giggles. "We're opting to continue with the previously successful and spontaneous hourglass debate; the in-laws won't have seen that coming." Rio let out a triumphant snort. Jeez. The annual set-up at Justin's folks' place sounded a bit too competitive. No wonder the boys had stopped at nothing to convince him and Alice that they needed to spend Christmas in Glastonbury.

And it had been a fun-filled affair, which had also helped to mask River's disappointment over the final stop in Godney. Oh, that had been revelry and joy and every inch of community spirit at the outset. But it had ended with his friend's broken heart. Paper hats off to Bruno for showing up at Heather and Terry's for Christmas tea at all. And yet, as promised, he'd arrived laden with traditional Italian desserts that made a mockery of Terry's packet trifle.

Spontaneity might have lent a helping hand to River's friends and their stage act, but it was time to clean up his own, else change his middle name by deed poll. For River's sudden and unexpected burst of 'spontaneity' had done so much for so many, but at the cost of the emotions of his gingerbread supplier, and that didn't seem fair.

The thing was, this Zara and Bruno malarkey and the great potential everyone else could see – *huh, everyone else except Zara* – was like a scab that River, too, couldn't resist picking in the end. Why couldn't he have gently teased it at the edges like Alice and Hayley, though? Why did he have to go and rip it off full-throttle in front of all and sundry?

CHAPTER THIRTY-FOUR
Alice

THERE WERE NO words…

Christmas day had been a blast, all things considered, although for obvious reasons Alice hadn't quite gotten around to inviting Zara. And likely if she had, her cocoa supplier would not have RSVP'd.

Yep. She meant no. There were no words.

River and his well-meaning 'goodwill' antics could only be summed up as a rebel without a Claus.

CHAPTER THIRTY-FIVE
Bruno

THERE'S A LITTLE lay-by on the A38, just down the road from Bristol airport. That's where Bruno Lombardi parked his shiny red Mercedes on the morning of January the fifth. It's a hidden gem of a spot for friends and family – for happy-go-lucky lovers – to pull over and await the landing of their passengers on an inbound aircraft, so as to avoid the extortionate parking fees one has to shell out at the airport. You sit, you wait, you watch out for the aircraft to fly overhead, and you estimate the process of your person or people disembarking the plane's steps, passing border control, nipping to the loo, and grabbing their luggage, timing it just right so you can be in and out of the short stay car park in minutes, parting with pounds instead of notes.

Bruno wasn't picking anybody up, though. Bruno would have given every last penny, if only he was.

He'd checked the departure of the Bristol to Pisa easyJet flight, and he'd made a pilgrimage to wave Zara off as her plane tilted up into the sky, finally disappearing from sight into the wispy cotton wool clouds. He had to know, had to see with his own two eyes that it was over, that she really was gone. It was the only way he could accept it and try to move on.

His heart hammered as the second hand on his watch ticked closer to eleven twenty-five. Of course there were dozens of orange and white livery airbuses here, but he'd meticulously monitored the departures information online and he knew everything was running to schedule.

At eleven twenty-six there it was, a mighty bird powering through the air, carrying the woman he loved, its undercarriage glinting in the sunlight.

"Carry Zara safely to the land of my ancestors," he said with a sigh. "And if it doesn't work out for her highest good, bring her back home to me. I'll wait for eternity."

God, he'd never felt anywhere near this intensity of emotion for Pandora. It baffled him. How could he know it was love with Zara after just one short but very sweet, very *everything* kiss?

Well, he did. Some things in life just couldn't be explained, and the effect Zara had on him was one of them. That's when Bruno let himself cry, pressing his head to the wheel. He knew he needed to let it all out before he returned to the farm and the rest of his existence, without the love of his life.

CHAPTER THIRTY-SIX
Zara

THE FINAL STOP had been on Godney's moors. Nothing about this escapade had come out of a textbook so it didn't surprise Zara in the slightest that Christmas Eve's fun and frolics would take place in a hamlet rather than a village. Another farmer had given River and Alice the green light for the use of their field, except this one apparently came with a magnificent haybarn which Zara could already imagine strewn with the kind of fairy lights you'd see at a bohemian wedding. If she hadn't known any better, she'd have wagered that Alice wanted to test the water as a possible venue for her big day.

But something else about this stop was different too. From the moment Zara got out of the Ka, everyone looked familiar. Not just the 'staff', who of course really had become very familiar over the past few weeks. No, Zara was sure she recognised the clientele too. Sure, there would be some Glastonbury locals here, Godney was just down the road from the town, after all. But still. Somehow there was some serious *déjà vu* going down.

Stepping into the field only further confirmed it. Where had she seen these people before, and where had she seen their costumes?

Of course! It took her a moment to make the connection, but it was the flash mob dancers again. How cool of them to come here and mark the occasion of the final stop of the gingerbread and cocoa tour! What an epic finale.

The further she walked into the field, the farther away she appeared to repel the dancers though, until collectively they came to an abrupt halt, lining up opposite Zara in such a way that she wondered if they might break into a haka. Weird. Weirder still, now a song started to play, the dancers elongating their frames to pirouette to 'Baby It's Cold Outside'. Blimey, these guys were quite incredible, up on their tiptoes in their pointe shoes and taking Zara back to her handful of years at the ballet *barre* as a child. Surely River didn't have the budget to enlist the help of a dance school twice in a month?

Zara stood in a trance trying to figure out what was going on. How she could weave her way around them to drop her goodies off at the van without ruining the performance? The politest thing seemed to be waiting until this part was over. But as Dean Martin's voice began to sing about starlit eyes, one of the dancers became mysteriously entranced by Zara's, leaping through the air to take her in his arms and lead her through the now parting ballerinas.

This was not the way she'd envisioned herself slipping in and out of today's shenanigans, dammit. And now she'd had to abandon her trolley and her precious boxes of perfectly moulded chocolates, melts, stirrers, and all of those carefully layered mason jars filled with DIY hot cocoa mix Christmas presents – the latter a new addition that she was particularly proud of.

With the moor fast filling up, she could hardly play party pooper in front of the growing audience. At some point this debacle would end and the slender but deceptively strong guy would put her down, choosing somebody a little more spirited for a dance partner.

Alas Zara was soon to realise that was wishful thinking. In just the same fashion as the dancers had peeled away to reveal River Jackson on bended knee to Alice in Glastonbury high street, here in this giant field they *grand jetéd* to the sides, revealing a table for two beneath the mistletoe in a very twinkly-lit hay barn. Zara laughed nervously, simultaneously furious with herself for not pre-empting one final matchmaking mission – although who could ever imagine something as over-the-top as this? – and giving in to the pressure, as the dancer led her to a Bruno who looked good enough to eat. She took the seat opposite him and tried to remain cool, fully aware her cheeks were matching the shade of the dancers' slippers.

"Zara, I'm sorry." The colossal chocolate pools of Bruno's eyes made her heart melt, flooring her. It was just as well she was seated. "None of this was my idea, per se, and yet when River suggested it... well, I knew it was perfect and I had to take a chance, even if it meant you'd end up hating me forever."

Hate? How she wished she could loathe the man sitting in front of her. Unfortunately her feelings were rooted on the opposite end of the emotional scale.

"Look, I know you're going away and I know you won't change your mind about that but please do me the honour of dining with me... and then later, maybe a dance?"

Woah. This Zara had not been expecting. Jackson was such a bloody sneak! All that nonsense she'd heard him bleat to Hayley when she'd eavesdropped on their conversation from the inside of the van in Watchet. In fact, River made Hayley look positively angelic now. What a stunt to pull! She couldn't have felt more mortified. And how very apt that the great rocker himself was nowhere to be seen. Zara was as peaceful in nature as any of Glastonbury's hippies, but frankly, at that moment in time, she could have decked River Jackson for this party trick.

Yes, she was head over heels in love with Bruno but he simply couldn't be her destiny, not when she'd already decided that lay somewhere else. Somewhere 1500ish miles away.

Too many people hung on her every movement, too many expectations enfolded her. Her palms began to sweat, her breathing became laboured and she feared she might suffocate in the misty moors air. She had to get out, had to get away. *She was going away.* What was the matter with the world? Why was everyone trying to trip up her future plans? *Give a girl a break.*

Think, Zara, think!

Okay then, she'd meet the crowd halfway, grant them a mini performance. It was Christmas Eve, she conceded. This way she might make it a little easier for herself. Mentally she attempted to realign, brushing herself down, hardly able to believe the move she was going to make next. But it had to be this way. Short and sweet. It wasn't fair to string the notion of romance along with three courses of aphrodisiacal food – or whatever in God's name River thought he'd have a bevy of waiters serving her and Bruno.

Zara shuffled her chair closer to Bruno, gasps ringing out around them as the legs of her seat kept getting stuck in the grass and threatening to topple her into his lap. Bruno's doting dark eyes approved of her proximity. He pressed his lips together in anticipation of the tender moment that was nearing him.

Zara took a deep breath and reached for his hand, trying with all her might to share the parting sentiments she couldn't speak aloud via touch. Words would sting too much. Tears pricked at her eyes, yet bizarrely she fought back chuckles too. This was such an other-wordly situation to find herself in. Even by Glastonbury standards! Unfortunately, Bruno's senses completely misinterpreted everything, lifting Zara's hand (taking her back to that steamy and seductive bare chest episode in the camper van) and pressing it to his lips.

His velvety, sensual and utterly kissable lips.

She felt her eyelids flutter in the most natural (and yes, corny) of responses, embers dancing in her lower stomach, ready to flood the rest of her body until she was a goner.

No, no, no. Enough. She couldn't sit here a moment longer! It was unfair to him, to her, to the both of them. The audience would probably think it was unfair to them too. The audience could jolly well fuck off.

Finally, though, and perhaps as predictably as any great romantic movie scene, Zara succumbed to Bruno's touch. It was the thumb that did it. Zara had always dreamt of someone engaging in that whole thumb stroke charade with her face. In umpteen years of dating and relationships, it hadn't happened yet. But then Bruno only flipping moved his thumb to her lips. Then she'd melted, hopelessly and helplessly, as if he were the sun shining on a fresh attempt to cake herself in snow. Two mouths moving closer and closer until the point of no return. Oh, how the crowd roared at the perfection.

One could put it down to the mistletoe, true. But Zara had been fighting this for weeks. Fighting with herself, not Bruno, she realised with startling clarity. Punishing herself, not giving her feelings a chance.

But none of that mattered, she realised all over again as she came up for air. It was too late. All of this would have to fizzle out even faster than a Christmas Day Buck's Fizz going flat.

Zara mouthed 'sorry' to the man of her dreams, staggered backwards, felt her heart shatter at his pained expression, abandoned her trolley and supplies in the middle of the field – for she'd never need any of them again – and sprinted to her car without looking back.

NOT ONLY HAD Zara's dreams reflected her regret over Bruno and the sadness and embarrassment etched over his face, ever since that night in Watchet she'd also been racked with a guilt that played out in her nightmares over the teen whose name they never did uncover. How pathetic that she was sitting on a six figure sum in the bank when she could have put it to good use and helped others. Not that she wished to try and emulate Jamie Oliver's past scheme to support the young and unemployed who came from poor backgrounds. She could never hope to pull off anything that megalithic. But she could have done something, and that in turn would have fuelled her own business endeavours. The boy's plight was like a slap in the face. Squirreling her finances away had been pointlessly selfish, even if she hadn't intended to spend any of that money on herself.

Zara gulped as her suitcases vanished behind the black rubber flaps of the conveyor belt and into the belly of the airport. The finality could have crushed her, but somehow she managed a smile for the bespectacled bald guy on the check-in desk, retrieving her passport and boarding card. Now to the escalator and departures lounge. She took her place on the moving stairs, envy coursed her veins as she played voyeur to the holidaymakers off skiing, and the travellers returning to Paris, Edinburgh, and Jersey after their festive break. Even the business folk *en route* to Frankfurt and Brussels seemed more buoyant than she was. Sure, nerves would be par for the course for anybody setting out on an intrepid new life adventure to Italy. But shouldn't she be feeling the tug of excitement too? More to the point, should she be feeling such utter devastation at everything she'd left behind?

"Shit!" she whispered to herself. "What am I doing?" she hissed. A couple of kids giggled at her as they passed on the moving stairs and she glared at them.

Zara took up residence on one of the airport's banks of plastic, immovable chairs and threw her head in her hands. She couldn't go through with it. Everything about Lucy's offer suddenly seemed completely inauthentic. Even taking into account the generous salary and free accommodation. All of which was the opposite to Glastonbury, to the life Zara was proud to live there, happy to live there.

TWINKLE, TWINKLE, LITTLE BAR

Home is where the heart is, and the heart is where the magic is.

The stark truth was this: the only time Zara wanted to visit Italy now was with Bruno at her side; cosying up together on a gondola in Venice, driving around the serpentine bends of the rugged Amalfi coast in a convertible, throwing coins into the Trevi fountain in Rome and feeding one another the lushest and tastiest of gelati.

She may have only kissed him one and a half times, but it was in the unspoken silences between them that Zara knew Bruno was her North Star. That's why she refused to step back on the escalator. That's why she took herself to the coffee shop next to Arrivals, pulling out the notebook of scribbles for her dream Glastonbury-inspired foodie business (she couldn't have contemplated travelling without it), looking up the name of that road where they'd dropped the lad off in Watchet on her mobile phone and jotting it down so she could see if he fancied an apprenticeship. And that's why she remained at the little round table until the tannoy called out her name to remind her she was holding up a flight.

"Oh, my God! Oh, my cases!"

Zara drained the rest of her coffee, pushing away the guilt at delaying two-hundred-and-however-many passengers with her dithering, and ran to the customer service desk as fast as her legs would carry her.

THE BUS BACK to Bristol's city centre (which would lead her to a connecting bus back to Glastonbury) was pulling away from its stop when Zara jumped up and down like a loon, waving frantically, trying to catch the driver's attention.

The moustachioed male frowned but pulled over, her lack of baggage ironically her saving grace. Zara knew it was highly irresponsible, but she'd felt it symbolic to leave her cases on the tarmac at the airport, where they'd undoubtedly been removed from the aircraft. Come what might when she returned to Glastonbury, she wanted to leave as much of the old Zara behind her as possible. Besides, after ninety days in lost property, UK airports often auctioned off abandoned luggage, with the proceeds going to charity. What could be more perfect?

She stepped onto the bus, avoiding the eyerolls of the passengers who were keen to get home, put the kettle on, and chase away the end of the holiday blues. She sighed as she took the last remaining double seat, wedging herself next to the window, wondering what the hell she was going to do once she returned to Glastonbury. No home, no business, no transport. She could only hope whichever hotel she chanced upon booking into for the foreseeable future wouldn't be declaring that there was also 'no room at the inn'.

It's funny how a split second can alter the course of your life, although in the case of saying *arrivederci* to Italy, to be fair, Zara had been granted a forty-minute window of opportunity to change her mind back in that coffee shop.

"Let me off, let me off!" she now screamed, jumping to her feet.

Her fellow passengers tutted at her, no doubt muttering expletives under their breath. But Zara couldn't give two hoots and kept pressing every bell she could find in the bus's aisle as she semi-ran, semi-lurched forward, determined to jump out the door.

"I said, stop the bloody bus!" she yelled.

"Gladly," the driver shouted back at her amidst the uproar of the passengers, who hadn't factored an emergency stop into their journey. "What a pain in the arse you've been since the moment I laid eyes on you, young lady!"

He pulled the bus over. On the opposite side of the road was the red Mercedes Zara had spotted, in the split second before she got to her feet and insisted on being liberated. It was Bruno's car; it had to be. Zara thanked the driver profusely. He sped away before she could change her mind, alas not before splashing her gorgeous cherry-red coat with a poo-brown muddy puddle, eliciting guffaws and flipped birds from some of the gawking passengers.

"Oh, bollocks to the lot of you!" Zara cried. She felt like she was in one of those endlessly hopeless romcom scenes, except nothing about this was remotely funny.

But not even the soiled coat predicament, now added to the lost luggage predicament, could bother her for long. Not when something – or rather someone – more important was on her mind. On her mind... and now pulling out onto the road, where he and his adorable quiff were about to drive off in the opposite direction.

Lord, she was in the middle of the biggest nightmare, now completely stranded. Tail between her legs she'd have to return to the airport and call Hayley to pick her up. Yes, she could opt for a city taxi firm, but what was the point? She might as well get the told-you-so lecture over with at the outset so she could slink back to Glastonbury, keep a low profile and try to rebuild her life. She doubted the car had been Bruno's anyway, just some dumb and wishful figment of her imagination. How many chances did she expect the guy to give her, when she'd behaved like the world's biggest bitch?

Reluctantly, Zara readjusted her backpack, stuffed her cold hands into her pockets and meandered back along the grassy verge in the direction the bus had come from. The thrust of a nearby jet engine revving up for take-off was almost deafening as she passed the airport's perimeter, no longer visible as it once had been, now cordoned off with hedgerows, tall trees and the highest of security fencing. Cars whooshed by in either direction. She could feel the motorists' sympathy, but she didn't need it. She was back in control of her messy, imperfect, loveable life, and at long last. Glastonbury was where she truly belonged. She only hoped her handful of friends would forgive her for running away from them.

A stylish red car slowed right down to the side of her, then. Zara was too scared to look at it properly. Her heart said it was Bruno, that she'd been right about the quiff-topped male she swore she'd sped past, sitting stationary in his fancy vehicle while she was on the bus. Her head said it was a chancer thinking they might hit on her.

Time slowed to a series of hazy slow motion movements. Zara heard the window go down first, the yank of the handbrake, the smooth voice drifting into the crisp air.

"What on earth are you doing here? I thought I was seeing things. It is you, isn't it? At least it looked like the most beautiful girl on the planet that I clocked in my wing mirror, hopping off a bus in the middle of the countryside. I had to turn back on myself at the next roundabout to check I wasn't daydreaming."

Her heart thumped. She didn't dare look to the side in case what she was experiencing was a mirage. But since the car had stopped, she halted in her tracks too. Just in case miracles still happened.

"What... why... well?" She put her hands on her hips, which was ridiculous. This was a time for humility, not her usual Zara capers. "How'd *you* appear on this road, more to the point?"

A tiny smile tugged at the side of her face and she could only hope she looked cute in profile so that if it was Bruno, he'd still feel the same way he'd professed on the twenty-fourth of December, before she'd trodden all over his heart.

"It's the longest story. Let's just say I had to come here today to pluck up the courage to face facts and start a new chapter."

Oh. He'd let her go. She began to fairy-step forward. It was too good to be true. She wasn't unwittingly starring in a budget version of *Bridget Jones' Diary* after all.

The car crawled along, its hazard warning lights now flashing, and with them a spark of hope that a mutual desire was still alive.

"The last story was a tale of horror, the stuff of nightmares," said the guy who sounded distinctly like Bruno. "I'm hoping this one is more of a contemporary romance. At least that's the way it could bill itself, if the main character doesn't encounter any more horrifically awkward meet-cutes."

"And what if I told you I'd changed my mind about Italy. Could I be a part of it?"

Finally she turned to him. Fleetingly but intensely they

drank one another in and then Bruno mimicked thoughtfulness, hand to chin, looking her up and down. His sexy eyes and smile rendered Zara a hot, wobbly mess who was just about ready to fall backwards into the hedge.

"In that elegant red jacket, sweetheart, you look like the whole new book. I'll take you off the library shelf and devour you any day of the week."

Their joint laughter permeated the air, Bruno very much howling *at* himself. Which was a relief. No woman wanted to endure that level of cheesiness… every single day… for the rest of her life.

"I'm coming home," Zara said with a shy but hopeful smile.

The look of love, the degree of emotion on Bruno's face in that moment in time was impossible to describe. She could pluck a hundred words from a dictionary and none of them would come close to summing it up. All Zara knew, with every inch of her being, was that it was the same face that would greet her at the end of an aisle in a few years' time. Preferably in Tuscany.

That's when she finally twigged how utterly slow on the uptake she'd been all along. So fixated on her imaginary queue of future Italian lovers. Bruno wasn't just Bruno. He was Bruno *Lombardi*, wasn't he? She wasn't sure of his surname's etymology and its geographical roots, and she didn't care whether his family hailed from north or south. But *Mamma mia!* Her Italian Adonis had been under her nose all this time. No wonder he'd offered her Italian lessons.

"Pinch me!" Bruno cried as he opened the door for Zara, stealing a searingly hot kiss. He pulled back out onto the main road. "From now on January the fifth will always be celebrated with cocoa and gingerbread, the new foods of love."

"Oh, really? Where are we going to do that, then?" asked Zara, barely able to contain herself that he'd mentioned the L word.

"We'll just have to start this exciting first page of our new story *together* in the only way possible, at the nearest purveyor of said goods. Destination Cafe Ritazza, Bristol airport!"

Zara giggled as she squeezed his thigh. "Easy, tiger."

Bruno's hand briefly enveloped hers, leaving Zara in no doubt that tame cocoa and gingerbread would be leading to slightly wilder activities by the time the sun had set.

How imperfectly perfect. The final scene of her old story would be the beginning of her new one. There was just one more thing they'd need to tag onto the event.

"Erm, Bruno? I might just need you to take me to the January sales for a spot of clothes shopping…"

"Would this involve the lingerie department?"

He playfully arched a brow and licked his lips. Zara flushed at the recollection of that taut chest. At this rate they'd be skipping the cafe and heading to the closest airport hotel.

"Uh-huh," she replied, "briefly followed by the jeans, skirts, shirts, dresses, trousers, hats, jackets etcetera. Oh, and the shoes, and I guess I ought to buy myself another pair of trainers."

"Looks like you've got yourself a deal… as long as we throw in some stilettos and boots."

"I'm game if you are." Zara couldn't resist leaning in and kissing him on the neck. Bruno quivered, batting her away playfully so he could focus on the road. Oh, the things she was going to do to the world's sexiest Santa Claus tonight. "Just one stipulation for that shopping list: definitely no more Wellington boots."

THE END

ABOUT THE AUTHOR

Isabella May lives in (mostly) sunny Andalusia, Spain with her husband, daughter and son, creatively inspired by the mountains and the sea. She grew up on Glastonbury's ley lines and loves to feature her quirky English hometown in her stories.

After a degree in Modern Languages and European Studies at UWE, Bristol (and a year working abroad in Bordeaux and Stuttgart), Isabella bagged an extremely jammy and fascinating job in children's publishing… selling foreign rights for novelty, board, pop-up and non-fiction books all over the world; in every language from Icelandic to Korean, Bahasa Indonesian to Papiamento!

All of which has fuelled her curiosity and love of international food and travel – both feature extensively in her cross-genre novels, fused with a dollop of romcom, and a sprinkle of magical realism.

Isabella is also a Level 4 Pranic Healer and a stillbirth mum.

You can keep up with her Foodie Romance Journey series by signing up for her newsletter: https://bit.ly/3x5Haee ... and at the following hang-outs:
www.isabellamayauthor.com
Twitter – @IsabellaMayBks
Instagram – @isabella_may_author
Facebook – IsabellaMayAuthor

Also published by Isabella May:
The Cocktail Bar
Costa del Churros
Oh! What a Pavlova
The Ice Cream Parlour
The Cake Fairies
The Chocolate Box
Bubblegum and Blazers

Printed in Great Britain
by Amazon